What Readers A

86 Bloomberg Place

What Readers Are Saying About 86 Bloomberg Place

"Melody offers Chick Lit readers a bouquet of colorful characters. Kendall and her Bloomberg roommates are guaranteed to brighten up your reading hours. Lovely!"

Robin Jones Gunn, best-selling author of the Sisterchicks® novels and *Peculiar Treasures*

"Melody Carlson is a master storyteller who deftly captures the heart and yearnings of young women. Readers will connect with the ladies of Bloomberg Place as they strive to find their place in this big world."

Rachel Hauck, author of *Sweet Caroline*

"This fun romp with the Bloomberg Place girls has it all—snappy dialogue, complex relationships, and a fantastically diverse cast of characters that kept me reading nonstop!"

Camy Tang, author of *Only Uni* and *Single Sashimi*

"As the 'Bloomberg Girls' weather the challenges of friendship together, they discover the joys of forgiveness and restoration."

Melanie Dobson, author of *Together for Good* and *Going for Broke*

spring broke

spring broke

Melody Carlson

86 Bloomberg Place

David C Cook®

transforming lives together

SPRING BROKE
Published by David C. Cook
4050 Lee Vance View
Colorado Springs, CO 80918 U.S.A.

David C. Cook Distribution Canada
55 Woodslee Avenue, Paris, Ontario, Canada N3L 3E5

David C. Cook U.K., Kingsway Communications
Eastbourne, East Sussex BN23 6NT, England

This story is a work of fiction. All characters and events
are the product of the author's imagination. Any resemblance
to any person, living or dead, is coincidental.

LCCN 2008942922
ISBN 978-1-58919-107-5

© 2009 Melody Carlson
Published in association with the literary agency of Sara A. Fortenberry

The Team: Andrea Christian, Erin Michelle Healy, Amy Kiechlin, Jaci Schneider,
and Susan Vannaman
Cover Design: The DesignWorks Group, Charles Brock
Interior Design: The DesignWorks Group
Cover Illustration: Rob Roth

Printed in the United States of America
First Edition 2009

1 2 3 4 5 6 7 8 9 10

122708

To Jennifer Bird,
a dear friend with a compassionate heart.

mc

One

Megan Abernathy

"I'm starting to get seriously worried about Kendall," Lelani said as she stirred milk into her coffee. "She hasn't been herself lately."

"She's been pretty bummed," Megan admitted quietly. She knew it was unlikely that their unpredictable landlady would be up at this hour—especially after she'd gotten what looked like a lifetime supply of puppy potty pads for Tinkerbell last week. Still, Megan didn't want to take any chances of being overheard.

"I think Valentine's Day was especially hard on her this year." Lelani put the milk carton away and shook her head. "She said it was the first time she'd never gotten a valentine from anyone."

"I gave her a valentine." Megan reached for a mug. "She didn't even say thank you."

Lelani smiled. "I know, you gave them to all of us, and that was some good chocolate. But you're not a guy."

"Kendall needs to learn to be happy without a guy." Megan poured coffee into her mug. "I heard that if you can't be happy without a guy, you will never be happy with one."

"I agree." Lelani nodded. "But I think Kendall's bummed about more than just not having a guy. She's starting to freak because she's beginning to show."

"Yeah. When I got home from work yesterday, I found her crying because her favorite jeans were too small." Megan stirred some sugar into her coffee. "I told her that she could borrow some of mine, but that didn't seem to help." To be honest, Megan thought tight jeans seemed fairly minor in comparison to being pregnant, unemployed, and unmarried, but to Kendall it was a major crisis.

"It doesn't help matters that Matthew Harmon is treating her like a stalker now."

"You can't really blame him," pointed out Megan. "If you think about it, she sort of did stalk him when she popped down to Tinsel Town and tried to put the move on him at his wife's birthday party."

"I know." Lelani frowned. "Still, it seems like he could show a little more compassion. It's not as if she got pregnant on purpose."

Now, Megan knew this was a tough issue for Lelani, and she didn't want to step on her toes. By now all the housemates were aware that Lelani had been through a similar situation before she left Maui. But as a result, Megan felt that Lelani had a tendency to be extra hard on dads who weren't willing to bear their share of the responsibility. These guys got blamed for everything, but Megan knew it took two people to make a baby.

"To be fair to Matthew," Megan began cautiously, "Kendall isn't a hundred percent certain that it's his baby." As far as Megan was concerned, this was just another bone of contention. Kendall had finally admitted that she'd slept with more than just one guy last fall. Not only had she been stupid, she'd been careless. Okay, Megan knew it was unkind to judge Kendall like that, so she never expressed these thoughts out loud, but it's how she felt underneath it all. And it was just one of many reasons that Megan felt that sex outside of marriage was a foolish mistake. "And even if it is Matthew's child, it's not like she can make him drop everything and come to her side. Although I'm sure she could force him to pay some child support. What a mess." Megan downed the last of her coffee.

"It's no wonder that she's depressed. Being single and pregnant is never easy. I guess we should be more supportive of her. Especially when she's as down as she's been these past few days. I kept thinking she'd bounce back."

"It seemed like she had more resilience earlier on." Megan rinsed her mug and placed it in the dishwasher. "Remember how upbeat she was when the pregnancy test turned out to be positive?"

"Being pregnant can play havoc with your hormones," explained Lelani. "And your emotions. I remember having moments of unexplainable happiness during my pregnancy. But then I'd get blue—really blue. It's kind of a rollercoaster ride."

"So we just hang on tight and hope that she stays on the track?"

Lelani smiled. "And try not to say the wrong things."

"Tell me about it." Megan lowered her voice again. "The other day Kendall was talking about terminating her pregnancy. I was just minding my own business. I mean, she knows how I feel about abortion. She knows how we all feel. So then she looks me in the eyes and asks me what I would do if I were in her position."

"Seriously?"

"Yes."

Lelani's brow creased. "What did you tell her?"

"That first of all, I wouldn't be in her position, since I don't plan to have sex until I'm married."

"I have to agree with you on that now." Lelani shook her head. "Although I didn't feel that way before."

"So I told her that I'd definitely have the baby, but that I'd probably adopt it to a loving family."

"And?"

"She fell totally apart."

"Oh."

Megan looked at the kitchen clock. "Well, I better get to work. Cynthia's gone this week and Vera has been stressing over absolutely everything. I wouldn't dare be one minute late lest she fly into a rage."

"Despite the fact that she makes you work overtime?"

Megan made a half smile. "But, oh, I'm so lucky to have this job." She imitated Vera's voice. "'Hundreds of young women would love to be in your shoes, Megan.'" Megan looked down at her Cole Haan loafers. "Of course, Vera would then make fun of my practical shoes and suggest I wear something a bit more stylish."

"You *lucky* girl!" teased Lelani.

Still, as Megan walked to work, she did feel lucky. Or maybe just blessed. And as the morning sun shone down, Megan felt truly optimistic for the day ahead. Oh, sure, Vera could be a witch. What else was new? But this was one of those rare late-winter days with hints of spring in the air. The plum trees that lined Bloomberg Place had burst into pale pink blooms, and the sunny faces of daffodils were making their cheerful appearances. Spring had always seemed a promising time of year to Megan. New life, freshness, the hope of things to come.

Of course, that's probably not how Kendall felt these days. Despite the new life that was growing within her, Kendall seemed more confused and worried and troubled than ever. And why shouldn't she be? A surge of empathy rushed through Megan. Poor Kendall!

As Megan turned onto Main Street, she felt a stab of guilt for not being kinder and more understanding toward her perplexing friend. Naturally, she couldn't help but disapprove of Kendall's lifestyle and choices. But at the same time, she should be careful not to condemn her. And she did want to help Kendall. But how? Often it seemed that Megan's words only irritated her. And for that reason, Megan had been trying to keep her mouth shut. Really, other than praying for Kendall, there seemed little Megan could do.

As Megan got closer to the design firm, she spied the homeless lady who often waited for her. By now Megan knew that her name was Margie. But she hadn't been around much during the past few weeks.

"Hello," called Margie, grinning widely to expose her missing tooth.

"Where have you been?" asked Megan as she fished inside her bag. She usually kept a couple dollars or McDonald's gift certificates handy, but since Margie had been gone, she'd gotten out of the habit.

"I've been sick."

"Really?" Megan extracted a five from her wallet.

"I stayed at the shelter for a while. A lady there took me to the free clinic and they gave me some medicine."

"So you're okay now?"

"Oh, yes. And darn glad to be out of that nasty shelter." She frowned. "So noisy and dirty in there. I can't stand it."

Megan had never asked Margie too much about herself. In fact, Margie had never said this much before. "So ... where do you stay now?"

Margie gave her a mysterious smile. "Oh, you know ... here and there."

Megan handed her the five.

"Oh, God bless you, dear child!" cried Margie.

"God bless you too."

Megan entered the design firm, a lavishly decorated place with expensive furnishings, authentic art, and pretty much useless accessories.

Not for the first time, she noted the sharp contrast between this fancy place and poor old Margie's world. To be honest, Megan sometimes felt totally disgusted by the entire decorating business—so much money wasted on making someone's overly priced home into a showplace. But then, it had never been Megan's career goal to land here. Hopefully she would secure a teaching job by next fall. In the meantime, she was thankful to be gainfully employed. Certainly, she wasn't getting rich. But she made enough to pay her bills.

As Megan hung up her coat, she noticed Margie still standing on the sidewalk out front, gazing up at the sky with an expression of wonder and delight. Megan wondered why it was that some sweet people like Margie wound up homeless, while others like mean Vera Craig ended up rich. Although to be fair, Margie seemed content with her lot in life. Compared to grumpy Vera, Margie seemed downright happy. Go figure.

Megan went straight to work on a floor plan that Vera wanted finished by two o'clock so that she could present it to Helen Ferguson. So far it was coming along just fine. But a little before noon, Megan's phone rang. To her surprise it was Kendall—and she sounded extremely distraught.

"I need help!" cried Kendall.

"What's wrong?"

"I'm—I'm in trouble."

Okay, that went without saying, but what did Kendall really mean? "What is going on?" Megan spoke slowly and clearly. "What happened, Kendall?"

"I need you to come home"—Kendall broke into fresh sobs—"right now!"

Megan glanced at the clock. It wasn't quite time for her lunch break, but this sounded dire. "Okay. I'm on my way."

Megan grabbed her bag and her coat and headed out to the reception area.

"Early lunch?" Ellen, the receptionist, frowned at her.

"Kind of an emergency. But I'll make up the time."

"I'm sure that Vera will be pleased to hear that." Ellen tossed a warning look.

Megan felt sure that Ellen wouldn't tell on her, although if Vera asked, Ellen would probably be honest. Megan pushed those thoughts from her head as she hurried out and jogged the six blocks back to 86 Bloomberg Place.

She was about halfway there when she realized that she should've gotten more information from Kendall. Perhaps Kendall was having some kind of medical emergency—maybe something was wrong with the baby. But in that case she would've called 9-1-1. Or maybe it wasn't that serious. Maybe she just wanted Megan to drive her to the doctor's or the hospital. Fortunately Kendall had a car, since Megan did not.

Then Megan wondered why Kendall hadn't called Lelani instead. They seemed to be closer. But Lelani was harder to reach at Nordstrom. Employees weren't supposed to take personal calls while on duty. But what about Anna? Kendall could've called her. And Anna did have a car.

In a crazy way, Megan felt honored that Kendall would call her in a time of crisis. She just had no idea what to expect once she got home. So Megan prayed as she jogged the last block. And, with a sharp pain in her side, Megan hurried into the house to find Kendall sitting in the living room. Still in her bathrobe, she had Tinkerbell in her lap and tears running down her cheeks.

"What's wrong?" Megan asked breathlessly as she sat down on the sectional next to Kendall. "Are you okay?"

"No. I'm not okay."

"What is it?" Megan placed a hand on Kendall's arm. "Is something wrong with the baby?"

"No, that's not it."

"What is it then?"

"I'm broke."

Megan's hand slipped off Kendall's arm and she sat up straighter and just stared at Kendall. "Huh?"

"I'm broke and a debt collector just showed up and—and it was horrible!"

"That's why you called me at work?" Okay, as kind and understanding as Megan had wanted to be earlier this morning, as sympathetic as she'd been feeling toward Kendall, as much as she'd prayed for her, Megan wanted to throttle her! Kendall had sounded like she was having a life-and-death emergency—and she had called Megan at work simply because she was broke? Like that was big news? Since when had Kendall not been broke? They all knew that her finances were a complete and nearly hopeless disaster. That's why she'd taken in renters to start with. Good grief!

"I—I just thought you could help me," sobbed Kendall. "You're so—so sensible."

"What is it you *thought* I could possibly do?" Megan knew that her voice sounded harsh and angry. Okay, she *was* angry. This was ridiculous! Besides, hadn't she already attempted to help Kendall sort out this mess? Hadn't she helped her to start making the minimum payments and suggested ways to consolidate her bills? But Kendall hadn't listened. Instead she'd gone out and accumulated even more debt. In her pathetic attempt to snag Matthew, she'd opened additional high-interest-rate accounts and made more ridiculous purchases. Some things she hadn't even used. Not to mention buying all the accessories for her dog. And while they all thought Tinkerbell was cute, they also questioned the sensibility in the additional expense of feeding—not to mention clothing—a pet.

"I don't know what you can do." Kendall turned and looked at Megan with watery blue eyes. "I just thought you might have some ideas. You're so much smarter at this stuff than me. What do you think I should do?"

Megan knew what she'd like to tell Kendall to do. But then she remembered that she was a Christian and she was supposed to be patient, kind, loving…. So she took a long, deep breath and steadied herself. "Fine. At least you're willing to admit that you're broke, Kendall. They say the first step to recovery is acknowledging you have a problem."

"I have a problem," Kendall said in a tiny voice.

"You have a lot of problems."

Kendall nodded sadly. "I know."

Of course, Megan doubted she could help Kendall with all of her problems. In fact, Megan felt doubtful she could help her mixed-up housemate with much of anything. Really, only God could help someone like Kendall. But then Megan spied one of Kendall's latest shopping conquests, an absurdly expensive Hermès bag that she'd gotten on sale after the holidays, now lying on the floor by the coat rack like a discarded piece of rubbish.

"I think I'm getting an idea." Megan remembered how her mother used to entice her to help with spring cleaning with the offer of a little extra cash.

"What is it?" Kendall looked up hopefully.

"We'll have a garage sale."

"A garage sale?" Kendall looked disappointed. "Are you serious?"

"Totally." Megan grinned. "It's a great way to make some money while you do some spring cleaning."

"Spring cleaning?" Kendall frowned. "That sounds like work to me."

"But it's work that pays off." Megan stood up. "You get a clean house and then you use the money from the garage sale to pay your bills."

"I don't know." Kendall still looked doubtful. "What could I possibly sell in a garage sale?"

Megan eyed that costly designer handbag again. "Oh, I'm sure we could find a few things, Kendall." Then Megan told Kendall to think about it and that she needed to get back to work. She controlled herself from adding, "Someone has to work around here." But as she left, she couldn't help but shake her head. Really, what would it take to knock some sense into that girl?

Lelani Porter

"Why don't you just go back to Maui and see her?" Gil looked at Lelani with an intensity that was slightly unnerving. "Emma is your daughter. You have every right to see her if you want."

They had met at Demetri's Deli for lunch, and Lelani had been stealing glances at a baby across the aisle. Dressed in pink corduroy overalls with bunny buttons, she appeared to be about the same age as Lelani's baby. The mother seemed oblivious to the baby sleeping sweetly in her stroller, but Lelani was captivated by the child—staring at the dark lashes on the rosy cheeks, the sweet little pinched-up lips. Once again, Lelani wondered what her own daughter might look like now. Emma would be almost nine months old.

And, not for the first time, Lelani wondered why her mother never sent photos of the child. How difficult would it be? They had a state-of-the-art digital camera, and her parents knew how to send photos online. But in their rare conversations, her mom always made excuses. They were too busy. Caring for Emma took up a lot of time and energy. The business was demanding this time of year.

But as time passed, Lelani began to doubt these pretexts. For one thing, Lelani knew that her mother had help. With a nanny, housekeeper, groundskeeper, and cook, her mother couldn't be that busy. Lelani began to draw her own conclusions. She had a pretty good idea why her mother was acting like this. She simply wanted to erase Lelani from Emma's world. She hoped that time and distance would eventually separate Lelani from Emma permanently. Perhaps from Lelani's parents as well. It had taken Lelani months to come to grips with this harsh reality, and she had never spoken openly of it to anyone, not even Gil, but she suspected she was right.

"I'm sorry," she told Gil. "I know I must seem distracted."

He nodded and reached for her hand. "And I don't blame you one bit, Lelani." He smiled sadly. "Sometimes I wonder how you do it."

"Do it?"

"Keep up such a strong front when I know that a part of you is hurting inside."

She sighed. "A strong front? Do you really think so?"

"Not so strong that I can't see through it."

"It's just that I thought … by now…." Lelani paused to take a breath. She didn't want to cry, but for some reason she felt close to tears. Of course, it was that baby. She shifted her chair so not to be distracted by it and looked directly at Gil. "I just figured that after this long—I mean it's been nearly nine months. I just thought I'd be over it. I thought I'd be able to move on."

"And forget that you have a child?"

"No, of course not. But that I'd be able to think of Emma as my parents' child … my little sister."

"And that's what your parents are hoping?"

"I'm sure they believe that's exactly what I've done."

"So, really, Lelani, why don't you just go back there? Visit your parents and see your daughter—and figure out how you really feel about the situation."

"You make it sound so easy."

"It is easy. Just ask for time off. Book the flight. And go."

"But when I get there?"

"One step at a time, Lelani."

She sighed and looked at her watch. "My break is almost over."

"And you're glad, aren't you?" His dark eyes twinkled. "You can escape me and my nonstop pestering."

She shook her head. "No. I don't want to escape you, Gil. But sometimes I just want to escape myself."

"Are we still on for dinner tonight?" He helped her with her jacket.

"You're sure you want me there?"

"Absolutely. The sooner my mother figures out that we're really a couple and that she can't scare you off or drive us apart, the easier life will be for everyone."

"Okay." They were out on the sidewalk now, about to go their separate ways.

"I'll pick you up around six." He leaned over and kissed her. "But, really, Lelani, think about taking that trip back home. It seems like you need to resolve this one way or another. Hanging in limbo is making you crazy."

"I know."

"And if I thought it would help matters, I'd offer to take time off from the restaurant and go with you."

"You would?"

"Sure. If it would make it easier for you."

She considered this. As tempting as it sounded, it might only complicate things if Gil came along. She just wasn't sure what to expect from her parents. On one hand, they were gracious people; on the other hand, they were still disappointed in her. "Thanks," she told him. "I'll think about that."

He grinned. "I mean it's not like you'd have to twist my arm to go to Maui. I've been to Oahu before and that wasn't exactly a hardship." Then he got more serious. "But it would probably be more fun to go there under happier conditions."

"For you and me both." She looked at her watch again. "I better run. See you around six."

As Lelani hurried back to Nordstrom, she tried to imagine what it would be like to have Gil accompany her to Maui. What would her parents think of him? How would they treat him? Would they assume that her involvement with him was her way of relinquishing parental rights to Emma? Would they encourage the relationship, pointing out that she and Gil could have other children? Or would they perceive his presence as some kind of threat? She could imagine that. She could just see her mother's dark eyes filling with dramatic fear. Then she would feign a helpless expression for her husband, the same dad who used to stand faithfully by Lelani, drawing him in to play her protector.

That seemed the most likely possibility. Her mom was territorial and slightly paranoid. She would assume that Gil and Lelani had come to snatch Emma away. Lelani wasn't a fool. She knew how much her mother loved that baby. She'd seen it in her eyes right from the very start. It was no secret that her mother had always wanted more children. In some ways it seemed that Lelani's mistake had turned into her mother's reward. Not that her parents ever said as much. If anything, they acted as if they had rescued Lelani from her own foolishness.

As a result, she was being punished—sent to the mainland for bad behavior. In some ways it was laughable. But not quite. And she knew that the longer she stayed away, the more time that lapsed between the already infrequent notes and phone calls, the harder it would be to return. Even now it seemed nearly impossible.

As Lelani put her bag in her locker, she overheard several female coworkers gently pestering Mr. Green about taking time off. This wasn't surprising, since a few of the part-time employees were also college students and still lived for the madness of a spring break in some "exotic tropical paradise." Just the same, it was irritating to hear their phony sweetness, their sugar-coated words as they attempted to cajole him into granting their wishes. They competed with each other in a slightly flirtatious way—very irksome, since Lelani was well aware that these same girls talked freely about him behind his back, calling him Mr. Mean, among other things. They loved to ridicule his clothes, poking fun at an outdated tie or slightly worn shoes. But the main reason they picked on him was because Mr. Green ran a tight ship, played by the rules, and didn't put up with slackers.

"And how about you, Lelani?" Mr. Green asked her in a pleasant voice.

"What's that?" She turned and smiled at him.

"I don't see you clamoring for a vacation. And you didn't take any time off during Christmas," he reminded her. "Don't you have any plans for spring break? You know what they say about all work and no play."

Something about the expressions of those catty girls made Lelani pause to reconsider her answer. Something about the way they looked at her, slightly askance, as if they were thinking, *Why would Lelani need time off? A workaholic like her couldn't possibly have any kind of a life.*

"You're probably right, Mr. Green," she said slowly. "I think it's about time I had some down time. I'd be happy to take a week off during spring break. Is that a problem?"

He smiled and shook his head. "Not at all. I'll put you down."

Meredith, a particularly snotty girl, looked at Lelani with slightly narrowed eyes. "Really?" she said suspiciously. "And what are you planning to do for spring break?"

"I think I'll go home for a visit," said Lelani.

Mr. Green nodded with even more satisfaction. "Well, I must say I feel a bit jealous now, Lelani. Maui sounds delightful right now. Especially since we've had such miserable weather this year. I'm sure you'll have a wonderful time."

"Your parents live in Maui?" This came from Margot. She was one of Lelani's friendly coworkers, and she'd paused to listen as she put her purse away. "I absolutely adore Maui. My husband and I go over there about every five years or so. Although I think it's been around six now. Where do your parents live on the island?"

"Western Maui." Lelani told Margot. "Not far from Lahaina, near Baby Beach."

"Oh, you lucky, lucky girl," gushed Margot. "I wish I could fit into your suitcase and come along."

Lelani laughed. "Well, with airport security what it is, I wouldn't recommend it."

As Lelani left the employees' lounge and headed down to work, she couldn't help but feel slightly smug. It was probably wrong of her, but it had been fun to watch the expressions on the girls' faces switch from catty superiority to what seemed like open envy. Not only had Lelani snagged some precious vacation time, but she actually had a rather cool place to go.

But as soon as Lelani slipped behind the cosmetics counter, her self-satisfied smile faded. This joke was on her. She had just asked for time off to go home, but she had no intention of actually doing such a thing. How could she? What would she say to her parents? What if they told her the timing was bad? Her mother would surely invent some kind of excuse to keep her away. And so what would Lelani do during that week off? Hide out in Kendall's house to avoid being seen by any of her coworkers, who would enjoy making jokes at her expense?

And what about the week's loss of pay? It wasn't as if this was paid time off. She'd managed to save up a bit of money, but it would be eaten up by her phony-baloney vacation. Oh, why hadn't she considered these things when she'd been showing off for the girls she usually considered to be foolish? She was just as bad as they were. Just a proud and silly fool who had just gotten stuck with a week of no pay and nothing to do. Brilliant.

Lelani's shift ended at five. As she walked home, she tried to think of a way to gracefully decline her time off. She could make some excuse, like she'd been unable to book a flight, or that she'd decided to wait until a later date to attend a friend's wedding, or that she'd forgotten a previous commitment here on the mainland. But no matter which story she concocted, it sounded lame … and it was a lie. And Lelani had discovered long ago that deception only gets a person into deeper trouble. Not that she always remembered this, which had been made obvious by her stupidity this afternoon.

When she got to the house, she opened the front door to be greeted by piles of junk heaped all over the living room. Kendall was coming down the stairs with a cardboard box in her hands and Tinkerbell dancing around her feet.

"What's going on?" Lelani asked Kendall as she picked her way across the cluttered floor. "What is all this old stuff doing all over the place?"

"I brought it down from the attic," huffed Kendall as she set the dusty box on the dining room table. "I'm exhausted."

Lelani frowned as she hung her Ralph Lauren jacket on the hall tree. Then, reconsidering, she took the jacket back. Already the living room smelled musty and dusty and she didn't want it to absorb the odors. "Spring cleaning?"

"Getting ready for a garage sale." Kendall opened the box and exposed a bunch of old magazines.

"Oh?" Lelani nodded as if this was a great idea. "This weekend?"

Kendall's mouth twisted like she was thinking. "I'm not sure when exactly. Megan is helping me with it. She just told me to start finding things to sell."

"So … are you going to leave all this, uh, *stuff* in here?"

Kendall looked puzzled as she surveyed the messy room. "I hadn't really thought about that yet."

Now Lelani noticed a beat-up bird cage. "You know, this is kind of cool, Kendall. I might buy it from you."

"Really?" Kendall looked hopeful.

"Sure. I think it would be cute cleaned up. I saw one almost just like it made into a floor lamp."

"A floor lamp?" Kendall didn't look convinced.

"If you decide how much you want, let me know."

Kendall nodded. "Sure. I'll see what Megan says. She's the garage-sale expert."

"Really?" Somehow Lelani hadn't thought of Megan in quite that way. But it would be interesting to hear the rest of the story. "Well, I need to get ready. I'm going out tonight."

Kendall sighed. "Some people have all the fun."

Lelani couldn't help but laugh. "Some people might say that you've already had more than your share of fun, Kendall."

Kendall kind of smiled. "Yes, I suppose that's true."

Lelani hurried off to her room, worried that Kendall might think about what she'd just said and take it the wrong way—or maybe it would be the right way. Lelani wasn't even sure, but she didn't want to go there. Instead, she opened her closet and stared at its rather sparse contents, hoping to spot something that would be perfect for this evening with Gil's family. Naturally, that was not happening. Most of her clothes were either for work or more appropriate for Maui. Not that she wanted to think about Maui at the moment. Besides, her Maui clothes weren't warm enough. Despite a few signs of spring, the damp air still felt chilly to her.

Finally, she pulled out a red Tadashi dress, a cast-off from Kendall, who decided that she didn't look good in red. But perhaps it was too dressy for tonight. Lelani held it up in front of the mirror and frowned. It showed more skin than she felt comfortable with around Gil's mother. But, if she topped it with the pretty black cashmere cardigan that she'd found on the markdown rack, it might be acceptable for a family dinner.

Tonight was a fiftieth wedding anniversary celebration for Gil and Anna's maternal grandparents. The Castillos had flown up from Southern California, and it would be Lelani's first time to meet them. She had tried to beg out, but Gil wouldn't take no for an answer. As it was, Lelani hoped to play the wallflower. She knew how these family gatherings could get. If Gil or Anna or any of the unwed cousins brought a date along, it was assumed that the relationship was very serious. Several of the meddlesome aunts considered this their free pass to inquire as to whether a date had been set. Or they might actually grab Lelani's left hand to search for a ring. It all got a little tedious after a while. Gil had told her to take his relatives in stride, but that was easier said than done.

"Your prince is here," called Kendall as she tapped on Lelani's door.

"Thanks," said Lelani as she turned off the light and emerged.

"That's what you're wearing?" Kendall frowned at her outfit.

"It's that Tadashi dress you gave me," said Lelani in defense.

"But with a sweater?" Kendall shook her head as they went into the living room where Gil was waiting. "You look like a librarian or a school teacher."

Lelani just smiled. "Thank you very much."

"If Lelani looks like a school teacher, I want to be teacher's pet," teased Gil as he hugged her. "I think she's hot."

Kendall waved her hand. "You guys are so corny. You deserve each other."

"What's going on in here?" Gil asked as they made their way around the boxes and strange items.

"I've been bringing things down from the attic." Kendall smiled proudly.

"It looks more like the attic threw up, and it landed in the living room." Gil made a face as they gave an extra wide berth to a box coated with dust and spider webs.

"Kendall's having a garage sale," Lelani informed him as the door opened and Megan walked in. "And it was her idea."

"Huh?" Megan looked at them and then at the piles of junk behind them. "What is all this?"

"Apparently it's your garage sale," Lelani said quietly.

"My what?" Megan looked past Lelani and Gil over to where Kendall was opening another dusty box and peering inside.

"Oh, Megan," called Kendall. "Look at all the great stuff I found."

Megan tossed Lelani a worried look, then made what appeared to be a very forced smile. "Where did you find all this?"

"In the attic," proclaimed Kendall.

"And you brought it all down here?"

"Yes." Kendall nodded. "And now I am exhausted."

"And we're going to keep all this junk in the house?" asked Megan in a slightly higher pitched voice. "Until the garage sale, which is going to happen when exactly?"

"That's up to you," said Kendall as she flopped onto the couch, causing a stack of dusty old magazines to tumble onto the floor.

"Hang in there," Lelani whispered to Megan. "Maybe we can all work together to move it out to the garage tomorrow."

"Let's hope so," said Megan quietly.

"Have a nice evening," called Lelani as she and Gil made a quick exit.

Once outside, Gil started to laugh. "Kendall is a real nut case."

"She's kind of impulsive."

"Megan looked like she wanted to scream or punch someone."

Lelani nodded. "Well, it's kind of shocking, you know, to come home after work—to what you consider to be your home, because you're paying rent and you do your share of work to keep it clean—"

"Not to mention all the work you girls—along with your generous friends—put into that place to get it looking that good."

"Exactly. So to find it looking like a garbage dump, well, it's a little disconcerting." Lelani laughed as Gil helped her into the cab of his pickup. "And I'm sure Megan was totally flabbergasted. I mean, can you imagine working in interior design, helping to put together the swankiest houses, and then to come home to that mess? This will probably be harder on Megan than on any of us."

"I don't know," he said when he got behind the wheel. "Anna probably won't be too thrilled to see that junk either. She has dust allergies."

"Oh, great."

Gil didn't say anything as he drove through town. And Lelani was quieter than usual since she was still feeling freaked over her spring break vacation dilemma. But finally Gil cleared his throat as if he wanted her attention.

"I'm sorry," she said. "Did you say something? I guess I was off in la-la land, as my old fifth-grade teacher used to say."

"No. I didn't actually say anything, but I was about to warn you about something."

"Warn me?"

"Yes. My grandmother is ... well, she's eager to meet you."

"Is that bad?"

"The warning part is that my grandmother is very old-fashioned and pretty outspoken too."

She nodded. "I see." She controlled herself from mentioning that sounded a lot like his mom. But then, they were mother and daughter.

"So please don't let anything my grandmother might say offend you, okay?"

She kind of laughed. "If it's any consolation, I was already sort of bracing myself."

"Is that why you were being so quiet?"

"No."

"Something wrong?"

"Not exactly."

He was pulling up in front of his parents' house, and it looked as if the circular driveway was already filled with cars, so he just parked along the street. "This will be better for making a quick getaway," he said as he helped her out of the pickup.

"A getaway?"

"You never know about these family get-togethers."

"I'm sure it'll be fine," she assured him. "And if it's any consolation, I'm not the least bit worried about any of your relatives."

"You haven't met *Abuela* yet."

"Abuela?"

"Spanish for *Grandmother*." He grimaced slightly. "Keep in mind she is my mother's mother ... and that old saying about the apple not falling far from the tree."

Lelani chuckled but didn't admit that she'd already made that assumption.

Gil pointed to Edmond's car. "Looks like Edmond and Anna are already here."

"But not parked in the getaway section?"

"Anna must not have warned Edmond about what he's getting into." Gil smiled as he opened one of the big double doors.

"Bienvenido!" said Gil's father as they entered the foyer. He shook Gil's hand and, to Lelani's surprise, gave her a big bear hug.

"Thanks." She smiled. "Or should I say, *gracias*."

"De nada." He lowered his voice. "And I hope you will not allow my mother-in-law to rub you the wrong way." He stepped back and winked and, although his warmth was refreshing, Lelani now knew she was in for a long evening.

Three

Anna Mendez

"You've put on weight, *mi'ja*." Abuela Castillo released Anna from a tight hug, then grabbed both cheeks with her wiry fingers, tugging in the same painful way that she'd been doing since Anna was four.

Anna extracted herself, stepped back, and smiled stiffly. "Thank you, Abuela, you're looking well too."

"You know, mi'ja, short Latinas need to watch their figures." Now Abuela pinched Anna's arm as if testing for doneness. "Before too long they get as wide as they are tall. I remember when you were little, Anna, we called you Gorda. It was cute and funny then. But it wouldn't be so cute and funny now."

"No, it wouldn't," said Anna. "I'll keep it in mind."

"And who is this?" Abuela's overly plucked eyebrows arched sharply as she peered curiously at Edmond.

"I was trying to introduce him to you, Abuela, but you—"

"This is the boyfriend?" Abuela stepped closer to him, staring as if he were a scientific specimen. Hopefully she wasn't going to grab his cheeks too.

"I'd like you to meet Edmond Dubois—"

"Dubois?" Abuela frowned. "Are you *French*, Mr. Dubois?"

He grinned. "My grandfather on my father's side was French."

"Do you *speak* French?"

"Actually, I do speak a bit—"

"How about Spanish?" she demanded.

"*Sì, Señora Castillo, yo hablo Español—poco-poco. Como estás?*" And then he continued trying to impress her with his one year of high-school Spanish, but Anna could see Abuela was not the least bit amused.

"That's okay, Edmond," Anna said quickly. "As you can see my grandmother is fluent in English."

"Fortunately." She scowled and looked at Anna now. "What happened to your other boyfriend—what was his name?"

"You mean Jake the Snake?" asked Anna.

Abuela actually smiled now, but in a slightly wicked way. "Oh, he may have been a snake, Anna, but he was a handsome snake."

Anna looked helplessly to Edmond, wishing she hadn't brought him tonight. But he seemed totally at ease and still smiling.

"May I congratulate you, Señora Castillo," he said pleasantly, "on your fifty years of marriage. But I couldn't believe that it was possible when I first saw you tonight. I'm sure you must've been a young child when you married because I could've mistaken you for Señora Mendez's sister."

Abuela's eyes lit up and she tilted her head coyly. "Yes, I have been told that I am aging gracefully."

"Your husband is a lucky man."

Abuela laughed and turned to Anna. "Well, he may be a gringo, but he does have some charms, doesn't he?"

Anna linked her arm in Edmond's. "Yes, he does. And now, if you don't mind, I'd like him to meet Abuelo."

"Yes, yes, go on your way. I see my handsome grandson coming in the door now anyway. Oh, that Gilbert, he is such a—"

Abuela grabbed Anna's arm just as she was trying to get away. "Who is that with him, Anna?"

"That's Lelani," said Anna. "Just like Mama told you. She's Gil's girlfriend."

"She's not Latina," snapped Abuela.

"No one said that she was." Anna's patience was wearing thin now. "She's Hawaiian. Her parents still live in Maui."

"And she is very beautiful, is she not?"

"Yes." Anna sighed. "And she's very nice too. She's one of my roommates."

"But Gil isn't serious about her, is he?"

"Why don't you ask Gil, Abuela?"

"Because I'm asking *you*, Anna. Please, do not be disrespectful to your elders."

"I don't really know if Gil is serious or not."

"This is very sad for your parents, very sad and very disappointing for your whole family, mi'ja."

"What is very sad and disappointing?" Anna sighed and shifted her weight to the other foot.

"That you and Gil have chosen outside of your own culture."

"Chosen outside of our culture to do what?" Anna heard the sharpness in her voice, but couldn't help it.

"For courtship." She sighed dramatically. "For marriage, for children. So very sad that you break with traditions."

"Abuela," said Anna with impatience. "Not that anyone is talking about marriage here, but this is the twenty-first century and your notions about marriage are outdated and old-fashioned." She tossed Edmond an apologetic glance and he just chuckled.

"In my day, young people did not *date*." She looked directly at Edmond, saying the word with disgust.

"How did you get to know Señor Castillo?"

"He courted me." She nodded her head firmly.

"Why is that different than dating?" persisted Edmond.

"Because he first had to ask my father for permission. And the understanding was that courtship would likely lead to a proposal of marriage."

"That still doesn't seem different from dating."

"And I suppose that you have a chaperone along when you are alone with my granddaughter?" She glared at him now.

"Well, no. But that's not really—"

"You see, young man, that is my point. You young people are—"

"Excuse me, Abuela," said Anna as Gil and Lelani came their way. "I think Gil would like to introduce you to—"

"My favorite grandson," gushed Abuela as she grabbed Gil into a tight hug, speaking in Spanish and then finally releasing him. "Oh, you are even more handsome than the last time I saw you, *mi'jo*." She reached up and slapped him on the cheek now. "You are a devil."

He looked innocently at her. "A devil? Why is that?"

She turned and looked at Lelani now. "Because of this one."

Now Gil quickly and politely introduced the two women and, although Anna wanted to escape her grandmother, she couldn't pull herself away. It was kind of like watching a train wreck about to happen. Plus, she thought it might make Edmond feel a bit better to see that poor Lelani would probably get an even worse torture than he had.

Anna tossed Lelani a sympathetic look as her grandmother began to grill her about her heritage and her family. "Is Porter a Hawaiian name?"

"No. My father isn't a native Hawaiian. He moved there in the seventies and liked it so much that he decided to stay."

"Is your mother Hawaiian?"

Lelani nodded. "Yes."

"So if you married my grandson and had babies, they would be … what?"

"Our children," offered Gil.

Abuela gave him a scornful look. "Yes, but what would their heritage be? What culture would they embrace? Who would they belong to?"

"They would belong to us," said Gil easily. "Not that Lelani and I are considering marriage right now, thank you very much." He put an arm around Lelani's shoulders.

"I suppose I do understand." Abuela nodded in a knowing way.

"You do?" Anna was surprised that Abuela's beloved Gil was getting off so easily.

"Yes. Of course, Lelani is a beautiful young woman. And a young man likes to—how do you say?" She held up her hands as if at a loss for words, which seemed unlikely. "Play the field? Sow his wild oats? I don't know how to put it politely. But I do know that young men often spend time with a beautiful woman before settling down with someone who is … acceptable."

Gil's eyes darkened. "I don't like to contradict you, Abuela, but Lelani is much more than that to me." He turned and looked directly at Lelani now. "And if she would ever consider having me, I wouldn't hesitate to ask."

Lelani's eyes opened wide, but she said nothing.

"Oh, you are not serious, mi'jo," cajoled Abuela. "It's only that I have offended you. And you are such a gentleman to leap to your lady's honor. But you know your poor old Abuela … she speaks her mind."

"That's the truth," Gil spoke calmly, but Anna could tell he was irked.

"Now, Lelani," said Abuela smoothly, as if trying to iron out the wrinkles she'd just created, "tell me more about yourself. Do you have brothers or sisters?"

Lelani glanced at Gil uncomfortably, then answered slowly. "I am an only child."

"An *only* child?" Abuela nodded as if adding this up. "So may I assume your family is not Catholic?"

"They don't belong to any organized religion."

Abuela looked shocked. "Oh."

"But they are good people," inserted Gil.

"You've met them?"

"No, but I know they're good people because Lelani is a good person." Gil turned and smiled at her.

"And what does Lelani do?" inquired Abuela.

"I work in a department store," said Lelani quickly, "selling cosmetics."

Abuela laughed. "And I suppose that women buy them in hopes that they will look like you after they use them."

"I don't make any promises." Lelani shrugged.

"So you are a store clerk." Abuela did her best to look unimpressed.

Anna could take no more. "It might interest you to know, Abuela, that Lelani was in med school in Hawaii. She only has a year or two more to complete it." She looked at Lelani. "Right?"

Lelani just nodded.

"Medical school?" Abuela looked skeptical. "To become a doctor."

"A pediatrician," said Gil proudly. "And she will probably—"

"Why did you quit?" Abuela's eyes were focused tightly on Lelani now, watching her closely. Almost as if she wanted to trip her up.

Lelani took in a slow breath. "Do you really want to know?"

"Of course. I would not ask if I didn't."

Lelani glanced at Gil now and he just nodded, but the corners of his mouth curled up ever so slightly, as if he was going to enjoy this.

"The reason I quit med school was because I got pregnant."

It seemed the whole room fell quiet. Anna looked nervously to where her mother had been talking to her aunt. But now their eyes were focused on Lelani and Abuela, waiting.

"You have a baby." This was more a statement than a question and Abuela looked satisfied now, as if she had just won this little sparring match and was about to receive some kind of trophy.

"I *had* a baby. That baby lives with my parents in Maui now."

"So ... you *abandoned* your baby?" Those thin brows arched more sharply than ever.

Lelani's face seemed to pale and she looked slightly confused.

"That's not how it is," said Gil quickly.

"Oh, it's not?" Abuela looked at him with mock sympathy. "How is it then?"

"Lelani's baby is being cared for by—"

"By her mother," finished Abuela. "Meanwhile Lelani is here selling makeup and acting as if she didn't have a care in the—"

"It's not like that. Lelani is—"

"Lelani is a beautiful woman who had a child, a child that was obviously born out of wedlock, and she is a selfish young woman who abandoned that child to her mother to raise." Abuela shook her head. "Very disappointing." And before Gil or Lelani could say another word, Abuela turned and walked away. And everyone began murmuring and Gil guided Lelani to a quiet corner, where Anna and Edmond joined them.

Anna looked at Lelani. "Don't take our grandmother too seriously—"

"It's all right," said Lelani quickly. But tears glistened in her dark eyes and her chin was trembling. "What Señora Castillo said was true."

"But Lelani," said Gil. "She doesn't even know you."

Lelani turned to Gil now. "I think she does know me, Gil. Maybe she knows me even better than I know myself."

"But she's—"

"She's right," said Lelani firmly. "Everything she said was absolutely true."

"But—"

"I'm sorry," Lelani said to Gil. "Would you mind if I called a taxi and—"

"I'll take you home," said Gil.

"No. It's a family celebration," said Lelani firmly. "You have to stay."

"After what my grandmother said to you? No way!"

"Yes, Gil. If you go now, it will only look like I've taken you from—"

"I *want* you to take me," pleaded Gil. "Please, please, take me away from all this madness and—"

"No." She put her hand on his arm and tears streamed down her cheeks. "Please, stay. Do it for me. Do it for your family and your parents. Be strong."

"Edmond will take you home," said Anna.

"I will?" Edmond peered curiously at Anna.

"Won't you?"

"No." Lelani shook her head. "I'll call a taxi, Anna."

"No." Anna firmly pushed Edmond now. "Please, take her home."

"But, Anna," tried Lelani, "The last time your boyfriend took me home you and I nearly came to—"

"This is Edmond," said Anna with confidence. "He is a gentleman. He's not Jake the Snake."

"Gee, thanks," teased Edmond.

"You know what I mean," said Anna. She smiled. "I can trust you."

"True."

Anna turned back to Lelani. "Besides, we're past that now. We buried that hatchet long ago."

Lelani nodded as she opened her purse and extracted a Kleenex to wipe her eyes.

Anna looked up at Edmond. "Do you mind taking Lelani home?"

"Not if that's what you really want."

Anna nodded. "Thanks."

"Lucky you," Gil said to Edmond. "Wish I were in your shoes."

"Never mind," said Anna. "Both of you better run while you can."

Gil handed Edmond his truck keys. "Here, take my truck so you can get out."

"That's right," said Lelani. "Your car is boxed in."

So Edmond handed Anna his keys. "Yeah. We'll switch them around later."

They were all outside now, and Anna wished she could run away with them. Instead, she watched as Gil took Lelani aside and kissed her. Then to her surprise, Edmond came over and gave Anna a quick peck. "See you later, Princess," he called as he and Lelani made a dash to Gil's pickup.

"Guess it's just you and me now," said Gil as he put an arm around Anna's shoulder and walked toward the front door. "Let's take 'em on, sis."

"You got it!"

They were barely back in the house when their grandmother approached them again. "Where are your guests?"

"You mean Edmond and Lelani?" asked Gil.

Abuela glanced around the room as if hoping to spy them.

"They left."

Her arched brows lifted higher. "Without saying good-bye?"

"Yes, Abuela," said Anna. "You hurt Lelani's feelings. I asked Edmond to take her—"

"I hurt her feelings?" Abuela's hand touched her chest as if she were shocked. "I only said what everyone knew was true. Does the truth hurt so much?"

"It hurts when it's wielded like a sword, Abuela." Gil shook his head. "You don't even know Lelani, but you feel comfortable cutting her to shreds."

"Cutting her to shreds?" She blinked. "What an imagination you have."

"We all witnessed it, Abuela," said Anna firmly. "You treated Lelani horribly."

Now their grandmother frowned sadly, as if she'd been deeply wounded by their accusation, although Anna knew this was unlikely. "I cannot believe how my own grandchildren can speak with such disrespect. Such a way to treat your elders." She glanced over to where their mother was watching with wide eyes. "I thought my daughter had raised her children better than this."

"Our parents raised us to think for ourselves," said Gil. "And to respect people for who they are, not what their heritage is or what—"

"Enough!" Abuela held up her hand. "I cannot bear to hear you speaking with such disrespect."

"But it's the way you spoke," persisted Anna. "It's the way you treated our guests."

"And like cowards they have run away," pointed out Abuela with a victorious glint in her dark eyes.

"We encouraged them to leave," said Gil. "But don't think they've left for good, Abuela. In fact, if I have my way, Lelani will be around for a long, long time."

"Are you suggesting you plan to marry that girl?" demanded Abuela.

"I'm suggesting that this is my life," he told her, "and I will live it as I think is best. And if I choose to spend my life with Lelani, there is nothing you can do to change that. So you might as well just get used to it, Abuela."

She just stared at him now.

"The same goes for me too," added Anna. "If and when I decide to get married, I will marry whomever I want to marry. And no one will stop me."

Abuela used an unladylike Spanish expression and the room became very quiet.

"And since everyone seems to be listening," continued Gil, "you may as well know that Anna and I are making our declaration of independence."

"That's right," said Anna. "No one is going to tell us who we can or cannot marry."

Now several of the cousins clapped quietly. But some of the older, more conservative relatives simply looked on with expressions that ranged from concern to disgust.

"And if any of you don't like who we chose," said Gil, "then we just won't invite you to our weddings."

Anna smiled as some of their relatives, particularly the older women, reacted as if hurt or appalled. "Like that's going to happen," she said quickly. "Naturally, we would never leave anyone out. Not that either of us is planning to get married anytime soon."

"I'm just saying," continued Gil. "If you love me, you better love the girl I'm going with too."

"Same goes for me," said Anna.

"So …" Tia Elisa came over to Anna's side with a sly look in her eye. "Let me see if you got anything on that ring finger yet?"

Anna threw back her head and laughed loudly. "Trust me, when and if that happens, you'll all be among the first to know." She glanced at her mother now. "Right?"

With a glum expression, her mom nodded. But at least she nodded, and she didn't even say anything, almost as if she were surrendering. Or perhaps it was just hopeful thinking on Anna's part. But somehow, despite all the stress and pain and tears, Anna felt that she and Gil had made a little headway tonight.

Four

Kendall Weis

"I'm not putting up with this anymore!" Kendall dropped the box that she'd been carrying and planted herself in the doorway to the garage with her hands on her hips. She stared angrily at her three housemates, wishing she'd never invited them to come live with her. Really, they were all just a big pain in the behind. What had made her think she needed them in the first place? She sat down on the garage step now and, placing her elbows on her knees, she jutted out her chin and glared at them. "Why is everyone picking on me?"

"We're not picking on you," said Lelani calmly.

"In fact, we're actually helping you," pointed out Megan. "I'd think you might be a little more appreciative."

"You act like you're helping me, but the whole time you're making mean comments."

"What mean comments?" asked Megan. She looked slightly irritated now, and Kendall knew that if she made Megan, the organizer, unhappy, this whole garage-sale idea might go by the wayside. But on the other hand, Kendall wasn't sure she cared. Why should she care? And why should she, Kendall Weis, be having a garage sale in the first place? It was nuts. She couldn't even remember why she'd let Megan talk her into it. In fact, it seemed like there were a lot of things she couldn't remember. Maybe pregnancy did that to a person. Was it possible that the child growing within her was absorbing brain cells?

"What mean comments?" asked Megan again.

"Huh?" Kendall looked blankly at her.

"You accused us of picking on you and making mean comments," Megan reminded her.

"Oh, yeah."

"Like what?" persisted Megan.

"Like what Anna said a few minutes ago. She thought I wasn't listening, but I heard her. And I may not always show it, but I do have feelings."

"I only asked why all this stuff had to come down from the attic when it's obvious that you won't be having a garage sale for at least a week or more." Anna's voice sounded irritated now. "Sorry if I offended you."

"I already told you guys." Kendall glanced over to where Megan was shoving some boxes closer together to make room. "It's all Megan's fault."

"My fault?" Megan dropped the box with a loud *thunk*.

"I hope my grandmother's china wasn't in there," snapped Kendall.

"Your grandmother kept china in the attic?"

"You never know." Kendall folded her arms across her chest, trying not to notice how her waist seemed thicker today than it had been yesterday. How was that possible? But that wasn't the only thing; now her breasts were starting to ache. Being pregnant was not for the faint of heart. And maybe it wasn't for Kendall either.

Still, there was the Matthew factor to consider. Oh, sure, he'd acted like a jerk when she informed him, but all that could change when he discovered that he was actually the father. Hopefully it would be a boy. Fathers seemed to like sons.

"So why is this all my fault, Kendall?" Megan was standing in front of Kendall now. And although her tone sounded fairly pleasant, she still looked somewhat aggravated, and she had a funny looking dark smudge of dirt on the tip of her nose, although Kendall didn't think now was the right time to mention it.

"Because you're the one who told me to get some things together for a garage sale," Kendall explained in her most patient voice.

"I didn't mean to empty the attic into the living room." Megan shook her head as she reached for the broom. "Even a child would know better than that."

"Now you're calling me a child?" Kendall felt like a pot that was beginning to boil. "Real nice."

"I'm not calling you a child," Megan backtracked. "I'm sorry. I think I'm just tired."

"Why not call her a child?" sniped Anna. "She acts like one."

Kendall whirled around and glared at Anna now. "You should talk, Princess!"

"Princess?" Anna laughed. "You are calling me princess? That's rather incongruous."

Kendall hated it when her friends used big words. It was like they wanted to trip her up. Usually she just ignored them, but sometimes she wanted to buy a dictionary—and throw it at them. "See," said Kendall. "You're proving my point. You're all mean and bossy and you all think you're better than me."

Kendall started crying. She hadn't really wanted to cry, but most of the time she couldn't help it these days. It seemed like her emotions were all over the place. She knew it had to do with being pregnant—kind of like having a constant case of PMS. But, really, why did women put up with this stuff? Why wasn't there some kind of magic pill that would make her feel better? Or maybe just make it all go away?

Lelani handed her a wrinkled tissue. "It's not used," she said.

Kendall wiped her eyes and blew her nose.

"I'm sorry," said Anna. "I didn't mean to say that." She pushed her dark curls away from her face. "Sometimes I'm just like my mom and grandma … things come pouring out of my mouth and then I'm sorry later."

Kendall nodded and sniffed. "Yeah, but I guess it was kind of true. I suppose I do act like a child sometimes. A child having a child. Pretty lame, huh?"

"Having a child might help you to … well, to grow up," suggested Megan quietly.

"You mean *if* I keep the child." Kendall sat down on the step again. "But I'm still not sure."

"Not sure about what?" asked Anna.

"About whether or not I'll have this baby."

"You mean you're still considering an abortion?" Anna frowned like she was seriously disappointed in Kendall.

"I know it's against your religion to get an abortion." Kendall sighed. "But it's my body and my choice. A woman's right to choose."

"What about the baby's right?" asked Anna.

"You mean the fetus," Kendall corrected her. She'd done some reading online. "Until the baby is born, it's called a fetus."

"It's only called a fetus when you're thinking about killing it," said Anna stubbornly.

"You're not killing it," explained Kendall, "you're terminating the pregnancy."

"What planet are you from?" demanded Anna. "You have a *baby*—an unborn child—in your womb. It is alive and well, and if you don't kill the poor child, it will probably grow up to be a beautiful human being someday." She frowned now. "Well, I guess that all depends."

"Depends on what?"

"On whether the child's mother decides to grow up first!" Anna pushed past Kendall and stomped into the house, slamming the door behind her.

"What a little hothead," said Kendall.

"Abortion is a pretty emotional issue." Megan was sweeping the garage floor now. "And not just for Catholics either."

"Yeah, yeah." Kendall waved her hands to show she was tired of this conversation. In fact, she was just plain tired, period. "Please, spare me. I know where you stand on this whole thing, Megan."

"You may know where I stand, but I have to agree with Anna. When I hear you using terminology like *fetus* and *termination*, it's all I can do not to scream. Seriously, Kendall, that's crazy. Anna is right. It's not a fetus, it's a baby. And to terminate your pregnancy is just a gentle way of saying you're killing your baby."

Kendall pressed her hands to her ears. Why did her friends—or were they her friends?—insist on torturing her like this? "Stop!" she yelled. "I can't take it."

Lelani put a hand on Kendall's shoulder. "Come on," she gently nudged Kendall toward the door to the kitchen. "Let's go inside."

Kendall just nodded, allowing Lelani to lead her into the house and then to sit her at the dining room table, where Kendall burst into fresh tears. She bent over and buried her face with her hands, sobbing almost uncontrollably. "Why is this so hard?" she muttered again and again. Finally, thinking she was alone, she looked up to see that Lelani had brought her a glass of water and was now sitting across from her.

"Do you want to talk?" asked Lelani in a quiet voice.

"I don't know." Kendall took a long swig of the water, then used the nearly disintegrated tissue to blot her eyes.

"It's obvious that you're still very conflicted about your pregnancy, Kendall."

"Obviously." Kendall tried to decipher what Lelani was saying. Conflicted meant you were in conflict, so maybe that was true.

"And you know that I know it's not easy," continued Lelani.

"I know."

"If it's any consolation, I'm still conflicted myself."

Kendall blinked. "You mean you wish you'd had an abortion?"

Lelani just shook her head. "No. That's not what I mean."

"What then?"

"Meaning I'm not sure I did the right thing to leave my child with my parents. I'm still not sure."

"Oh."

"But that's not what you need to hear."

"What do I need to hear?"

Lelani kind of smiled. "I don't honestly know. But I know what I'm going to tell you."

"What?"

Lelani folded her arms on the surface of the table and sighed. "When I got pregnant, I was in med school."

"I know. You already told me."

"Yes, let me finish. Because I was in med school, there were a lot of options for *terminating* a pregnancy, as you like to say."

"What do you call it?"

"I call it an abortion."

"That's such an ugly word."

Lelani pressed her lips together and nodded. "Yes. But it's an ugly procedure too."

"I thought you just went into a clinic and they did a quick procedure and then you left. The baby is gone. No big deal."

"That's not true. It is a big deal. It's hard on your body. And, depending on how far along you are or which procedure you have done or the skill level of the person administering the procedure, it can actually have some serious side effects or complications."

"Like what?" Kendall was not convinced. No one had told her anything like this. The sites she'd gone to online made it seem like no big deal. One site said it was similar to having a tooth pulled, only you could still eat afterward.

"Like with any type of sedated surgery, there can be complications with the anesthesia. Or there can be problems with hemorrhaging or possibly a perforation of the uterus. Or a bladder or bowel injury as a result of—"

"Enough!" cried Kendall. "You're as bad as Anna." She stared at Lelani in horror. "Seriously, what is wrong with you people?" Kendall was seized with an irrepressible urge to go lose herself in a mall. Although buying clothing was no longer much fun. Nothing fit right anymore. And she was not the least bit interested in maternity clothes. Still, that left shoes … and handbags!

"I'm sorry." Lelani stood now. "I was just trying to give you a medical perspective."

"But you were grossing me out."

"Sorry. But to be honest, from a doctor's perspective, an abortion isn't pretty."

"So you're totally opposed to abortion?"

Lelani's brow creased. "Not totally. For instance, if the woman's life was endangered, I would absolutely agree."

"What about her social life?"

"Very funny." But Lelani wasn't smiling.

"Any other reasons?"

"Of course. If it were rape or incest ... I would absolutely see it differently. Although I've heard the statistics of pregnancies as a result of rape are rare."

"So your reason for opposing abortion is more medical than religious?" Kendall felt a dash of pride for putting out what seemed a fairly intelligent question.

"It's more personal than medical."

"Huh?"

"Well, before I got pregnant, while I was in med school, I thought abortion was acceptable. Like you, I thought it was only about a woman's right to choose."

"But you changed?"

"Being pregnant changed everything." Lelani's espresso colored eyes sparkled, and not for the first time Kendall was somewhat amazed as well as slightly jealous over her beauty. And yet Lelani didn't even seem to know how gorgeous she was. "Having a baby growing inside of me made me take a second look."

"Me too," admitted Kendall. "I keep staring at myself in the mirror and I can't believe how my body is changing."

Lelani laughed. "Not like that."

Kendall waved her hand. "Yeah, I knew that. I was just joking."

"I meant I began to view abortion differently. And when the father of the baby, a man who happens to be a doctor, wanted me to *terminate* my pregnancy, I got very defensive." She shook her head. "He tried that whole bit about it being just fetal matter and the sooner you get rid of it the better."

Kendall nodded. That's exactly what Amelia had told her. She was the only one besides her roommates who knew about the pregnancy. Amelia had strongly urged Kendall to get rid of it—and to do it quickly. In fact, Amelia was one of the sources who acted like it was no big deal.

"But I did some research." Lelani's eyes lit up. "By the way, what trimester are you in?"

"Huh?"

"You know. How far along are you?"

Kendall looked up at the ceiling and attempted to calculate. "It's been about three months."

Lelani looked slightly alarmed. "You're just starting your second trimester, Kendall. That means, statistically, you're at an even greater risk if you have an abortion."

"Meaning what?"

"Meaning that the rate of complications, as well as the mortality rate, increases along with the duration of the pregnancy."

"English please."

Lelani nodded. "The longer you wait to have an abortion, not that I recommend it, the more dangerous the procedure becomes. A lot of doctors won't perform one after the first trimester."

Kendall took in a sharp breath. "You mean it's too late?"

Lelani just looked at her, then let out a long, sad sigh.

"What?"

"I just don't think you've really thought things through, Kendall."

"Duh. Would I even be in this place if I had? Some people think I'm impetuous and fun and a risk taker. But I know that some think I'm a stupid airhead. Sometimes I'm not too sure myself."

"Getting pregnant can be a serious reality check."

"You got that right." But even as Kendall said this, she realized that she didn't like reality very much. Just then Tinkerbell jumped into her lap and whined to be let out. "Well, this little baby is good training for me, right?"

Lelani nodded and stood now. "For sure."

Kendall got up and headed for the front door, then paused. "But I have one question for you, Lelani."

"Yes?"

"Why did you leave your baby with your parents in the first place?"

Lelani frowned but didn't answer.

"I mean if you knew you really didn't want to have a baby. Like if you were so certain that you didn't want to be a mother and raise a child, then why didn't you just find someone to adopt your baby? I've heard that there are millions of couples out there who can't have kids, and some will even pay good money for a baby. Why didn't you just do that instead?"

Lelani simply looked at her. But Kendall couldn't read her expression.

"I mean, if you didn't want to be reminded of the whole thing, if you wanted to be free and single and all that, which I can by the way totally understand, then why did you leave your baby with your parents? It's like you'll never get away from the whole thing. I mean you'll go home, and there's your little mistake staring you in the face. Seriously, what's the point?"

Lelani held up her hands in a hopeless gesture, and Kendall knew that she'd gotten her. Not that she'd wanted to get her. Mostly she was just plain curious. But it seemed that the brilliant Dr. Lelani Porter had just run out of answers.

Five

Megan

"I would *love* to go out tonight," Megan told Marcus when he called later that afternoon. "Anything to get away!" Then she explained about Kendall and the garage sale. "I wish I'd never opened my stupid mouth." She spoke quietly as she slipped through the still-cluttered living room and down the hallway to her bedroom. "It's like I created a monster."

Marcus chuckled. "Oh, don't take too much credit. Kendall was a monster long before you knew her."

Megan laughed as she kicked off her clogs, peeled off her dust-encrusted sweats, and sat down on her bed. "I didn't mean Kendall was a monster. It's the garage sale idea that I'm regretting."

"Yeah, I'm having a hard time imagining Princess Kendall having a garage sale."

"Try imagining how the house looks after Kendall emptied the attic. We've been trying to help her sort things out, but it's a nightmare. I must've been suffering temporary insanity when I suggested a garage sale." She flopped back onto her pillows.

"My grandmother used to be a garage-sale freak," he admitted. "And a couple times she talked me into helping her out, but as I recall garage sales are a lot of work."

"Yes. And we all know Kendall does not particularly like work."

"So, what are you going to do?"

"I told her that we could just call the Salvation Army and ask them to pick the junk up."

"And?"

"She wouldn't hear of it. Somehow she's gotten it into her head that it's all very valuable."

"Is it?"

Megan sighed. "Who knows?"

"You said it's stuff from the attic?"

"Yes. Her grandmother's things."

"And her grandmother is okay if she sells them?"

"Good question."

Marcus laughed. "Poor Megan. You had no idea what you were getting into when you connected yourself to someone like Kendall."

"Well, at least I met you." Megan smiled. The last couple of months with Marcus had been surprisingly good. Especially considering that she thought they were history before the holidays. But when he gave up his Christmas day to help serve the homeless at the mission, her opinion of him had changed considerably. Since that day, not only had he willingly attended church with her on Sundays, he had also gone with her to volunteer at the soup kitchen several times. He honestly enjoyed helping out, and she enjoyed working together with him. It was fun seeing him caringly interacting with needy people. His natural way of chatting with an unwashed, unshaved street person only made her like Marcus more. It was like they were on the same page. Or nearly.

"So you're still happy that Kendall brought us together?"

"Pretty much so." She smiled to herself.

"Okay … while you're happy about that, do you mind if ask you something?"

Megan sat up. His voice sounded somewhat serious. "What?"

"Well, I ran into an old friend from high school—Jeremy Sutter—and he told me about this church he's going to … and it sounds interesting."

"What kind of interesting?"

"Well, for one thing it's downtown, not far from the mission and soup kitchen. In fact, a lot of the members are involved in helping out with those things."

"Sort of like my church."

"Yes. But this church sounds different too."

"How?"

"Jeremy called it *postmodern,* and he said there's a focus on art and music and culture. You never quite know what to expect, he said, but it's nothing like a traditional church. Like sometimes they'll do something theatrical. Or have a slide show of art with a poetry reading. And they even have dancing—"

"They *dance* in church?" Megan tried to wrap her mind around that.

"I don't know how it is for sure, Megan. But Jeremy said it's very cool and he thought I'd like it. And the music is supposed to be really good. Anyway, he invited us to come tonight."

"Tonight? Church on Saturday night? Is it an SDA or—"

"No. I don't think it's a denomination exactly. And, according to Jeremy, tonight is more like a coffeehouse kind of gathering. They have music and somebody talks."

Megan's gut response was to say, "No way." She wanted to tell him that she had no interest in visiting another church and that she was perfectly happy in the church that her parents had belonged to for decades, the church she'd attended her whole life, the church where she'd been baptized and where she knew almost everyone by first name and they knew her. If it wasn't broken, why fix it?

But then she remembered how Marcus had been reluctant to come with her to church last fall, and how they actually broke up over this very thing. That's when she realized that she owed it to him to at least give this church, or whatever it was, a try.

"Okay," she said lightly. "It'll be interesting to see what that church is like."

"Great. I'll pick you up a little before seven."

As Megan showered and dressed, she thought about her relationship with Marcus and how it had been changing these past couple of months. In fact, they'd gotten to the place where she actually referred to him as her boyfriend. But even so, she wasn't positive that he was "the one." Not that she knew that he wasn't. The truth was she was very attracted to him. She liked almost everything about him. She always enjoyed herself when she was with him. So what was the catch? She still wasn't sure that he was a Christian. When they talked about it, he would assure her that he believed in God and believed in Christ. And he just didn't seem to think there was much else to it.

"But do you pray?" she'd asked him.

He'd shrugged and said, "I don't know. How do you define prayer?"

So she simply said, "It's just talking to God." But he still acted unsure. "Do you ever read the Bible?" she'd asked then.

"I've read *parts* of the Bible," he told her.

"But do you read it now?" she pressed. "Do you read it regularly? Do you sense God speaking to you through it?" Once again, he seemed unsure.

"Not exactly."

After that, she never brought it up again. But it had bothered her then. And it still bothered her now. More than that, it bothered her that he wanted to take her to some strange postmodern church. She wondered what her mother would think. Since she had a couple hours before Marcus would be here, she called.

"Megan," said her mother happily, "I was just thinking about you."

"Why?"

"Oh, I was going through old photos, sorting them out, boxing up the ones I thought you might like to have, as well as a few other old things."

"Wonderful." But Megan's tone was sarcastic.

"You don't want them?"

Megan laughed. "No, that's not it, Mom. I *do* want them. It's just that I don't want to hear about any dusty old things right now." Then she quickly explained about Kendall and the old boxes and junk from the attic, and how the whole house was still a mess from it.

"I think that sounds like fun!"

"Seriously?"

"Especially if the things from the attic are old. You know my favorite PBS show is *Antiques Roadshow*."

Megan nodded. "Yes, I nearly forgot."

"Do you think Kendall would like some help going through her things? I have a few books that could help her to place values and prices."

"Are you serious?"

"Certainly."

"Oh, Mom, that would be a true godsend."

"I can only give her a couple of days—and not until Wednesday and Thursday—then I'll be leaving on Friday."

"I almost forgot," said Megan. "You're going to British Columbia next weekend."

"Yes, I'm so excited. It's my first time to go up there."

"It's so great that you're traveling a lot, Mom."

She sighed. "Yes, although I'd always planned to do these trips with your father, you know, after he retired and all."

"At least you're doing them," Megan pointed out. "And I just know that Dad is happy about that. He's probably looking down from heaven, saying, 'you go, Linda!'"

"Yes, I think you're right."

There was a long pause, and Megan knew if she was going to ask her mom, she better just get it over with. "I wanted to ask you about something."

"What is it? Anything serious?"

"Well, it has to do with church. I know how you and Dad were always glad that I continued going to your church. I mean, so many other kids quit going or switched churches. And I know you guys were married there and I was—"

"Yes, Megan, I know all that. But what are you saying? Have you decided to go somewhere else?"

"No, of course not."

"Oh, what then?"

So Megan explained about Marcus's invitation and how he called it a postmodern church and how Megan wasn't too sure. "But I agreed to go tonight, just to try it out."

Mom laughed. "Well, what's wrong with that?"

"I don't know. I just didn't want you to feel badly."

"Oh, sweetheart, I think it's great that Marcus is looking for a church that he feels comfortable in."

"Meaning you don't think he's comfortable in our church?"

"No, not exactly. But he mentioned once that he doesn't really like his parents' church that much. And I sort of suspected that our church is similar."

"So?"

"So, maybe he needs something different."

"But a postmodern church?"

"As long as they worship God and believe in Jesus, really, Megan, does it matter?"

"I can't believe you're so casual about it."

"I know. I used to be such a stick-in-the-mud when it came to churches and religion. But I suppose that getting older … and losing your father … well, I suppose that changes a person."

"So you're not concerned that I might join some strange church where people dance up and down the aisles?"

"They dance in the aisle?"

Megan chuckled. "Well, I'm not really sure, but I just wondered if you'd be concerned."

"Not concerned exactly. Because I know you have a good head on your shoulders, Megan. And I know you take your relationship with God seriously. But I suppose, if you did decide to join this dancing church, well, I might like you to invite me to visit occasionally—just to see what it's really like."

"I don't think they actually dance," admitted Megan. "But Marcus said it was different."

"Sometimes different is good."

Megan considered this. "I guess so. As long as God is in the center of it."

"Marcus is a sensible guy, Megan. I can't imagine him wanting to go to some crazy church."

Megan nodded. "You're absolutely right."

"Anyway, let me know how it goes."

"I will. And I'll tell Kendall that help is on the way."

"Good. Tell Kendall to give me a call if she'd like me to drop some of those books off for her. And tell her to tune into *Antiques Roadshow* on Monday night. That can be her homework."

"That's about the only kind of work that Kendall likes to do," said Megan. "Fixing microwave meals and vegging out in front of the TV." Megan hadn't told her mom, or anyone else, about Kendall's pregnancy yet. Kendall had asked her housemates to keep it quiet. As far as Megan knew, even Kendall's own family was still in the dark. That wouldn't surprise her, since Kendall's communication with them was sparse at best. Megan's theory was that Kendall's relatives avoided her even more than she avoided them—probably because they knew she would hit them up for money again.

Megan told her mom good-bye, then went to the kitchen to fix a quick bite to eat before Marcus came. Kendall and her little dog were nowhere to be seen, but Megan guessed they were holed up in Kendall's room, probably watching one of Kendall's favorite reality TV shows.

"Going out tonight?" asked Lelani as she joined Megan in the kitchen.

Megan nodded as she swallowed a bite of leftover pizza. "You too?"

"Yes." Lelani poured a glass of water. "The condition of this house doesn't exactly entice one to stay in."

"I hear you. And, if it makes you feel better, I'm really sorry that I ever suggested this stupid garage sale."

Lelani shook her head. "Anna was having a sneezing fit and decided to go to her parents'. My guess is she'll stay the night."

"Lucky girl."

"You could always stay with your mom, couldn't you?"

Megan glanced at the garage-sale junk that was still scattered throughout the kitchen. "It'd be easier if I had a car for getting to work. But since this is all kind of my fault, I suppose I better stick it out to the end."

"I've never had or been to a garage sale," admitted Lelani. "But it seems like a lot of work for what I'm guessing isn't a lot of money."

Megan kind of laughed. "Probably. To be honest, when I suggested it to Kendall, I thought it would be something to keep her busy, and a way for her to earn a few hundred bucks—you know, to keep her collectors at bay."

"Yeah, right."

"But more than that, I thought it might make her realize that people have to work to make money. And maybe it would even inspire her to look for a real job."

"One with medical benefits."

"Wouldn't it be too late for her pregnancy?"

"Probably. But it might help out if she has complications. And at least the baby would be covered when it's born."

"Assuming it will be born."

Lelani frowned. "Yes, assuming."

Megan didn't want to talk about that now, and so she picked a grimy old metal colander out of a box on the counter. "Do you think anyone will really want to buy this?"

Lelani peered at it. "It might be collectible."

"That reminds me." Megan put it back in the box, then told Lelani about her mom's offer to help. "She's actually into this kind of stuff. And she has books and everything."

"That's great. I was wondering about the logistics of all this. I mean do you price every item, or do you just throw it out there and let people tell you how much they want to pay for things?"

"The way my mom used to do it was to clean and price everything. And then she would organize it to look like a store."

"Will she do that for Kendall?" Lelani looked hopeful.

Megan shook her head. "Unfortunately, she can only spare a couple of days."

Lelani sighed. "Too bad."

"But I promised to help Kendall, so I better not back out now."

"Kendall actually offered to cut me in on the profits if I'd keep helping her."

"She offered to cut you in?" Megan felt slightly betrayed now.

"I'm sure she'd give you a piece of the action too." Lelani picked up an old electric coffee pot. "Here, you can have this."

"Thanks a lot."

"But, seriously, maybe Kendall should give us something in return for our help." Lelani brightened. "Like a week or two of free rent?"

"Hey, that sounds good to me," admitted Megan.

Lelani looked hopeful now. "And that might make up for my week off."

"What week off?"

"Oh, I stupidly accepted a week off during spring break."

"Are you going somewhere?"

Lelani shook her head. "That's just the problem."

"Then why did you—"

"Mr. Green was being pestered by some girls for time off and he asked me if I wanted spring break and I said yes."

"I'm sure you could use a break, Lelani."

"To do what?" Lelani set her glass in the dishwasher. "In fact, that's what my coworkers asked, and I blurted that I was going home to Maui."

"Oh, that sounds lovely."

"Except that I'm not."

"Oh."

"I only said that to make them jealous."

"I'm sure it worked."

"Yes. It worked on them, but now I'm stuck with a week off, no pay, and no place to go."

"Why don't you go home to Maui?"

Lelani's brow creased. "You know, I've actually been thinking about it. And Gil has been encouraging me to go."

"Why don't you?" Megan said earnestly. "You've said how much you'd like to see Emma. Why not just use that week to go over there. All it would cost you is airfare."

Lelani nodded without answering.

"Seriously, Lelani. It's like it's meant to be. You have the time off. And didn't you say once that you have an open-ended return fare ticket?"

"To get back there. But then I wouldn't have the fare to come back here."

"Oh. Right."

Lelani's eyes brightened. "But it would be so good to see Emma."

"Then do it!" Megan grabbed Lelani by the arm. "Come on, just do it!"

Now Lelani looked directly at Megan. "I'll tell you what, I'll do it if you'll come with me."

"Me?"

"Yes!" Lelani looked excited now. "You're such a strong person, Megan. If you would come with me, I think I could handle it."

"Seriously?"

"Absolutely."

Megan considered this. Spring break in Maui didn't sound half bad. And she knew she could afford it. She still had money in her savings from her dad.

"Will you come?" begged Lelani. "Please?"

"I'm not sure."

"All you'll need is airfare. We'll stay at my parents'. They have a separate guesthouse and everything. It's right on the beach and—"

"Yes!" said Megan eagerly. "I'll come."

Lelani threw her arms around her and hugged her tightly. "Thank you! Thank you!" And then Gil was there to pick up Lelani, and Megan was left to wonder at what she'd just agreed to do. Still, Maui in March … how bad could it be?

Six

Lelani

"You seem in good spirits tonight," said Gil as he helped Lelani into the cab of his pickup.

She just smiled, watching as he hurried back around to the driver's side and hopped in. Then he turned and looked into her eyes. "I was worried that you'd be mad at me."

"Why?" She continued to smile.

"Why?" He frowned. "Remember last night? My grandmother?"

Lelani just laughed. "Oh, that's over and done, Gil. Anna filled me in on what happened afterward, and I think that it's all for the best. In fact, I'd been trying to come up with a way to lay all my cards on the table. Your grandmother just helped me."

"If it's any consolation, my dad and grandpa think you're wonderful. They loved how you stood up to Abuela and just spoke the truth. Most people in our family are afraid of her."

"Including you and Anna?"

"Not me. I've always been able to wrap my grandmother around my finger. But Anna, well, that's a different story. Still, I think it helped her to see your boldness. She stood up to all of them after you and Edmond made your getaway."

"Good for Anna." Now Lelani frowned.

"What's wrong?"

"I just hope … well, that I can be that strong when I stand up to my own parents."

"And is that happening any time soon?"

"Actually …" Lelani told him about her plans to go to Maui for spring break. "And I couldn't have done it if Megan hadn't agreed to go too."

Now Gil looked slightly hurt as he started the engine.

"I needed someone to help me be stronger," she told him. But she could tell that wasn't helping. "And I would've asked you, Gil," she said.

"Really?"

"But my parents …" She shook her head. "They're a little old-fashioned."

Gil sort of smiled now. "Oh, I wouldn't know anything about that."

"No, I figured you wouldn't." She sighed. "But it's going to be hard enough to go back there and figure out this thing with … Emma. But taking my boyfriend—" She stopped herself now.

"It's okay," he said eagerly. "You can call me your boyfriend."

"It's just that I've never done that before."

He frowned again. "And you don't want to now?"

"That's not it."

"You're just not as into me as I'm into you?"

"No." She turned and looked at him as he drove. "No, that's not it at all."

There was a long silence as Gil drove toward the city. Lelani bit her lip as she struggled over what it was she wanted to say. And yet it felt like the words were tied into tight little twisted knots and wedged inside of her. Even if she could unleash them, she knew she had no idea how they would come out or what they would even mean.

"Sorry," he said as he slowed down for a stoplight. "I didn't mean to pressure you."

She reached over and laid her hand on his arm. "That's not it, Gil. It's just that I still have so many things to figure out. So much baggage. Sometimes it's hard for me to know how I feel about anything."

"Including me?"

She took in a deep breath, centering herself, preparing herself to be honest with him. "This is how I feel about you, Gil: You are the best friend I have ever had. And I am continually grateful for your friendship. You mean more to me than I thought was even possible."

"Honestly?" He brightened now.

"Honestly." That was the truth. And it felt good to *speak* the truth. If only it was always so easy to *know* the truth.

⋙●⋘

Sunday afternoon, the roommates continued trying to sort, clean, and organize all the junk that Kendall had retrieved from the attic. But Kendall, as usual, was dragging her heels.

"I'm tired," she complained as Lelani brought yet another box to where Kendall had been posted at the kitchen sink. Her job was to wash, dust, or wipe down the objects that seemed worthy of putting in the garage sale. But the piles on the dirty side seemed to be growing more quickly than the piles on the clean side.

"We're all tired," Lelani pointed out. "And everyone except you has to go to work tomorrow, Kendall. So don't complain."

"Besides, this is your garage sale," Megan reminded her.

"But it was your idea," protested Kendall.

"Then maybe I should take a cut from the profits," Megan threatened. And that seemed to quiet Kendall. At least for the moment.

Megan returned to the garage, and Lelani picked up a wet rag and began washing an old kerosene lamp that was blackened on the inside and covered with dust and grime on the outside. But it had a nice shape to it and, as far as Lelani could see, no cracks. "This lamp is kind of pretty," she said to Kendall, who was using the sink sprayer to clean an encrusted metal object that Lelani couldn't even recognize.

"Pretty ugly, you mean?"

"Whatever." Lelani continued to scrub.

"Maybe if you rub it hard enough a genie will appear," teased Kendall.

"And I would wish for what?"

"A million dollars."

"Why settle for just a million?" asked Lelani.

"You're right. A billion. That should last me awhile."

Lelani didn't say anything.

"I know you think I'm stupid."

"I never said that."

"But you do."

"What makes you think that?"

"Because you're so smart. You went to school to be a doctor and it sounds like you could have made it through." Kendall made a face now. "Except that in a way you were as dumb as me. You got pregnant."

"So you think getting pregnant is sign of a lesser intellect?"

"Back in high school, I always heard that smart girls didn't get knocked up."

"That's a lovely way of putting it."

"Okay then, pregnant."

"What about our mothers? Were they stupid?"

"Not if they found themselves a rich man first. That's what my mom did. Otherwise, I'm sure my dad wouldn't have married her."

"Are you saying your mom got pregnant in order to get your dad to marry her?"

"Oh, they don't talk about it, but when my parents celebrated their twenty-fifth anniversary—years ago—I realized that my oldest sister's twenty-fifth birthday was only five months away. I was in grade school then, but it didn't take long for me to figure that one out."

"And your point is?"

"I don't know." Kendall pushed a strand of blond hair away from her face. "I guess I'm just rambling."

"So how are you feeling?" Lelani began carefully. "About the baby I mean?"

"Besides fat?"

"Yes, besides fat."

"And besides tired?"

"Yes." Lelani grew irritated. "I mean how are you feeling in regard to carrying your baby to term?"

"You mean am I still thinking about terminating my pregnancy?"

"Yes."

"I don't know."

"Oh."

"I thought I should go in and meet with someone tomorrow."

"Meet with someone?"

"You know, like Planned Parenthood or one of those places that doesn't cost much. I don't have any health insurance and I can't really ask my parents to help me out with this."

"Oh." Lelani took in a deep breath. "And what will you ask about when you go to—wherever it is you decide to go?"

"I don't know. But I heard they offer counseling."

"So what will you tell them?"

"That I'm not happy about this. That I'm too young to be a mother. That I don't like what it's doing to my body, not to mention my social life."

Lelani set down the kerosene lamp with a thud.

"Careful there," warned Kendall. She looked at the lamp. "Hey, that looks really nice. Do you think it might be valuable?"

Lelani considered this. "Well, you didn't think it was worth much before I cleaned it, did you?"

"Not really." Kendall picked up the lamp and looked more closely. "But this looks like a different lamp."

"Some things increase in value when we perceive them as such."

Kendall frowned and set down the lamp. "Couldn't you speak in plain English, please?"

Lelani reached over and turned off the water. She handed Kendall a dishtowel and said, "Come here, I want to show you something." Then she led Kendall to her bedroom and set her down on the comfy rocker.

"Hey, this is more like it," said Kendall as she sighed and leaned back.

Meanwhile, Lelani turned on her laptop. She Googled "photos of unborn babies" and waited for some Web sites to appear. Then she went to one and searched for a photo of a twelve-week-old baby in the womb. Lelani had seen images like this before, but this photo was so clear, so sweet, that she couldn't help but gasp. "Oh, my!"

"What?" demanded Kendall. "What are you doing?"

"Have you ever seen photos of unborn babies?"

"Huh?"

Lelani put the computer in Kendall's lap and pointed to the image. "See those fingers, those toes, that little leg?"

Kendall just nodded.

"That's what your baby looks like right now."

"My baby?" Kendall looked puzzled. "Right now?"

"These are photos of babies that are almost exactly the same age as the baby that's growing inside of you, Kendall. Look at how well formed they are. Isn't it amazing?"

Kendall was looking. And she did seem amazed. She just stared and stared and, without saying a word, Lelani clicked onto more images. "Aren't they beautiful?" Lelani said finally.

Kendall just nodded. "They look like tiny people."

"They are tiny people. They're babies who are growing and developing and getting ready to be born."

Kendall didn't say anything, but she reached down and touched her stomach. "I've never seen pictures like that," she admitted.

Lelani removed the laptop and sat on her bed. "So, do you see why Megan and Anna and I have a hard time when you call it a fetus, or fetal tissue?"

Kendall nodded again. Now she was rocking gently in the chair with both hands on her stomach. "I just never imagined anything like that, Lelani. I remember girls looking at pictures like that in school, like in biology or something, but I was always kind of grossed out by them. I never wanted to look. Like I thought ignorance was bliss, you know?"

"Not exactly." Lelani sighed. "I've always been fascinated by science and things like that."

"One of those brainy girls."

"Yeah, one of those brainy girls who got pregnant."

Kendall smiled. "Yeah, whatever."

"So, do you still want to talk to someone about having an abortion?"

Kendall just kept rocking now, looking down at her midsection as if trying to see the baby tucked within her. "I don't know."

"I mean it is your decision," said Lelani. "And I can't tell you what to do. But I just think it needs to be an informed decision. You know?"

"Yeah." Kendall stood slowly now, as if she was very tired. "I guess so."

"Why don't you go have a rest?" she suggested.

"Really?"

"Yeah. You've worked pretty hard. I think I can finish up the things in the kitchen."

"Thanks."

Lelani knew that Kendall was still torn. But maybe those photos would help her to see things differently, the way that lamp, which had looked worthless to Kendall, suddenly appeared valuable when it was clean and shiny. Not so much different from a so-called fetus of unformed tissues compared to a real live baby with delicate fingers and toes.

"Let me guess," said Megan when she discovered Lelani was working by herself in the kitchen. "Kendall wimped out again?"

"I told her to take a break." Then Lelani told Megan about the online photos.

"Wow, that was a great idea," said Megan. "Did it change her mind?"

"Not yet. But I don't think it hurt anything."

"I told my mom about going to Maui," Megan said as the two of them cleaned up the remaining items in the kitchen.

Lelani nodded. A part of her was glad to hear Megan's enthusiasm. But another part of her wished that she hadn't invited Megan. That way it would be easier to forget about the whole thing.

"My mom's travel agent is trying to find me a good deal on airfare. She wanted to know which airlines you fly on."

"Hawaiian. They used to have a direct flight from Portland to Maui, but I think it's through Honolulu now. Then you take an interisland flight."

"So should we book our flights together?" asked Megan eagerly.

"Yes." Lelani nodded. "Of course."

"My mom said the sooner we book them, the better the rate will be. How about if I give her agent your phone number?"

"That's perfect."

"I'm really looking forward to this," gushed Megan. "I mean I wasn't so sure at first, but I realized that was nuts. This is going to be great." Now Megan's face clouded over slightly. "Except for one thing."

"What's that?"

"I hope I can get time off. I mean I've only been there six months."

"Oh." Lelani wasn't sure whether to feel worried or relieved. "So, when will you know for sure?"

"I plan to ask tomorrow. I just hope that Cynthia is there."

"Because Vera would say no?"

"It's always hard to predict what Vera might say or do."

"Well, let me know how it goes."

"I won't book my flight until I know I have the time off," Megan assured her.

"But it's spring break," Lelani reminded her. "Flights might already be booked."

Megan frowned. "Well, I'm praying that's not the case."

Lelani just nodded, but she wondered if that was a prayer that God would answer. Or, if he did, if he would say no. Lelani wasn't used to that kind of an answer. "I'll be praying too," she told Megan.

"Good," said Megan. "If we're meant to go, God will kick open the doors."

"And if we're not …"

Megan sighed. "Well, I hope that's not the case. But if it is … well, then there'll be a reason for it."

When Lelani went to bed that night, she did pray. Her prayer probably sounded vastly different from Megan's. Megan was probably praying with optimism and hope. But Lelani knew that her own prayer was draped in anxiety and dread. She just hoped that God wouldn't be confused by these two contradictory prayers originating from beneath the same roof. But surely God was much smarter than that!

Seven

Kendall

Kendall had come to like Sunday evenings, because her housemates were usually home and they often rented a new-release flick and sat around in their pajamas to eat junk food and watch it. It reminded her of high-school days, and she found the whole thing very comforting. Especially after she discovered she was pregnant and her social life (rather dating life) had steadily deteriorated. Not that she'd told any of her friends, but it was like they could sense something had changed. Or maybe they just noticed that she'd developed an unattractive muffin top over the waistband of her jeans. Not that she was wearing jeans these days. They were all too small. She'd moved on to sweats.

It was almost eight thirty and Kendall had on her favorite *I Love Lucy* pajamas, and Tinkerbell had on her pink bed jacket, the popcorn was popped, and the chick flick was ready to roll. But where was everyone? Then she remembered that Anna was at her parents—thanks to Megan's brilliant garage-sale idea—an idea that had gone south just a few hours ago, shortly after Kendall had gotten up from her nap. As usual, Megan blamed everything on Kendall: the garage sale and Anna's allergies and the messed-up house and probably even global warming. Naturally this all resulted in a big old fight.

"What do you mean you never called your grandmother?" Megan demanded after Kendall let that little kitty out of the bag. "You promised you would do that, Kendall. It's not like I've asked you to do a lot. You could at least have done that. Here we are going through all this junk, up to our eyeballs in dust and grime, and it's entirely possible that your grandmother doesn't want any of it sold. Maybe she's willed it to someone or promised a museum or whatever. Seriously, why haven't you called her yet?"

"I just haven't gotten around to it," Kendall had answered casually.

Then Megan, acting like a total idiot, grabbed a pad and pen, drew a big circle, and wrote the words *to it* inside the line. "Here," she'd said hotly as she shoved the paper at Kendall.

"Huh?" Kendall studied the silly note.

"Now you've got *a round to it*."

"Very funny." Kendall crumpled the paper, then made a comment that she now regretted. "I can't believe this is all you guys have gotten done," she'd said to distract them from her grandmother, which was really none of their business anyway. "At this rate we won't have this garage sale until next Christmas."

That was all it took. Tempers flared, words were said, Kendall burst into tears, but they didn't even take pity. And the stupid fight resulted in both Lelani and Megan totally bailing on her. Acting like they were the ones who'd been offended, they washed their hands and grabbed their coats and bags and, just like that, they abandoned Kendall. Like they expected her to work alone, cleaning and sorting all that junk with absolutely no help from them. "Well, fine!" Kendall had snapped at them, acting like she didn't care and telling them that she didn't need their help and could handle the whole thing by herself. But after about an hour, she had given up on it. Not just the cleaning and sorting, but the garage sale too. Really, what was the use? And now the house was

still cluttered with all that junk—the junk that would need to be hauled
back up to the attic. Maybe Kendall could hire someone. Not that she
had money. Oh, she'd think about that later.

As she dug into a pint of chocolate-mint ice cream that had Anna's
name written on tape across the lid, she vaguely wondered where Lelani
and Megan had taken off to. It was past five when they left, and a lot of
things closed by then. But as she polished off the last bite, disposing of the
evidence and rationalizing that Anna was gone now anyway so why should
she care, she figured Megan and Lelani would return before long. After all,
what could you really do without a car? Although there were the buses and
the metro. Not that Kendall had ever stooped to use them. Just the idea of
sitting on one of those grimy seats with strangers was rather frightening.
Still, she expected that they'd be home soon.

One good thing about her roommates, so far anyway, was that they
didn't tend to hold grudges. Not like some of her friends, or even family, who could stay mad for weeks, months, even years. And so Kendall
really expected Megan and Lelani to pop in at any moment. They'd
probably even apologize, and if she was lucky they'd have food with
them.

But finally it was nine and Kendall went ahead and turned on the
movie. She'd go ahead and start it without them. They'd be sorry when
they got here to see it was half over and they'd missed out. But watching the movie by herself with Tinker was just not that fun. Besides, it
turned out to be pretty lame, which was not all that surprising since
Megan had picked it out. Eventually Kendall gave up on it, turned the
TV off, and went to her room.

As usual, her room was messy. Clothes that were too small were
tossed everywhere. Shoes and handbags—even designers ones that she'd
paid big bucks for—were tossed around like broken toys she'd gotten

tired of. And, really, that's how it felt. She'd go out and buy some delectable designer piece and feel like she was queen of the world. But just a week later, sometimes within the same day, she'd see that pricey item and simply shrug and wonder why she'd felt it was so wonderful before. And now it was just part of the junk that was messing up her room. She picked up a used potty pad, carefully wadded it up, and took it to the bathroom to dispose of. That way she wouldn't have to smell it.

Of course, the bathroom was nearly as messy as her room, and already the trash can was overflowing with puppy pads, but Kendall just stuffed another on top. It was no surprise that the bathroom looked this bad. Anna, the neat freak, had been gone for a couple of days now—long enough for Kendall to leave her mark. Not that she particularly liked her mark anymore. If anything, she'd grown to appreciate Anna's cleaning skills. And sometimes she even attempted to imitate her.

But why bother now? Besides the bathroom and bedroom, her whole house was messed up. Even her friendships with her housemates seemed pretty messed up. Her life was equally messed up. And at this rate, it could only get worse.

Kendall took out a bottle of pills that her shrink had prescribed for her when she thought she was having anxiety attacks at night. She'd never been the depressed, gloomy type, but as she looked at those little blue pills, she wondered how hard it would be to end it all. Could she even do something like that? Or, what if she attempted *something like that* and she messed up? It wouldn't surprise her—what hadn't she messed up lately? Or what if she survived an overdose and somehow messed up the baby? Not that she planned on keeping the baby.

But what if the baby really was Matthew's? She was 99 percent certain that it was. And what if things for him changed? What if, like gossip rags predicted, his marriage to Heidi ultimately failed? And what if he got back together with Kendall only to discover that his precious son had been damaged by her foiled suicide attempt? And what if he got mad and dumped her as a result? How would she feel then?

She shoved the bottle back into the medicine cabinet and slammed the door so hard that the old leaded mirror in the front of it cracked right down the middle. Great, now she would have seven years bad luck. It figured.

Kendall looked at herself in the damaged mirror. The crack went right down the middle of her face, making her nose look twice as big and slightly deformed. She leaned forward and stared at herself with a sense of twisted amusement. And although she normally had no sense of metaphor or irony except for what she'd picked up during her brief stint as a film major, she wondered if this split face in the mirror might be a true reflection of who she was.

"Or not!" She bent down and scooped up Tinkerbell, turned off the light, and went to bed.

Eight

Anna

Monday morning, Anna decided that it was better to breathe dust and suffer an asthma attack at Kendall's than to remain at her parents' home for one more night. Oh, her dad was fine. But her mother, still under the influence of Abuela Castillo, was another story. Anna had assumed that things in her parents' home would calm down and return to normal when her grandparents went to stay with another one of their lucky children. But Anna had been wrong. The more time Anna's mother spent with Abuela, the more Mama came down on Anna. And since the grandparents were staying for another full week, Anna knew she needed to run for her life. She'd gotten up early and packed her things, but to her surprise, her mother was up even earlier. And she had cooked breakfast!

"I don't see why you are so sensitive," her mother said as Anna shoveled in another spoonful of *huevos revueltos*. "I was only asking."

"Asking?" Anna swallowed the bite. "You and Abuela ask questions like the Spanish Inquisition."

"Anna." Her mother frowned at her. "Where is your respect?"

"It's the truth. The way you treat Edmond is humiliating."

"I only asked out of concern for the children."

"What children?" Anna glared at her mother.

"If you were to marry Edmond, you would surely have children."

"Who said I'm going to marry Edmond?"

Her mother smiled in relief. "Hopefully that won't happen."

Anna wiped her mouth with her napkin. "I don't know, Mama. The more you try to push me away from Edmond, the more I'm drawn to him." She took a quick sip of coffee. "I'm thinking maybe I'll run away and elope with him tonight." Anna pointed to her suitcase by the door.

"Anna Consuela Maria Mendez!"

"See what you drive me to do, Mama?"

"I know you're joking with me." Her mother made a sad expression. "But it's not kind, Anna. It's not like you."

"Do you think you're being kind when you say mean things about Edmond?"

"I only asked where your children would go to church, Anna. Why is that such a mean thing? Young people in love, they forget the practical things. And I heard Dr. Phil say that there are only a few things that destroy a marriage." Her brows drew together as she held up one finger. "I think the first one was money. And I'm not sure about all of them, but I know that religion was in there."

"And how about meddlesome in-laws?" asked Anna. "Was that on the list?"

"So you are thinking of marrying Edmond?"

"No." Anna shook her head as she stood up. "I'm not thinking of marrying anyone at the moment. I'm thinking about not being late for work."

"You think about what I'm saying to you, Anna. If you don't ask these questions early on, you find out the answers too late."

"Yeah, yeah." Anna was slipping her coat on now.

"Remember your Tio Roberto. He married that Baptist girl.

Everything seemed just fine until they had children. Then she wanted to take them to her church. He wanted them to go to his. It got ugly, Anna."

"I know, Mama." Anna reached for her suitcase. "And it didn't help that Tio Roberto was having an affair with Vanessa either."

Her mother looked shocked. "Who told you that?"

"Everyone in the family knew about it."

"But you were just a child."

"Even as a child, I had ears, Mama." Anna leaned over and kissed her mother's cheek. *"Adiós!"*

Anna sighed as she slipped behind the wheel of her little red Cooper. Ah, freedom. What had she been thinking of to go back home again? And even if she had to get a particle mask and one of those electric air-filtering machines for her bedroom, it would be worth it to escape her mother's tirades.

Of course, Anna knew this latest paranoia over grandchildren and where they would go to church was partially Anna's fault. She'd let the cat out of the bag last night when she told her mother that she had a wedding to attend the following weekend. And she'd only mentioned this in order to escape her cousin Eva's baby shower. It would be the third baby shower since Christmas, and Anna couldn't bear to sit and watch another one of her pregnant female relatives opening another pastel package containing bibs or booties or baby blankets. Enough was enough.

"Who's wedding?" her mother had asked with suspicion.

"Edmond's mother," Anna had casually informed her. "It's a small, intimate evening wedding and I feel honored to be included."

"I didn't know that Edmond's mother was single. Did Edmond's father die?"

"No. Edmond's father is alive and well in Pasadena."

"Oh?" Her mother's brows had arched sharply, a warning that things could get ugly.

"Edmond's parents divorced when he was quite young. His father remarried years ago and Edmond has a couple of half siblings."

Her mother looked even more surprised now. But the reason Anna had disclosed this much was to paint Edmond's mother in a better light. Unfortunately, it didn't seem to be working. "Anyway, Betsy—that's Edmond's mother—has been single for a long time. She put all of her energy into working and raising Edmond on her own."

Anna's mother nodded with a slight look of compassion. "She sounds like a strong woman."

Anna smiled. "She is. And now she has finally met the love of her life. A very nice man named Phillip Goldstein." Okay, as soon as it was out, Anna wished she'd had the foresight to withhold a little information.

"Goldstein? Isn't that Jewish?"

"Yes, Mama. It's Jewish. Are you prejudiced against Jewish people now?"

"No, no, of course not." Her mother's brow creased deeply.

"Well, good."

"So … is Edmond Jewish too?"

"No. Edmond is Episcopalian."

"Oh? Edmond is Episcopalian and his stepfather is Jewish? Is his mother perhaps Greek Orthodox?"

"Actually, I don't know. But it seems that she is Episcopalian too."

"But she will be changing to Jewish now?"

"It's not like that, Mama."

"What is it like then?"

"I don't know. But you make way too much of it."

Her mother sighed then. "Perhaps you're right. At least they will have no children."

"Actually, Phillip has a son, a sweet kid named Ben, who's eleven or twelve."

"So is this Ben Jewish too?"

"I would assume."

"Unless he is confused by his stepmother's religion, and then perhaps he will convert to Episcopalian."

"Probably not."

"But don't you see, mi'ja? You hurt your children when you bring two different religions into the home." And so it had gone on. Her mother ranting and lecturing about culture and religion and values and children until even Anna's dad could take it no more. Both he and Anna had gone to bed early to escape the endless tirade. But Anna's poor dad was still subjected, because Anna could hear them arguing into the night—just one more reason for Anna to leave in the morning. It was bad enough to suffer her mother's temper for her own choices, but it seemed unfair her father should suffer as well.

To be fair, Anna suspected that having Abuela Castillo around had brought out the worst in her mother. It was as if her mother was regressing. And the less Anna saw of it, the happier she would be. It was her intention to stay away for a while. Or at least until the final farewell gathering for her grandparents next Sunday. That is, if she was invited. After the rumors circulated that she was skipping Eva's baby shower to attend her boyfriend's mother's Jewish wedding, well, who knew what might happen? Maybe they would excommunicate Anna from the family. But probably not.

Nine

Megan

Megan practiced her speech in her head as she walked to work on Monday morning. Of course, if Cynthia was there, which was unlikely since she was starting a big job up in Astoria this week, there would be no need. But if it was just Vera, Megan would have to do her best to convince the woman that she deserved some time off. Not that she expected it to be paid time off, since she hadn't been there a year yet. But she really wasn't making that much money and, besides, who would be into decorating during spring break? Moms would have kids underfoot. Grandmas would be planning excursions with their grandchildren. Really, it just made good sense. Right?

"Wrong," Vera told her as she stepped into her private office, firmly closing the door behind her.

"No go?" asked Ellen. Naturally, the receptionist had heard the whole pitiful thing.

"No." Megan sighed. "I guess I'll have to call Cynthia."

"Well, don't call her until after lunch. She told me she plans to be in a consultation with the homeowners all morning."

"Thanks for the heads-up."

"Did you hear it's another ten-thousand-square-foot house?" Ellen shook her head. "What's up with these rich people building these huge houses? Haven't they heard that the new rage is to build green?"

Megan smiled. "It's hard to imagine a house of that size being green, but I suppose it's possible."

Ellen glanced over to where Vera's door was still shut, then lowered her voice. "Don't say you heard it from me, Megan, but I think Vera is planning to take some time off about the same time you were asking for. Maybe that's why she was so stubborn."

"Or maybe she just can't help herself." Megan considered how peaceful the office would be with Vera gone for a week. It almost tempted Megan to stick around this place in her absence. That in itself would feel like a real break. Except that Megan really wanted to go with Lelani to Maui. And she'd promised. No, she couldn't give up. Not without a good fight.

Megan was relieved to get her work done without interruption. Monday always meant lots of ordering and checking on orders and paperwork, but Megan managed to get it all done by noon. She was just getting ready to head out to meet her mom for lunch when Vera stopped her.

"I just thought you'd like to know that I spoke to Cynthia, Megan."

"Oh?" Megan slipped on her jacket and waited.

"I told her you wanted to take spring break off."

"You did?" Megan frowned. Which way was this going to go?

Vera made a catty smile. "Cynthia agreed with me. We'll need you in the office since I'll be gone that same week. Sorry."

"So there's no chance?"

"No. And, if you'll recall, your employment agreement stipulates that you won't have any vacation time until you've been here a full year."

"You mean if I stay a full year," snapped Megan. "Now, if you'll excuse me, this is my lunch break." And, not waiting for a response from Vera, Megan walked out and stomped down the steps and down the walk.

"You don't look very happy."

Megan turned to see Margie at her regular post. "Hey, I didn't see you this morning," she said. "Is everything okay?"

Margie smiled and looked up at the sky. "Everything's fine. And if the rain holds off until nighttime, I'll be happy as a clam." Her brow furrowed now. "But you don't look happy as a clam. What's wrong?"

Megan had fished several ones from her purse. She handed them to Margie and just shook her head. "I wanted some time off, but it's not going to happen."

Margie thanked her for the money and tucked it inside her oversized man's parka. "That's why my life is so perfect." She smiled to reveal her missing tooth. "I don't have to ask anyone for time off."

Megan couldn't help but laugh. "That's true. Sorry to run, I'm meeting my mom."

"Tell your mother hello for me."

Megan nodded but didn't point out that Margie had never met her mom.

"Sorry, I'm late." Megan found her mom already seated at a quiet corner table.

"I took the liberty of ordering for you," Mom told her. "Salmon chowder and a garlic bread stick."

"Yum!" Megan slipped off her jacket and sat down. "You know what I like."

"And blackberry cobbler for us to split for dessert."

"I should probably pass on the cobbler if I want to look good in my swimming suit." Megan frowned. "Not that it's going to matter."

"What do you mean?"

"I might not get to go to Maui after all."

"Why not?"

"I asked for time off, and Vera told me no."

"But that's just Vera, Megan, what about—"

"Then Vera called Cynthia and told her why I shouldn't be given time off."

"Oh." Mom's brows lifted slightly. "And why was that?"

"Because Vera is already taking that week off. And because I haven't been there a year yet, and the employment agreement says no vacation until you've been there for a full year."

"But isn't that referring to a paid vacation? You weren't asking for paid time off, were you?"

"No." Megan brightened. "That's true."

"So, do you think Vera misunderstood?"

Megan rolled her eyes. "Probably not. But she might've made Cynthia misunderstand."

"So are you going to talk to Cynthia?"

"She's out of town until Thursday, and it sounds like she's pretty busy with a huge estate up in Astoria. I hate to be a pain."

"Well, I wouldn't wait longer than Friday to book your flight. Phyllis, my travel agent, said it's already hard to find two seats on the same plane. And I'm sure you and Lelani will want to fly out there together, won't you?"

"Of course." Megan paused as the waiter set their orders on the table. She and her mom bowed their heads for a quick blessing.

"I'm just saying you and Lelani should get your flights reserved as soon as possible, Megan."

"I know you're right. Especially for Lelani's sake. I'd hate to make her wait because of me and then end up not getting a flight herself." Megan shook her head as she stuck her spoon in the soup. "And now I have a confession."

"A confession?" Mom leaned over with interest.

"Yes, I snarled at Vera before I left the design firm. I acted like I might quit before my year is up." Megan took a bite, savoring the sweet flavors of salmon and cream.

"But, surely, you're not going to quit, are you?" Mom looked concerned. "You know what a tough job market it is out there. And really, it's a good job for you, sweetie."

"Good? In what way exactly?"

"Well, I think it'll look good on your resume."

"Like that matters."

"It does matter if you want to look for another job. They say that it's better to search for your next job while you're still employed."

"Who says?"

"Oh, you know, those talking heads on TV."

"Yes, yes, those brilliant talking heads."

"But I do think it's true, Megan. If I were interviewing someone for a job, I'd be more impressed if she was still employed. That would say that the person had come to me because she wanted to work for me, not because she desperately needed the work."

"That makes sense."

"And what about teaching jobs? Have you been putting in applications?"

"I heard that it was still too soon."

"Who told you that?"

"A teacher friend. She said they don't start really looking until after spring break."

"I'll bet there are exceptions, Megan. Like what if a teacher gets sick? Or has a baby? Or is forced to move? You never know. If I were you, I'd start looking around. You know what they say about the early bird."

Megan made a face. "But I don't even like worms."

"Very funny."

"Are you still planning on coming to help Kendall this week?"

"Sure."

"Because you might want to call her first."

"Why's that?"

So Megan explained about yesterday's fight and how Kendall announced this morning that she was scrapping the idea of a garage sale altogether.

"Do you think she meant it?"

"Who knows? I mean Kendall is pretty unpredictable. She often says one thing and then does something totally different."

"But you said she's broke and needs money."

"That's true. But Kendall doesn't exactly look at things like bills and working and responsibilities in the same way we do."

Mom made a wry smile. "That can get a girl in trouble."

"You got that right." Okay, Megan was thinking about the pregnancy as much as finances, but she'd been loyal not to mention Kendall's pregnancy to anyone, including her mom.

"Well, I'll give her a call and see what we can do."

"Thanks. And I'll warn you, she's a little bummed right now."

"Kendall?" Mom looked surprised. "She's usually such an upbeat person. I can't imagine her being too down."

"And she'll probably get even more depressed when she finds out that Lelani and I are going to Maui."

"She doesn't know?"

"No. We haven't told her or Anna yet. Anna will be home tonight, though. She called me before work. Apparently she and her mom have been into it."

"That's too bad. I hate it when mothers and daughters don't get along."

"Well, if you knew Anna's mother, you'd probably understand why. Right now, she's picking on Anna's boyfriend. She's worried they'll get married and the kids will be all mixed up because Anna is Catholic, Edmond is Episcopal, and his new stepdad is Jewish."

Her mom laughed. "That does sound like an interesting mix."

"According to Mrs. Mendez, it's a formula for disaster or World War III."

"Speaking of boyfriends and religion, how was Marcus's church?"

Megan broke her garlic stick in half. "It was actually rather nice. I was pleasantly surprised. The music was a jazz group. And the meeting was like a coffeehouse, a very cool coffeehouse, that was set up in the basement of this beautiful stone church in the old part of the city."

"Sounds interesting."

"It was. The guy who spoke was in his early thirties and has been a missionary in Latvia the past ten years. But he wasn't the least bit stuffy. Really, it was a very cool experience."

"So you think you'll go back there again?"

"I think so." Megan peered at her mom. "You really don't mind?"

Mom smiled. "Not at all, Megan. I think it would be great for Marcus, and you, to find a church that you feel comfortable in. Isn't that what it's all about?"

"I guess."

"And you can always come back to your old church to visit."

"And you can visit this church—I mean if we start going regularly. To be honest, we didn't really talk about it. But I could tell that Marcus liked being there. I've never seen him listen to a preacher with so much interest."

"That's wonderful."

"It's making me see him in a different light." Megan wondered how much she wanted to divulge to her mother.

"Aren't you glad you didn't give up on him?"

Megan smiled. "Yeah. Thanks for encouraging me not to, Mom. It seems like you were right."

"Well, time will tell. And what does Marcus think about you going to Maui?"

"He doesn't know yet."

"Do you think he'll mind?"

"He'll probably be jealous." Megan frowned. "Well, if I even get to go, that is."

"But if you do go, I'm sure he'll understand that a big part of why you're going is to provide moral support for Lelani."

"That and to have some good plain fun."

"Well, anyone who doesn't have fun in Maui shouldn't be allowed there."

"That's right. And, while we're on the subject … if I do get to go, do you think I can borrow your luggage? Or will you be off on some big new trip by then?"

"No big trip for me after we get back from Victoria. Although Phyllis just told me about a European tour that sounds tempting, but that wouldn't be until next fall."

Megan's lunch hour was winding down. "So, you'll give Kendall a call then?"

"I will."

Megan paused as she reached for her bag. She was tempted to tell her mom about Kendall's pregnancy simply as a forewarning about her mood swings but stopped herself. No, she would continue to respect Kendall's privacy. "Thanks for lunch, Mom." Megan gave her mom a hug. "I better get back before Vera thinks that I've really quit."

"And don't forget to start putting out teaching applications," her mom reminded her. "I really don't think it's too soon."

Megan brightened. "You're right. Hey, there could be a disgruntled art teacher out there right now who has suddenly decided to give up his job and take a pilgrimage to Tibet where he will study to become a monk."

Mom grinned. "It could happen."

As Megan walked back to work, she thought maybe it could happen. And maybe pigs could fly too!

"Is Vera back from lunch yet?" Megan asked Ellen as she hung up her jacket.

"Are you kidding? She never takes just an hour."

"Great. I think I'll give Cynthia a jingle."

"Good luck."

But when Megan called, she was dumped into Cynthia's messaging service. Unsure of how to put it, Megan simply asked for Cynthia to return her call at her convenience. "It's not any kind of an emergency," she said finally, "I just wanted to ask you something." Then she hung up.

As Megan continued to work, sifting through a pile of stuff that Vera had dumped on her desk, Megan couldn't help but feel like this was unfair. Because, like her mom had pointed out, it wasn't as if she was asking for paid time off. And she'd been a faithful employee, often going beyond what was expected to make a customer happy. And she often worked overtime without even being compensated for it. Really, how easy would it be for them to replace her? She was tempted to write a letter of resignation right now.

On the other hand, she knew that this job was valuable work experience, and her mom was probably right that it would look good on a résumé—especially if she stuck to it for more than just her "almost" six months. If she was smart, she would revise her résumé and start sending it out to the local schools. She should be checking out job Web sites and filling out applications to teach art … or to teach anything. Really, wouldn't any kind of teaching job be preferable to working for Vera?

Of course, Cynthia might be disappointed. Really, Cynthia had been great to work for. It was too bad that Cynthia was stuck with Vera. So what if Vera was well connected to wealthy homeowners in dire need of redecorating? Was it worth it? Sometimes Megan thought Cynthia had sold her soul to the devil just to make a successful design firm. And the sad part was that Cynthia had the talent to make it without Vera. But from what Megan could tell, Cynthia hadn't believed in herself or her ability. She had been impatient. She had wanted success early on. And she had gotten it. But she'd also gotten Vera. It seemed a high price to pay.

Megan hoped that she'd remember things like this when it came to making choices in her own life. Although she prayed about major decisions and tried to let God lead her, she still suspected there could come times when she, like Cynthia, might be tempted to run ahead of things—to break or slightly twist the rules to accomplish whatever it was she was trying to attain. But she hoped that wouldn't be the case. She hoped that she'd learn from the mistakes of others and not fall into those same traps herself. Still, sometimes the school of hard knocks taught the most memorable lessons. That is, if a student was paying attention. For someone like Kendall, maybe not so much.

Finally, the workday came to an end and Cynthia still hadn't returned her call. Megan was tempted to call again but knew that would appear pesky. So she turned off the light in her tiny office and gathered up her things to go home. Vera's office was dark too, and it looked like she'd already left, but Ellen was still at the reception desk.

"I just heard from Cynthia," she told Megan. "She said today was crazy, but she did get your message and will try to get back to you tomorrow afternoon."

"Thanks." Megan forced a smile. "See ya."

As Megan walked toward home, it began to rain. Naturally, she hadn't brought an umbrella. Most native Oregonians didn't carry one. Still, the idea of having something overhead to keep her dry was appealing. As she hurried toward Bloomberg Place, she prayed. First she asked God to make a way for her to go with Lelani to Maui. Of course, she asked him to close the door if he didn't want her to go. Next she asked God to help her find a job more suitable to who she was—something where she could make a difference in a person's life, not simply their dining room drapes. And, finally, she prayed for Kendall. She asked God to soften her heart toward this perplexing girl. "Show me how to be a better friend and to not be so judgmental," she prayed as she turned onto the walk that led to the house. The raindrops were falling in big splats now, and she hurried inside and shut the door against the wind.

She spun around and plowed smack into Kendall. Trying to recover, she nearly stepped on Tinkerbell. Megan hopped aside, and the little dog yipped and jumped behind Kendall with her tail between her legs.

"Sorry," said Megan. "I didn't see you two there."

"I cannot believe you!" Kendall glared at her in anger.

"I said I'm sorry." Megan peeled off her soggy jacket. "It was raining cats and dogs outside. I was just trying to get into the house. Sorry I ran into you. Are you okay?"

"No, I am *not* okay."

Megan frowned at her. "You look okay."

"Looks can be deceiving."

"What?"

Kendall waved her arms dramatically. "I try to wear a happy face, but underneath it, I am crying. My heart is broken."

"Huh?" Megan hung up her wet jacket and just stared at Kendall. Had she lost her mind?

"You and Lelani have tricked me, Megan. You have betrayed me."

"How?" Was Kendall going to rake them over the coals for walking out on her yesterday? Hadn't they already been there, done that?

"You two are going to Maui without me!" Then Kendall burst into tears, snatched up her little dog and ran up the stairs, slamming the door behind her.

Ten

Lelani

"Who told her about Maui?" Lelani asked after Megan had informed her of Kendall's tantrum. They were making spaghetti for dinner, thinking they might help to calm Kendall down about not being invited.

"I don't know who spilled the beans," said Megan. "But it sure wasn't me."

"It wasn't me."

"I don't see why she's so mad. It's not like she could even afford to go anyway. She doesn't have enough credit left on all her cards together to buy a ticket."

"Speaking of tickets." Lelani paused from washing lettuce. "Did you call the travel agent today?"

Megan sighed and shook her head. "I'm sorry." Then she told Lelani that she was still trying to get time off. "Cynthia promised to call me tomorrow afternoon, but maybe you should go ahead and book your flight now."

"Not without you." Lelani put the lettuce in the salad spinner and gave it a fast whirl. "I just don't think I can do it alone."

"What about Gil?"

"I considered Gil, Megan. But I don't think my parents would take me seriously if it looked like I'd brought home my latest boyfriend. You know?"

Megan nodded. "Well, I'm actually thinking about quitting my job."

"Because of this?"

"No, not just this. I really want to find a teaching job. And it's probably time to start applying."

"But to give up your job before you have something else? I mean even if you did get a teaching job, it probably wouldn't start until fall, right?"

"Probably."

"Well, please, don't give up your job to go to Maui, Megan. That'd be crazy."

"And, please, don't give up going to Maui because of me."

"Let's not worry about it." Lelani returned to making the salad. "I think it'll all work out just how it's supposed to."

"Well, I've been praying about it."

"Praying about what?" asked Anna as she joined them in the kitchen. "Hey, this looks like dinner, what's the occasion?"

"Maybe it's to welcome you back," said Lelani.

"Yeah, we did miss you."

"Not everyone did." Anna frowned.

"Meaning?"

"Meaning you should see the upstairs bathroom. It's a disaster area that smells like a kennel. Even the medicine cabinet mirror is broken. What went on here anyway?"

"Not much," Megan said as she opened a jar of Ragú. "Same old same old."

So Lelani quietly explained how Kendall hadn't been too helpful and how they'd gotten into an argument, finally leaving Kendall to her own devices in preparing for her so-called garage sale.

"Like it's going to happen." Anna scowled. "The whole house still looks like a garbage heap. And for nothing. Does this mean we all have to drag all this crud back to the attic now?"

"Maybe not," said Megan. "My mom still plans to come and help Kendall."

"I'm afraid it will take more than just your mother to help her." Anna shook her head in a dismal way. "That girl is a piece of work."

"But she's our piece of work," teased Lelani.

"And be warned," added Megan, "she's really mad now."

"Any special reason?"

Lelani glanced uncomfortably at Megan, then answered. "Actually, there is a reason. You see, I've decided to go to Maui for spring break, and I invited Megan."

"Cool," said Anna. Then a shadow crossed her face. "Did you invite anyone else?"

"You mean like Gil?"

"Maybe."

"No. I did not. I don't think my parents would appreciate it."

"Yours aren't the only ones."

"But Gil knows I'm going and he's very supportive of the whole thing."

"Wow, Maui sounds good right now. Did you see that rain?" Anna peered out the kitchen window to where the street was turning into one giant puddle.

"We didn't just see it," said Megan, "we both walked home in it."

"You should've called for a ride."

"So is this where the party is?" asked Kendall as she came into the kitchen.

Lelani smiled. "We're making spaghetti and salad. Do you want to join us?"

Kendall looked askance. "Oh, do you mean that I'm invited to join you? I thought maybe you were going to make a habit of excluding me from everything."

"Oh, Kendall," said Anna. "Don't get your nose out of joint. I'm not going either."

"And how does that make *you* feel?"

"To be honest, slightly envious." Anna made a face at Lelani. "Especially in light of today's lousy weather. But I do understand."

"That's big of you." Kendall flipped her hair over her shoulder, then bent down to smell the spaghetti sauce. "I suppose this isn't homemade."

Megan tossed Lelani an irritated look but fortunately didn't say anything.

"No, we working girls don't really have time to do homemade sauces. Sorry." Lelani glanced at the kitchen clock. "And if you'll excuse me, I want to call my mom. This is the best time of day to get her since the baby naps now."

"The baby naps this late?" Kendall looked skeptical.

"It's earlier in Hawaii." Megan turned to Lelani. "No problem. By the time you finish your call we should be about ready to eat."

"Thanks."

Lelani picked her way through the messy living room. Perhaps they should all offer to help Kendall get this junk back to the attic after dinner. No sense in letting it clutter up the whole house if she really didn't want to hold her garage sale. Plus, it might help them to get along better if they weren't living in such chaos.

Lelani went into her room, closed her door, took out her cell phone, and sat on the bed. What was she going to say? She'd tried all sorts of opening lines in her head. But they all sounded forced and stiff and suspicious. Maybe the best plan was to not have a plan. She pushed the numbers and waited for the phone to ring. She could imagine her mother, looking down at the phone, waiting for the caller ID to identify Lelani, then deciding whether to answer. But if Emma was napping, she might answer simply to stop the ringing. So when she picked up on the second ring, Lelani knew that Emma must be asleep.

"Hi, Mom."

"Lelani?"

"How are you doing?"

"Okay. How are you?"

"I'm doing well, Mom. Thanks."

"Good, good."

"How is Daddy?"

"He's doing fine. Busy with the shops."

"And baby Emma? How is she?"

"She's a little fussy just now. I think she's teething again."

"Oh." Lelani tried to imagine the tiny newborn Emma that she remembered now with teeth.

"How is your job?"

"It's okay."

"And the weather? How is the weather?"

"Pretty lousy." Lelani described the cold, wet rain.

"Oh."

"How about the weather there?"

"There's a breeze today. A few clouds. Mid-seventies."

Lelani sighed with longing. "Sounds nice." And now there was a long pause, and before her mother could say, "I'm very busy and I need to get back to …" whatever it was she did to keep so busy, Lelani went for it. "I want to come home, Mom."

"Why?" Her mother's voice sounded alarmed now.

"Just for a visit."

"Oh."

"I have the week of spring break off and I wanted to see you."

"Which week is that?"

"The third week of March."

"Less than two weeks from now?"

"That's right."

"Oh."

"I just really miss Maui. And I miss you too, Mom. And Dad." Lelani was careful not to add Emma to the list. That would raise suspicions.

"Oh."

"And if you don't mind, I'm bringing a friend."

"A friend?"

"One of my housemates, Mom. Her name is Megan. I think you'll like her."

"Oh, yes, I'm sure I would like her. But it's just that this isn't the best timing for us, Lelani."

"Why not?"

"Oh, you know … spring break … your dad is so busy."

"But he could take time off. He has lots of employees."

"I know, but he—"

"Why don't you just be honest, Mom?" Lelani couldn't believe she'd just said that. But since she started, she was determined to finish. "You don't really want me to come home, do you?"

"Well, that's not—"

"You'd be happy to never see me again, wouldn't you?"

"Oh, Lelani."

"I know it's true. You're ashamed of me. You've replaced me with Emma. You probably even tell people that she's your baby, don't you?"

"Lelani!"

"But I'm still your daughter too." Lelani was starting to cry now. "And your husband, he's still my daddy. And I-I have a right to come home—if-if I want to. I mean it's a free country and unless you've taken some kind of legal action against me, I am free to come and go to and from Maui if I want to."

"You're upset, Lelani." Her mother's voice was calm and cold. "Maybe you should call back when you're not so emotional."

"I just wanted you to know." Lelani sniffed as she attempted to steady her feelings. "I just wanted you to know that I *am* coming. And I'm bringing my friend Megan with me. And if we're not welcome in your house, we will simply camp on the beach. Maybe my father will take pity on me and throw us some food." Then Lelani hung up.

Oh, she knew she was acting childish. But that's how her mother made her feel. Like she was just a child. An unwanted child. It wasn't the first time that Lelani had been cut by her mother's words. And it probably wouldn't be the last, either. Lelani threw herself down on her bed and sobbed.

She must've fallen asleep, because she woke to the sound of someone tapping on her door. Then Megan called, "Are you okay?"

"Yes." Lelani sat up and blinked at the light. "I think I fell asleep. Come in."

Megan came in and then frowned to see Lelani. "You've been crying."

Lelani filled her in on the conversation. "It feels like she hates me, Megan. Like she wishes I'd died during childbirth so that she and baby Emma and my father could all live happily ever after."

Megan sat on the bed and put an arm around Lelani's shoulders. "I'm so sorry, Lelani. I don't even know what to tell you. Except that it's hard to imagine that any mother would really feel like that toward her child."

"It's hard to imagine, but true." Lelani took in a jagged breath. "Maybe I should just stay away … and forget about them … forever."

"What about your dad? I'm sure he still loves you."

"My mother influences him. And then there is baby Emma for him to pour his affection onto."

"Well, it's up to you whether we go to Maui or not." Megan paused. "But I think you need to go. Even if it's just to give them both a piece of your mind and to part ways."

Lelani's eyes filled with tears again.

"But I really don't think that's what will happen. I really think something good will come of it. And you can resolve how you feel about Emma. Think about it, Lelani. You've sort of left Emma hanging in the balance. I mean you gave your parents guardianship, but you didn't let them adopt her. They're probably living in constant fear that you'll take her away. And then they'll lose you both."

Lelani considered this. "That could be true."

"It just seems that you need to go. You need to figure this thing out. We've all seen you being haunted by your past, Lelani. Maybe it's time to face it."

"Maybe."

"Want to come to dinner now?"

"Sure. Sorry I fell asleep. I meant to help."

"It's okay. Kendall actually stepped in and set the table."

"So, she's not mad anymore?"

"I wouldn't go that far. But I do think she's been lonely."

"Maybe we can have girls' night in tonight," suggested Lelani.

"Yeah, I think Kendall would like that. Despite all her tantrums and complaining, I think she actually does like us. And I think she needs us too."

Lelani nodded. The truth was she needed her housemates too. Maybe even more than Kendall did. In fact, they were more like family to her than her own family. And following the conversation with her mother, it seemed that these girls would continue to be family for Lelani—whether or not she went home.

Still, it seemed that Megan had hit the nail on the head when she said that Lelani needed to go home to face her parents, to express herself, and to once and for all resolve the situation with Emma. It wouldn't be easy, but it needed to be done. It made sense. Perfect sense.

Except for one thing. Of course, Megan wouldn't get this because she had a great relationship with her own mom and she'd never actually met Lelani's mom. So she had no idea what the beautiful Alana Porter was really like, what she was capable of, and what truly motivated her. No one really did. Not even Lelani's father, who was devoted to his wife. Oh, he knew she had her faults, but he also knew how to overlook them. It was just better for everyone if he did. And like so many others, Will Porter remained under her spell.

Few people knew what a force Alana Porter was. And that's because most people never crossed her. Alana had learned early on to use her beauty, charms, and later her wealth to get her way. And she usually wielded her power so carefully and gracefully that no one really felt the sting of it. Or the chill. Everyone simply complied to her wishes, unaware that they'd been duped. Everyone except Lelani, that is. Even so, it took years before she fully grasped her mother's rare talent, and perhaps that never would've happened if Lelani hadn't gotten pregnant.

But Megan was right. The time had come to get this thing out in the open. It wouldn't be pleasant or easy, and if history was any indicator, Lelani would probably lose this battle too. At least she would fight. Anyway, she hoped she would.

Eleven

Anna

"I suppose you heard that your brother is taking the week of spring break off," Anna's mother told her. She had called Anna at work to apologize. At first Anna wasn't sure whether to be shocked or suspicious. Maybe both. Because, although her mother was calling to make sure that Anna was coming to her grandparents' farewell dinner at the restaurant on Sunday night, she actually invited Edmond to come along with her. Anna had told her she'd get back to her on that.

"Gil's taking spring break off?" Anna frowned as she flipped through her e-mail box. Because she was multitasking at work, she didn't feel guilty for having a conversation with her mother.

"Yes. The whole week. This will be the first vacation he's taken since he began doing books for us."

"So he's going to Maui?"

"Maui?"

"Or wherever." Anna saw an e-mail from a copy editor. "I need to get to work now."

"But what's this about Maui, Anna? Are you saying that Gil is going to Maui with Lelani?"

"No, I'm not saying anything. He's probably going skiing. I hear spring skiing is good this year and—"

"No, I think you're right, mi'ja. I'll bet he is going to Maui—with Lelani." Now she began speaking in rapid Spanish and Anna had to cut her off.

"I need to go now. Bye, Mama. And don't worry so much." Then Anna hung up and sighed. So when had this developed? The last she'd heard, Lelani had explicitly said that Gil was not going. Of course, Anna didn't know for sure he was going. Really, he might just be doing something else to occupy his time while Lelani was gone. That had to be it.

But when Anna got home from work and spotted Gil's pickup in the driveway, she decided to get to the bottom of it.

"Hey, Anna," said Gil as he hopped out of his truck.

"Hey," she called back. "Did you know there's a rumor going around that you're going to Maui with Lelani?"

He frowned. "Who told you that?"

She made a face. "Let's just say it slipped out."

"How?"

"Okay, maybe it was my fault. Mom said you were taking the week of spring break off and I wasn't really thinking and I asked about Maui."

He shook his head. "Oh, great."

"You mean you were going to keep your whereabouts a secret from your family?"

"Not exactly."

"What then?"

"I wasn't going to tell them until I was on my way there."

"So you really are going with Lelani?"

"Not exactly *with* her, Anna. I just happen to be going to Maui while she's there."

"But I thought she—"

"Here, this is how it went down." He lowered his voice as if he thought someone in the house might be listening. "Lelani called me last night and she was pretty upset."

"Why?"

"She's kind of freaking over how her parents are going to handle things."

"I thought that's why Megan was going?"

"But it's not a hundred percent for sure that Megan can get time off of work. Apparently her boss is kind of mean."

Anna nodded. "Yes. She's a witch."

"So Lelani went ahead and booked her flight in the hopes that things would work out for Megan, but then she got to thinking that she'd be stuck on her own if Megan didn't go. And Lelani and her mom don't exactly have what you'd call a good relationship, if you know what I mean."

"No, I wouldn't possibly know anything about difficult mothers, Gil."

"It sounds like our mom is a piece of cake compared to Lelani's."

Anna considered this. "Poor Lelani. She should've thought things through a little better before she started dating you."

Gil frowned. "Mom will come around about Lelani eventually, Anna."

"Yeah, like when pigs fly."

"So, after we got off the phone I decided to go to Maui. I'll stay in a hotel, and if Lelani needs me for moral support, I'll be there. And if she doesn't ..." He shrugged. "Hey, I'll still have a good time. I mean it is Maui. And the snorkeling is great and I've always wanted to learn to surf and I hear the whales are—"

"Okay!" Anna held up her hands to stop him. "Now you're making me seriously jealous, Gil. Enough."

"Sorry, sis."

"Well, I'm sorry that I kind of spilled the beans with Mom. I tried to cover it, but sometimes it's like that woman has some kind of ESP when it comes to her kids."

"I know."

"So, should I assume Lelani knows about all this?" They were at the front door now.

"Actually that's why I zipped over here after work. I wanted to tell her in person. I thought she should be home from work by now."

Anna pointed down Bloomberg Place to where a tall slender figure was coming down the street toward them. "Looks like you're timing's good, Gil. Here she comes." Then Anna went inside and left them to their vacation plans. Okay, maybe it wasn't exactly a vacation to Lelani. But it sure would be to Anna. The more she thought about it, the more jealous she did feel. Oh, it wasn't a jealousy that made any sense. Kind of like when Anna's best friend Mandy Peters broke her arm in third grade and ended up getting all this attention, and Anna wished she could break her arm too. In fact, she even jumped out of a tree, hoping that she'd injure herself.

Feeling jealous of Lelani's trip was equally ridiculous. It would be no fun to do the hard emotional work of seeing her parents and figuring things out with her baby girl.

Most of the time, Anna found it hard to believe that Lelani really had a child. It just seemed so out of character for someone as smart and sensible as Lelani. Now Kendall, that was a different story. But Anna knew it was true. Not only did Lelani have a baby, she wasn't sure that she wanted to continue letting her parents raise her daughter. Anna tried to imagine what Lelani's life would be like if she decided to be a mother to her child.

Would she be able to support herself and Emma? Would she continue to live at Bloomberg Place? What would Kendall think of it? And what about Kendall's baby? Would Bloomberg Place start looking more like a home for unwed mothers than friends sharing a house? Anna wasn't sure she wanted to live in a place like that.

And what about Gil? How would this change his life? And why hadn't he thought about this before he'd gotten so involved? Whether Anna's family could admit it or not, Anna felt pretty sure that Gil was in love with Lelani. She had felt that from the start. To be fair, other than the baby dilemma, Anna thought Lelani would make a lovely sister-in-law. It's just that throwing a child into the picture complicated things. And as far as Anna and Gil's mother was concerned, things were complicated enough already.

"You don't look very happy," observed Megan as Anna came into the house. "Bad day at work?"

Anna shook her head. "No. Just thinking." She wondered if Megan was aware of this latest development—that Gil might be with them in Maui. Or at least be nearby. "Did your boss give you time off for Maui?"

Now Megan looked unhappy. "Not yet. But I left her another message, specifically asking for that week off. At least she'll know that I want it."

Anna considered telling her about Gil, but since she'd already let one cat out of the bag today, she decided to keep her mouth shut. "So"—she glanced around the still-cluttered living room—"how's Kendall today?"

Megan kind of smiled. "She's actually a little more positive. My mom called her and talked about *Antiques Roadshow*, and now Kendall is certain she's going to become a millionaire from all her junk."

Anna laughed. "Yeah, right. I've seen that junk. She'll be lucky if she can get rid of it without paying people to haul it away."

"You never know. Anyway, my mom will be here to help her to sort through things and price them tomorrow and the next day. I've already put ads in the papers, and my mom's bringing signs and some tables and stuff."

"So we're really doing this thing?"

"Looks like it."

Anna nodded. "Good. It'll be nice to get this place back to normal."

"And then, if all goes well, Lelani and I will leave for Maui the following Saturday. She's already booked her flight, and I'm tempted to go ahead and book mine."

Anna just pressed her lips together.

"Are you feeling bad that you're not going?"

"No, I'm fine. Okay, I'm a little jealous, but I'll get over it."

"Not me," said Kendall as she came into the room. "I mean I'll get over it, but I'm more than a little jealous. I'm screaming mean green with envy." She made a face at Megan. "And I really think Lelani should reconsider the whole thing. I mean I have more in common with her than you do, Megan. I'm going to be a mom too. Shouldn't we moms stick together?"

"So you've made your decision?" Anna asked with hopeful relief. "You're not still considering an abortion?"

Kendall put a finger on her chin and looked uncertain. "I'm mostly sure that I'll have the baby. Not completely." Just then Tinkerbell started to bark to be let out. "But I'm determined to make up my mind by the end of this week. Lelani thinks I've already let it go too long. She said that not making a decision is like making a decision. I suppose that could be true." She turned to her dog. "I'm coming, Tinker. Sheesh, with you to keep me hopping, who needs a baby?"

Anna sighed and Megan just rolled her eyes.

"Sometimes I think that stepping into 86 Bloomberg Place is like stepping into a soap opera or Lifetime movie," said Anna.

Megan laughed. "Isn't that kind of like life?"

"I guess." Anna just shook her head as she went up the stairs. Having grown up with a mom who was fairly melodramatic, Anna had decided that she didn't particularly enjoy drama. Oh, it was okay on TV or the big screen or theater. But when it came to her own life, she liked things to be nice and even. Maybe that's why she liked Edmond so much. And so she decided to give him a call.

"Hey, Anna," he said happily. "You slipped away from the office before I could say good-bye."

"I was done with work and just wanted to leave. Sorry."

"So, how's life at Bloomberg Place? Is Kendall behaving?"

Anna often filled him in on the activities there. "She's okay. But I'm having attacks of jealousy over not going to Maui." So she told him about Gil.

"Why don't you go?"

She laughed. "Well, for one thing I haven't been invited."

"No one needs an invitation to go to Maui, Anna. You just buy a ticket, reserve a hotel, and go."

"Hmm." Anna considered this. "By myself? Isn't that a little pathetic?"

"I'd be happy to go with you."

"Right." Anna laughed. "That would send my poor mother right over the edge. She's already freaking over Gil and Lelani. Not that they'll be staying together."

"So if it weren't for your mother, would you consider going there with me?" asked Edmond hopefully.

"No," Anna answered firmly. "I wouldn't."

Now there was a long pause.

"Sorry," said Anna. "It's nothing personal. But if I go to Maui with a guy it'll have to be on my honeymoon."

"Are you proposing to me, Anna Mendez?"

She laughed. "No, I'm not. And, just so you know, I'm a little old-fashioned that way. I expect the guy to propose to me."

Now there was another silence and Anna got worried that Edmond might think she was hinting. "Not that I'm ready for anything like that," she said quickly. "Because I so am not. I was just saying."

"Hey," said Edmond. "I wonder if Gil wants a buddy to go with him to Maui. I mean if he's getting a hotel room, we could split the cost. And I can—"

"That's actually a great idea." Anna remembered Gil's talk of snorkeling and surfing. But what if Lelani was busy doing other things? The idea of Gil out there alone was a little scary. "Do you know how to snorkel?"

"Oh, yeah. And I'm a certified diver too."

"How about surfing?"

"I've done it a few times, but I'm not great."

"Sounds like you and Gil are a perfect match."

"Great. I think I'll give him a call." Edmond ended the conversation and Anna realized that now she was not only jealous of her brother going to Maui, she was jealous of Edmond as well. And to think she'd encouraged it. What had she been thinking?

"Hey, Anna?" Kendall poked her head in her room. "Can I borrow your shampoo?"

"Uh … yeah, sure." Anna nodded. Okay, she wanted to say no and to point out that her shampoo was expensive, and that Kendall always left the lid off and used too much, and why couldn't Kendall just buy her own anyway? But Anna didn't say any of that. Instead, she just sat there on her bed considering the fact that she'd be spending the whole week of spring break here with Princess Kendall. Just Kendall and Anna. Together for one whole week. No Megan or Lelani to balance things out or soothe Kendall's feelings or reassure her that her life wasn't over just because her size-four jeans didn't fit anymore.

And then it hit Anna: not only that, but now there was a very good chance that she wouldn't even have Edmond to run away and escape with. For all she knew he was talking to Gil right now, booking a flight to Maui online, and asking his uncle for time off. To make matters worse, Anna wouldn't even have her brother. Just Anna and Kendall. Anna groaned loudly and flopped back on her bed. This was so unfair!

Twelve

Kendall

Kendall did not feel like getting out of bed Wednesday morning. But then she'd never been much of a morning person—at least not since she was a kid. And mornings were even less welcome now that she was knocked up. Okay, her housemates had told her numerous times to quit referring to her pregnancy in such negative terms. Just last night Lelani had given Kendall the spiel that she was carrying a miracle inside of her body. Maybe it was something she'd learned in med school. But this little "miracle" had gotten Kendall up to hurl just a little past seven, and Anna had not appreciated it one bit when Kendall blasted past her to get to the toilet. However, Anna might've appreciated it even less if Kendall hadn't made it in time.

"Eeuw," Anna complained as she stepped back, holding her hair dryer as if it were a handgun. "Can't you do that somewhere else?"

Kendall had glared at her. "Like where?"

At least Anna had the good sense to apologize and ask if Kendall was okay.

"Define okay," Kendall had snapped back at her, snatching Anna's still damp bath towel and using it to wipe her face.

Anna then had the good sense to keep her mouth shut.

Of course, Tinkerbell wanted to go out. Kendall had reluctantly trudged down the stairs to oblige the dog. At least that meant one less puppy pad to change. She couldn't imagine what it would be like having to change baby diapers and, according to an ad she'd seen in some stupid baby magazine at the ob-gyn office yesterday, the average baby went through around five thousand diapers before it was potty trained. As she stood outside waiting for Tinker to do her business, she tried to remember what the ad had been trying to sell. Perhaps the idea that having a baby was ridiculous. In that case, she was buying.

Eventually, she fell back into bed again, and now she did not feel like getting up—ever. But someone kept knocking on the front door, incessantly ringing the doorbell, which had caused Tinkerbell to go into a barking frenzy that was not going to stop. And so Kendall dragged herself out of bed, pulled on her robe, which was looking ratty, shoved her feet into her pink bunny slippers, whose ears had been chewed to pieces by Tinkerbell, and once again she trudged down the stairs. Maybe she should consider forcing Lelani or Megan to switch rooms with her. How was it fair that a pregnant woman had to climb up and down all those stairs?

Kendall opened the door to see a middle-aged woman with an oversized bag smiling at her. Thinking she was selling something, Kendall prepared to tell her to take it someplace else, but then she realized it was Megan's mom.

"Remember me?" she said pleasantly. "I'm Linda Abernathy, Megan's mom."

Kendall nodded dumbly.

"And we were going to—"

"Oh, yeah." Kendall nodded. "I totally forgot. Uh, I wasn't feeling too good this morning and I—"

"Are you sick?" asked Linda as she pushed her way into the house. This woman actually reminded Kendall of Megan, the pushiness anyway.

"Not exactly sick, but sort of …" Kendall frowned as she looked at the junk that was still cluttered about the living room.

"Don't you want help with this?"

"Yeah, I guess so. I mean I need help, don't I?"

"It seems you do." Linda smiled again. "Why don't you go get dressed and I'll start going through things." She held up her bag. "I found some more books at the library that will help us to price some of the collectables."

Kendall felt slightly encouraged. "Do you really think there might be something valuable here?"

"Well, based on what you told me, the age of the home, how long things have been in that attic, it seems likely."

"Cool." Kendall nodded. "I'll go change."

"And I'll get to work," chirped Linda. "This is going to be fun."

Kendall wasn't so sure about fun, but if it was a way to make some money, Kendall was in. Her last viable credit card had been rejected at the gas station yesterday, and she'd been forced to spend her last bit of cash on a few gallons of gas. She really was desperate. As she pulled on the same sweats she'd worn yesterday—for the past week for that matter—she considered once again asking someone in her family for help. But she knew that would mean revealing to them her delicate (rather, indelicate) condition. And that would give them just one more thing to throw in her face. Plus, she still wasn't convinced that she'd continue her pregnancy.

If only Matthew would step up and be the man she had thought he was. If only he'd come to his senses and realize that Kendall, not Heidi Hardwick, was the woman he should be spending the rest of his life with. But the last time she'd tried to contact him, just days ago, he'd politely threatened to get a restraining order on her if she continued to pester him.

Then she'd just as politely threatened to go public with her pregnancy if he pulled a stunt like that. Now it seemed they were in a standoff. The only way to prove it was his baby would be to give birth and have a DNA test to determine paternity. Then she could either sue him for child support or hope that he'd figure things out and leave Heidi to marry Kendall.

Still, the more she thought about the possibility of Matthew giving up his high-profile Hollywood marriage, the less likely it seemed. Although she had tried, she had not forgotten her therapist's suggestion that Kendall, besides being narcissistic, might sometimes suffer delusions of grandeur. Well, who didn't sometimes? And what was wrong with believing that you were someone special? Wasn't that also called good self-esteem? Why did everyone have to make everything so complicated?

"Are you coming down, Kendall?" called Linda from the foot of the stairs.

"Oh, yeah." Kendall shoved on a pair of flip-flops. "Coming!"

Linda had already begun sorting some things out. And now she was holding a small stack of old magazines and grinning like they'd just won the lottery. "Do you know what these are?"

Kendall peered at the musty looking pile of periodicals. "Trash?"

"No, they're old hunting magazines."

"And?"

"And they are very collectable. Not just for the contents, but some people like to frame them and use them for wall art."

Kendall peered at the cover on top. A guy in a plaid shirt and Elmer Fudd hat was aiming a long gun at what appeared to be some kind of mountain lion that was about to leap down onto him. "Who in their right mind would put something like that on their wall?"

Linda just chuckled like she knew some big secret. "Oh, plenty of people. Especially here in the Northwest."

"Oh." Now Kendall was curious. "How much would one of these magazines go for? Like a hundred dollars?"

Linda laughed. "No, I don't think so."

Kendall frowned. "So how much then?"

"Well, depending on their condition and the demand, some could go for as much as thirty dollars. And they should all be worth a minimum of ten dollars each."

Kendall eyed the stack. "It looks like there's about twenty there. So would that be worth around two to three hundred dollars?"

"Quite possibly. But you wouldn't get that much for them unless you sold them directly to a serious collector. And, although Megan said she used the word *collectibles* in the garage-sale ad, she couldn't be specific about it. So the chances of getting the right person at your garage sale might be slim. Do you know anyone who knows how to sell things on eBay?"

Kendall thought for a moment. "Oh, yeah, I think Marcus knows how to do that."

"Marcus?" Linda looked confused. "You mean *Megan's* Marcus?"

Kendall smiled coyly. "Megan's Marcus used to be *my* Marcus."

"Really?" Linda looked skeptical but didn't question this.

And, although Kendall knew that Marcus would give the story his own spin, acting like he'd never been that into Kendall, he had to admit that he never would've met Megan if not for Kendall. Really, Megan should be more grateful!

"Well, let's continue sorting."

And so they worked together. Actually, Linda directed and Kendall tried to do what she was told, but by noon she was tired, and it looked like they had made no progress. "This place is still a mess," she pointed out.

"It's an organized mess." Linda pointed to a box of glassware. "If we hadn't sorted through, you'd never know that some of those pieces are rather valuable." She frowned. "By the way, Megan mentioned something about your grandmother, Kendall. Have you secured her permission to sell these things yet?"

Kendall looked down at the hardwood floor and shrugged.

"Kendall?"

"Well, she pretty much gave me the house. Why should she care about the junk in the attic?"

"Because some of these things might be mementos. It's possible that the value to your family members might be more than just monetary."

"Huh?"

"Does anyone in your family want to save any of these things?" Linda looked slightly irritated now. "You know, for sentimental reasons?"

Kendall waved her hand. "No one in my family is into old stuff."

"Are you certain?"

She nodded.

"Well, just to make sure, I'd like you to phone your grandmother, while I'm here." Linda sat down in one of the dining room chairs. "I refuse to help you anymore until you speak to your grandmother, Kendall."

"Fine." Kendall reached for the phone. "If that'll make you happy."

It took about six rings before her grandmother picked it up. "Hello?" Nana's voice crackled, then she loudly cleared her throat. "Who is this anyway?"

"Hi, Nana. This is Kendall," she said sweetly. "How are you doing today?"

"I've been better. What do you want, Kendall? If it's money, you can forget it. Your mother told me clearly not to give you one red cent."

Kendall controlled herself, forced a smile for Linda's sake, then continued. "Oh, that's not why I'm calling, Nana. I was just doing some spring cleaning, you know, and there was all this junk in the attic and I thought it might be a fire hazard—"

"A fire hazard?"

"Yes."

"Did you call the fire department?"

"No, there's not a fire now, Nana. But I wanted to clear things out—just to be safe. And then I thought I'd have a little garage sale and—"

"A garage sale?" The pitch in Nana's voice rose with interest. "I used to love going to garage sales. Why, you can get all kinds of nice things at garage sales. One time I found a perfectly good brass spittoon for only fifty cents. Can you imagine? Solid brass for fifty cents. Oh, my."

"So do you mind if I have a garage sale then?"

"And there was the time I found an old desk lamp just like the one my daddy used to have, back when I was a girl. Oh, it didn't work, but it was a beauty alright."

"Nana?"

"What is it?"

"Do you mind if I have a garage sale?"

"No. I like garage sales. I have an idea, Kendall. Why don't you come get me today and we'll go to some garage sales. Maybe I'll find another spittoon."

"I don't think they have any garage sales in this part of the week," Kendall told her.

"What day is it anyway?"

"It's Wednesday, Nana."

"Oh, phooey. I hate Wednesdays."

"Why?"

"They always have meatloaf on Wednesdays and it tastes just like old sawdust soaked in watered-down ketchup."

"Sawdust soaked in ketchup?"

"Yes. And the mashed potatoes are the nasty kind where you just add water and they taste like wallpaper paste. Why don't people use real potatoes anymore?"

"I don't know, Nana. Maybe I can take you out for a real dinner sometime."

"Oh, yes," she said eagerly. "We'll have to do it on a Wednesday since they have pot roast on Thursday and it's much better than meatloaf. And on Friday it's fish. Sometimes it's just those nasty little fish sticks that come frozen. But sometimes it's halibut. My, how I like a good piece of halibut."

So Kendall agreed to take Nana to dinner next Wednesday, although she knew Nana would probably forget about it as soon as they hung up. But Kendall told herself if she made enough money at the garage sale, she would go and take Nana out for dinner. Why not?

"So, she's okay with this?" asked Linda.

"Yeah, she's fine. She loves a good garage sale." Kendall noticed what looked like a brass spittoon amid some other junk in a big cardboard box. "Hey, that must be the brass spittoon Nana was just talking about."

"Did she want to save it?"

Kendall laughed. "No. She told me she got it for fifty cents at a garage sale."

Linda picked it up and turned it over and sure enough, there was a bit of masking tape with fifty cents marked on it. Linda peeled off the tape and studied the bottom of the spittoon. "That stamp makes me think this is fairly old."

"Do you think it's worth a lot?" asked Kendall eagerly.

"Well, certainly more than fifty cents." Linda frowned. "Let me do some checking on it."

By the end of the day, Linda had managed to find a number of treasures that she felt would do well on eBay. And she also helped Kendall to put prices on some of the older, less valuable things. Kendall went around trying to tally up what they'd marked and suddenly realized that having a garage sale wasn't such a bad idea after all. And then Megan came home.

"How's it going?" she asked her mom.

"Pretty well." Linda set aside a box of old kitchen things that they'd just finished pricing. "Although to get a good price, it would make more sense to sell some of these things on eBay. Kendall said Marcus knows how to do that, do you think he'd want to help?"

Megan shrugged. "Maybe."

"I also told your mom that Marcus was my boyfriend first," teased Kendall.

Megan rolled her eyes.

"You don't seem to be very happy today," Kendall pointed out. "Was your witchy boss in a mean mood?"

"Not much more than usual."

"How about giving you the time off to go to Maui?" her mom now asked.

"Cynthia hasn't returned my call." Megan frowned. "I don't know what to do."

"Maybe I should go to Maui with Lelani," suggested Kendall hopefully.

"You don't have any money," Megan reminded her.

"But I will." Kendall grinned at Megan's mother. "After we sell all this stuff. Did you know that some of those old magazines are really valuable?"

"I thought the *Life* magazines were only worth about five bucks apiece."

So Kendall told her about the hunting ones. "And if you add that all up, including the *Life* magazines and everything else, it's looking pretty good."

"Even so," said Megan firmly. "You cannot afford to go to Maui and pay off your credit card bills, Kendall. No way. No how. Not going to happen. Uh-uh."

"You are such a buzz kill, Megan."

Linda just laughed. "But she's right, Kendall. You need to pay off your bills before you start planning trips to Maui." She looked at her watch. "And I need to get going. I promised to meet my friend Karen for an early dinner tonight." She smiled at Megan. "Would you like to join us, honey?"

Kendall would never admit it—to anyone—but she felt a stab of jealousy just then. After spending most of the day with Linda, she had nearly forgotten that she was actually Megan's mom. Then suddenly Linda was inviting Megan to dinner but not Kendall, and it seemed all wrong.

"No, thanks, Mom. Marcus is coming to get me for a music thing at his church tonight." Megan kissed her mom on the cheek as she went out.

Kendall sighed loudly. "Marcus Barrett and church … I can't even wrap my head around it."

"Maybe you should come with us," offered Megan.

"Thanks, but no thanks."

"So you think you're going to get rich off the garage sale?" asked Megan in what sounded like a skeptical tone.

"I think it'll be worth the time." Kendall held up the spittoon now. "Your mom said this could bring as much as twenty-five dollars."

"Hmm." Megan didn't look convinced. "But I have an idea how you can make even more money, Kendall."

"How?"

"Sell some of your clothes and shoes and bags. Designer labels should bring in some quick cash."

"Sell my clothes?"

"You're not wearing most of them anyway," pointed out Megan. "And you won't be wearing them anytime soon. In fact, they'll probably be out of style by the time you can fit into them again. That is, if you can fit into them."

Kendall just stared at her. "You are so mean!" she shouted. And then she tossed down the spittoon and ran upstairs with Tinkerbell trailing behind her, went into her room, slammed the door, tripped over a Prada boot, and tumbled into bed.

Really, Megan could be so heartless sometimes. How dare she say such things about Kendall's beautiful designer clothes … not to mention Kendall's ability—or inability—to fit into them? How cruel!

Thirteen

Megan

"Wow, you've made real progress here," Megan told her mom and Kendall after she got home from work on Thursday. "It almost looks like you're ready for a garage sale."

"I think Kendall is just about set," said her mom. "Almost everything is priced. We've set aside the things that we think will fetch more on eBay."

"And the ads are in the paper today and through the weekend," said Megan.

"I have signs all ready to go," said Kendall. "And, you'll be pleased to hear that your mom helped me to pick out some clothes and shoes and things to sell too."

"We put them on a special rack," Mom explained to Megan.

"With a sign that says Designer Clothes," added Kendall. "I don't want anyone to think they can get my nice things for nothing."

"Yes," agreed Mom. "I told Kendall that if they don't sell at her garage sale, I know of a nice consignment center that would be happy to take them."

"There's just one problem." Kendall frowned, then looked sadly at Megan.

"What's that?" Megan pretended to be more interested than she felt.

"I'll be here all by my little lonesome," said Kendall in a baby voice.

"So?" Megan shrugged.

"So, I thought maybe you could get off work around noon and come help me." Kendall smiled hopefully.

"Yeah, right." Megan shook her head. "I can't even get time off for Maui. Do you honestly think I can get off for a garage sale?"

"I just thought maybe—"

"Sorry, Kendall." Megan just shook her head, then went to her room.

She had barely closed the door when she heard someone knocking. Thinking it was Kendall coming to beg, she answered with a grumpy, "What?"

"It's me," said her mom.

"Sorry," Megan opened the door. "What's up?"

"I don't want to intrude, but I just thought you could be a bit nicer to Kendall, Megan."

"Why?"

"Well, for one thing, she's pregnant and her feelings are a little unstable." Mom sat down on the chair across from Megan's bed.

"She told you about that?"

Her mom nodded somberly. "And it's not easy for her."

"Tell me about it."

"For another thing, you did promise to help her with the garage sale. And it was your idea."

"Yeah, my umpteenth idea for helping her to get out of debt. But does that mean I have to hold her hand through the whole thing?"

"Well, she is in a tough spot right now."

Megan didn't say anything. The truth was she didn't really care.

"And you never know how God might be using you."

Megan sighed. "Yeah, I know, Mom. But sometimes it's hard. Kendall is so good at playing the poor little victim. And you know she's the one who gets herself into these messes in the first place. I've already tried so hard with her."

"I know. Kendall and I had a very nice little chat this afternoon."

"About?"

"About the baby."

"And?"

"And she said that you girls have been encouraging her not to get an abortion."

Megan nodded and waited. Certainly her mother wasn't going to fault her for doing that. Megan knew that her mother was as pro-life as she was.

"It seems that Kendall has been listening to you girls. You've been a good influence on her."

"So, she's not going to have an abortion?"

Mom shook her head. "No. She assured me that she's not."

Megan smiled. "Oh, that is a relief. Thanks."

"But I still think she needs your encouragement."

"But I can't get off work tomorrow. I'm helping Vera with an install, and Cynthia is supposed to be back in the office and I just can't get off. Okay?" For no really good reason, Megan felt close to tears. "I don't know what I'm going to do about Lelani, Mom."

"So you still haven't gotten the okay from Cynthia then?"

"No." Megan frowned then punched her pillow. "It's just so unfair. I work really hard at a job I don't even like and then they treat me like—"

"Have you prayed about it, Megan?"

"Yeah, but not a lot. I guess I've mostly been complaining about it."

"Tell you what, I'll be really praying about it too. I think it would be wonderful if you could go, Megan."

"Wonderful enough to quit my job?"

Mom didn't answer.

"I know, I know. The job market is tough right now."

"Have you been checking out teaching jobs?"

"A little."

"I'm sure it'll all work out, Megan." Mom stood now.

"Yeah, I'm sure it will too." But, even as she said this, Megan wasn't so sure. For all she knew she might be working at the design firm forever. And the idea of ordering overly expensive furniture and helping to hang ridiculous drapes that would be out of style by next year was not very appealing. Wasn't her life supposed to have more meaning than this?

"If I wasn't going to Victoria, I'd offer to help with Kendall," Mom said as she opened the door.

"You've already done way more than enough, Mom." Megan stood. "I'll see what I can do about getting off work. For sure we'll all be around to help during the weekend."

Mom smiled. "Good. Because I think you were really right about having this garage sale. Between it and eBay and the consignment shop, Kendall stands to make a good deal of money. It should help out her finances considerably."

"Only if she uses it to pay her bills." Megan sighed.

"Well, hopefully you can help her with that too."

Megan hugged her mom now. "If I don't see you before you leave, have fun in Victoria."

"Thanks, sweetie. And let me know what happens with work and Maui."

"Even if Cynthia does let me go, I wonder if I can get a very good deal now."

"Just call the travel agent as soon as you know. Hopefully tomorrow."

"Hopefully."

Shortly after Megan's mom left, Lelani got home from work. Her first question to Megan was about going to Maui. "Did you get the week off?" she asked.

Megan explained her dilemma. "I don't know why Cynthia's being so difficult about it," she told her. "But she'll be in the office tomorrow and I plan to give her an ultimatum."

"An ultimatum?"

"Yes. Because it's taken her so long to get back to me, I'm going to tell her that if she doesn't give me that week off, I'm walking."

Lelani looked shocked. "Oh, Megan, don't quit your job for me."

"Why not? I don't like it anyway. And that would motivate me to get a teaching job."

"But what if you didn't get hired?" Lelani looked truly worried now. "I'd feel like it was all my fault."

Megan considered this. "Of course it wouldn't be. I'm just so frustrated."

Lelani kind of laughed, although her eyes looked unhappy. "Right now it looks like the boys and I are going to Maui."

"The boys?" Megan knew that Gil had decided to go in case Megan wasn't able to get off work. "Who else?"

"Edmond. Anna told me that he and Gil are going to share a room." Lelani shook her head. "And now Anna is jealous." She looked perplexed. "Do you think I should invite Anna to go?"

Megan wanted to say no way but knew that was selfish. "I don't know, Lelani. If I don't get to go, Anna might be good moral support for you."

"Not as good as you, Megan. You really are my first choice."

"Thanks." Megan gave her a halfhearted smile. "But in the same way you'd feel lousy if you thought I was unemployed because of you, I'd feel terrible if you had to face down your parents alone because of me. Maybe you should ask Anna."

Lelani seemed to consider this. "I suppose it would be nice for Edmond—and Gil—if Anna came. Even though she's not you, she can be feisty when she needs to be."

"I know she'd back you up, Lelani."

She nodded. "Yeah. You're probably right."

"So if you want to ask her, I'll totally understand."

Lelani said she'd think about it. But Megan figured that was probably as far as it would go for now. She suspected Lelani would wait until the weekend to see if Megan had gotten the time off. Still, Megan was perplexed. Would it really be a mistake to quit her job if Cynthia turned her down? Wouldn't it be a legitimate form of protest, considering how Cynthia had ignored her all week? She knew her mom was against it. And it seemed Lelani was too. Still, Megan was fed up. Just because she was trying to be a good Christian, did that give her bosses the right to treat her like dirt and walk all over her?

Fourteen

Lelani

"I'll bet you're counting the days until your trip to Maui," said Margot as Lelani punched out the time clock for her lunch break.

Lelani smiled and nodded. "Oh, yeah, I can hardly wait."

"Lucky you," said Margot.

But as Lelani went down the stairs, she felt anything but lucky. In fact, she was starting to feel downright worried and upset. It was bad enough that she'd decided to do this thing without carefully thinking it through, but now it really looked as if Megan would have to bail on her as well. Certainly, Megan didn't want to let her down, but Lelani had a feeling that she wouldn't be able to do much about it. And the last thing Lelani wanted was for Megan to sacrifice her job for this silly trip. That would be really dumb.

Maybe the smartest thing would be to cancel the whole thing. Sure, she'd lose some money on the ticket, but it would be a small thing compared to showing up at her parents and falling completely apart.

Of course, there was still Gil and Edmond to think of, but she hadn't asked them to book trips to Maui. They were big boys, they could handle it. And yet she knew Gil had only made his plans for her sake.

"Lelani!" exclaimed Anna as they nearly ran into each other on the sidewalk outside. "Where are you going in such a hurry?"

Lelani forced a smile. "I'm not in that much of a hurry, just thinking and not watching where I'm going. I was on my way to the Soup Pot for a quick lunch. How about you?"

"I was heading to Demetri's. But the Soup Pot sounds good. Especially since it's so cold today."

"Why don't you join me?"

Anna and Lelani hurried across the street and managed to beat the rush at the Soup Pot. They both ordered Manhattan clam chowder, then grabbed the last available table along the wall.

"You know I was thinking about you this morning," Lelani told Anna as their soup arrived.

"Why's that?" asked Anna.

So Lelani told Anna what Megan had said about inviting her to Maui.

"Seriously?" Anna's eyes lit up. "You would invite me to stay at your parents' home in Maui?"

"Sure. But, you need to understand that I'm not just inviting you for the fun of it, Anna."

"I know." Anna grew serious. "I understand about Emma and how it's weighing on you and how you need to sort it all out."

"I mean I'd hope that we could have a good time, but it might get a little messy and there are things about my family—particularly my mom—that might surprise you."

Anna actually laughed. "Hey, don't you remember my mom? Not to mention my grandmother?"

Lelani nodded. "Yes, I suppose you do understand."

"More than you know. And Gil told me a little bit."

Lelani frowned.

"Only to explain why he felt the need to go."

"Yes, that's sweet of him."

"So you're serious, Lelani? You're really asking me to go with you?"

Lelani nodded. "Yes. Absolutely."

"But what if Megan gets to go?"

Lelani just shrugged. "Although it doesn't sound likely, it won't be a problem. There's plenty of room in my parents' guesthouse."

"This is so great!" Anna was already opening her phone. "Do you mind if I call Edmond and tell him the good news? And maybe he'll start buttering up his uncle so I can get that week off."

"Go for it."

Lelani waited as Anna talked to Edmond, explaining this surprise invitation with more excitement than Lelani had seen from Anna in some time. And when she hung up, she was grinning.

"What?" asked Lelani hopefully.

"Edmond told me to start packing my bags, because he was almost positive it wouldn't be a problem getting the time off."

"That's great."

"I'll ask officially when I get back to the office." Anna looked at her watch. "Speaking of that, I should probably go. I wouldn't want to be late when I'm asking for time off."

"No, of course not."

Later that afternoon, as Lelani walked home from work, she called Gil to tell him the good news and how it looked like Anna would be going with them to Maui.

"What about Megan?"

"I just don't think it's going to work for her."

"That's too bad."

"Are you sorry I asked Anna?"

"No. She's my sister, why would I be sorry?"

"I don't know."

"I just know how much you wanted Megan to go with you, Lelani. And I know how she can be a great encourager to you. That's all I'm saying. But I also know that Anna is stronger than she seems. Sometimes she totally surprises me by how well she does under pressure. I think she'll be a great asset to you. And I know Edmond will be jazzed."

"She already told him and he sounds ecstatic."

"I just wish you sounded happier."

"Oh, I'm happy about Anna coming," she assured him. "I just think the whole thing in general is getting to me. And I feel badly that Megan isn't coming. At least I don't think she is." Lelani sighed. "You know, I'll just be glad when the trip is all over."

Gil laughed. "Now that's something you don't hear every day. Someone planning a vacation to Maui saying they can't wait until it ends. Too funny."

She kind of laughed. "Oh, you know what I mean."

Although he assured her that he did know, she wondered if he could possibly have a clue. How could anyone understand how confused she felt? She didn't understand it herself. If only she could figure out what was best—best for Emma, best for her, even best for her parents. But nothing about this seemed clear-cut or black and white. Although she'd been praying about it—or trying to—as Megan had suggested, sometimes she felt that she was just talking to the walls. Oh, sometimes she got an unexplainable peaceful feeling, but that was about it. She never got any kind of signal or direction regarding her daughter or her parents.

If only she knew how this whole thing was supposed to turn out. Or if there was any way to fix something that already felt so broken, so far gone, like it had spun out of control long ago when she'd let her guard down. Really, what was the point of trying to figure it out now? And what was the point of dragging three of her friends along for the show? The Let's Humiliate Lelani Again Show.

These thoughts were erased from her head as she turned onto Bloomberg Place. Instead of the usual quiet, fairly dignified lane, cars lined both sides of the street directly in front of 86 Bloomberg Place. Kendall's garage sale. Lelani hurried down the street and across the yard, where it looked like Kendall was about to lose it. Or maybe she'd already lost it.

"No!" Kendall was shouting at an overweight teenage girl. "You cannot buy that beautiful Chloé bag for three dollars! Can't you read? The price on it is fifty dollars."

"Fifty dollars for a purse at a garage sale?" complained the teen. "That's nuts!"

"That bag was ten times that much new." Kendall snatched the pink bag from the girl and clutched it to her chest.

"No one in their right mind would pay five hundred dollars for that," the girl retorted.

"Maybe she's not in her right mind," said the girl's friend. And several garage sale shoppers chuckled.

"Why don't you take a break," said Lelani to Kendall. "I think I can handle this."

Kendall looked truly thankful as she continued clinging to her pink Chloé bag. "Yes!" she said loudly. "Lelani knows how to sell things. She works at Nordstrom."

Lelani gave the onlookers a sheepish smile. Why did Kendall have to announce that to everyone?

"Well, your prices are too high," said an older woman. "Don't you know that this is a garage sale?"

"It's a different kind of garage sale," Kendall shouted as she went into the garage. "And if you don't like it, you don't have to shop here!"

"Well, I won't," the lady shot back at her and walked away.

Lelani did the best she could to calm the shoppers, but it was clear that their concept of a garage sale did not include high-priced designer goods. Even when Lelani tried to explain it to them, most didn't get it. A lot of them continued to be rude. Just when Lelani was ready to put things away and put out a closed sign, Megan came home.

"Thank goodness!" exclaimed Lelani when Megan came to see how it was going. "I don't know what to do." She quickly told her what was going on.

"I was worried about that," admitted Megan. "But maybe it'll be better tomorrow. My mom told me the bargain hunters come on Fridays."

"Should we shut it down for the day?"

"Why don't you take a break and I'll handle it for a while," offered Megan.

"Thanks, my feet are killing me."

As Lelani went into the house, she realized that she hadn't even asked Megan about whether Cynthia had given her an answer or not. This only made Lelani more certain that it wasn't going to happen. Surely if Megan was going to Maui, she would've told Lelani immediately. Or even called her on her cell phone. No, it was probably just as well that she'd asked Anna to go. Not that it mattered. The more Lelani thought about it, the more she knew it was a fool's errand anyway. Best to just get it over with.

Fifteen

Anna

Anna was ecstatic that Rick Erlinger had agreed to give her spring break off. She knew his decision had more to do with Edmond than her, but she was thankful just the same. Okay, it offended her a little when Rick made his comments. He asked her to his office at the end of the workday after she'd put the official request form in his basket.

"I don't normally approve of office romances," he said, "but since Edmond is my favorite nephew, I guess I can make an exception."

She'd been too stunned to respond with anything more than a quiet, "Thank you."

"But I'll warn you," he'd added, "don't bring it into the workplace, Anna. You're a good editor and I'd like to keep you around, but if things between you and Edmond should go south, you'll be the one looking for a new job. You understand that, don't you?"

She just nodded.

"Okay, then. As long as we're all on the same page here."

But as she left the building without even saying good-bye to Edmond, she wondered if this was such a great idea. It wasn't that she didn't trust Edmond, she did. And if things went south, as Rick had intimated, she knew Edmond would handle it like a gentleman. After all, hadn't they been through this before? Still, it was a little unsettling to think she might be putting her job on the line. But maybe she was overreacting.

After she got into her car, she called Gil and told him the good news.

"I already know," he admitted.

"Lelani told you?"

"Yeah, just a little bit ago actually."

"Did she sound happy about it?" Anna put her key in the ignition. "I realize I wasn't her first choice."

"No, she sounded fine. She's still pretty uneasy about the whole thing in general, but she seemed relieved that you're going, Anna. And I'm sure you'll be a comfort to her."

Anna hoped she'd be comfort to Lelani, but, to be honest, she also hoped that she'd have some fun along the way. After all, it was supposed to be a vacation too. At least she had assumed that was the case when she accepted the invitation. It wasn't like this was an expenses-paid trip. She'd have to cover her own airfare as well as buy a few things for the week. In fact, she decided to stop by the mall on her way home and do some quick shopping. Anna didn't usually go overboard with things like clothes and fashion, but for some reason—maybe it was the enthusiastic sales girl in the petites department of Macy's who kept telling Anna she looked fantastic in everything—Anna walked back to her little Cooper loaded down with bags.

By the time Anna got home, it was just getting dark, but she could still see the remnants of Kendall's garage sale—the empty tables in the driveway, price lists and signs posted here and there, and garage-sale signs stuck in the yard. The lights to the house were all out, almost as if no one was home. Anna wondered if it was Kendall's way of saying that the sale was closed for the day.

"What have you been up to?" demanded Kendall when Anna came into the house with all her purchases.

"Shopping," Anna told her as she struggled to close the front door with her foot.

"For what?" Kendall's eyes were wide with interest.

"For Maui." Anna made her way to the stairs now.

"You're going to Maui too?" demanded Kendall.

Just then Megan emerged from the kitchen with a confused expression. "What?"

"Anna is going to Maui!" cried Kendall. "You're all going to Maui. Everyone is going to Maui except me!" She had real tears running down her cheeks now.

"You're going to Maui?" Megan asked Anna.

"Lelani just asked me—"

"That's right," said Lelani as she came into the living room. "I was going to tell you, Megan, but the garage sale and—"

"I want to go to Maui too," sobbed Kendall. "Everyone has a life but me. This is so unfair." She sank down onto the sectional and continued to cry.

"So Anna is going too?" Megan asked Lelani.

Then Lelani quickly explained about her unexpected lunch with Anna. "And I just felt so sure that it wasn't going to work for you, Megan, that I went ahead and asked Anna."

Anna couldn't read Megan's expression. It was either hurt or anger, or maybe both.

"But if it works out for you to go," Lelani said, "it's okay. There's room for three of us in my parents' guesthouse."

"There's room for three of you," cried Kendall. "But not four? You won't even invite me to come with you too?"

"Don't worry, Kendall," said Megan. "I'm not going either. It's just going to be Anna and Lelani. Don't get all worked up for nothing."

"But I want to go too," protested Kendall.

"Cynthia said no?" Lelani asked Megan.

"Cynthia is still in Astoria. Something went wrong and she'll be there until tomorrow. But Vera continues to assure me that I will not be getting spring break off."

"I'm sorry," said Lelani. "I really wish—"

"But if there's room for three," said Kendall hopefully, "why can't I go with you and Anna?"

Lelani looked perplexed.

"Because you're broke?" tried Megan.

"Not anymore," proclaimed Kendall. "And this was just the first day of the sale."

"Even so—"

"You're not the boss of me," snapped Kendall. "If Lelani wants me to go to Maui with her, I can go. Right, Lelani?"

Lelani's dark eyes were wide. "I, uh, I don't—"

"No, you can't go," Anna told Kendall.

"Why?" demanded Kendall.

"For one thing, Lelani hasn't invited you to go. For another thing, like Megan said, you cannot afford to go, Kendall. You need to pay your bills with that garage sale money."

"That's right," agreed Megan.

"Now, if you'll excuse me," Anna puffed as she trudged upstairs, "I need to put these things away."

The three of them continued to talk as Anna hauled her purchases to her room to unpack and hang up and admire. Then she went online and began to shop for an airline ticket. To her shock and dismay, they were really expensive, about twice what she had available in her bank account. Anna had a Visa card that her parents had gotten for her in college, but they had always warned her that it was strictly for emergencies. She had heeded that warning and only used it a couple of times. She pulled the card out of her wallet only to discover that it had actually expired just a few weeks ago. Since the card had been sent to her parents' address, she suspected that replacement cards had probably been sent there too.

She called her mom, although Anna wasn't eager to explain that she and Edmond would be in Maui with Gil and Lelani. So she simply inquired as to whether any mail for the credit card had come to them.

"As you know, your father takes care of those things," her mom told her.

"Is Dad there?"

"No. But, tell me, Anna, why this sudden interest in that credit card? I know how you hate credit, mi'ja. Surely you're not having an emergency, are you?"

"No, Mom, it's not an emergency exactly."

"Not exactly? But perhaps a little?"

So Anna told her mother about Maui.

"Oh, Anna." Her mother's voice was laced in disappointment. It was the same tone she had used when Anna was ten and came home with grass stains on her pale-blue party dress after a birthday gathering where all the other girls had been wearing pants—just like Anna had told her mother they would be.

"What?" demanded Anna. "What is wrong with that?"

"Gil told me."

"Told you what?"

"That he and Edmond are going to Maui for spring break too. Certainly you're not going to Maui with your boyfriend for a week, mi'ja. What would people say?"

"Of course, I'm not going with Edmond, Mom. I'm going with Lelani."

"Lelani?"

"Yes. Didn't Gil tell you she was going?" Even as Anna said this, she knew she was in trouble—again.

"No, Gil told me he was going with Edmond. Is that not true?"

"Yes, it's true, Mom. Gil is going with Edmond."

"And you are going with Lelani?"

Anna didn't answer.

"My children must both think I am a fool."

"No, we don't."

Anna's mother started talking in Spanish. Rapid Spanish.

"It's not like you think, Mama," Anna said loudly. "Really. I am staying at Lelani's parents' house with Lelani. They are very old-fashioned—"

"Old-fashioned? Their daughter has a child out of wedlock and that's old-fashioned?"

"Mama, what about Alicia?" Anna reminded her.

"Yes, yes. But that's different."

"How is that different?"

"Alicia and whatever his name is finally got married."

"A year after the baby was born, Mama? How is that different?"

"It's different because they were not *my* children."

"Oh, Mama!"

Her mother launched into more Spanish, and Anna was tempted to shout a quick good-bye and hang up, but she knew she needed that credit card.

"Mama," Anna pleaded loudly. "You need to understand that it's not like you think. Lelani and I will be at her parents' and Gil and

Edmond will be at a hotel—probably on the other side of the island. It's no different than how we're living here. Can't you see that?"

There was a short stint of silence now, and her mother finally sighed. "If I could only be sure."

"Why can't you just trust your own children, Mama?"

"I do, but I know boys will be boys, and girls will be girls, and I was young once."

"Aha," said Anna. "That explains everything. Maybe I should ask Abuela about your youth?"

"Speaking of Abuela, Anna, are you and Edmond coming to the farewell dinner Sunday night?"

"Maybe." Anna thought this might be her ticket.

"Maybe?"

"Here's the deal, Mama. I need that credit card to pay for my airfare to Maui. Can you ask Dad if he has it? If not, maybe you can loan me the money."

"You're asking me to loan you money for a trip to a tropical island with your boyfriend, mi'ja? Do you think I'm a fool?"

"No." Anna's voice grew hard now.

"We'll talk Sunday, Anna. I have much to do."

"But I need to book the flight now," said Anna desperately. "The rates go up daily and there might not even be any flights left if—"

"Don't talk to me about this anymore, Anna."

"But, Mama—"

"Anna!"

"Fine. Good-bye, *Mother.*" Anna hung up and stormed downstairs, where Kendall, Megan, and Lelani were still talking about Maui and why Kendall needed to let it go. Not that they were having any luck.

"What's wrong with little Anna?" Kendall asked her in a snide tone. "For someone who's going to Maui, you sure don't look very happy."

"Maybe I'm not going to Maui," Anna snapped at Kendall.

"But you got the time off," Megan reminded her.

Anna looked at Megan, then shook her head. "Sure, I got the time off. But I just found out my Visa card expired and my mom refuses to help me with it."

Kendall actually laughed now. "So Anna's got the time off, but no money. And Megan's got the money, but no time off."

"And your point is?" asked Lelani.

Kendall reached for the tin box on the coffee table and opened it up to show a big pile of bills. "My point is that I've got the time off, and I will soon have the money." She waved the wad of bills at Lelani. "Pick me! Please, please, pick me!"

Lelani looked like she was on the verge of tears or a nervous breakdown. She held up her hands. "I can't even think right now." Then she turned and went to her room as Kendall continued to beg her.

"Please, Lelani," she called out. "You won't be sorry. I'm great on vacations and I promise that I'll be—"

"Don't you see that you're driving us all bonkers?" Megan told Kendall. "Can you please give it a rest?"

"Okay." Kendall straightened up her money and put it back in the tin. "I'll give it a rest for now. But when this garage sale is over, and when I've sold my things on eBay and at the consignment shop, and when I've paid down my bills, if I still have money left over, I think Lelani should take me to Maui."

"How about you let Lelani decide," said Megan quietly. "Now if you'll excuse me."

And then it was just Anna and Kendall in the living room, although Anna wanted to make a getaway too. But before she could, Kendall turned to her.

"I know how you can make some money, Anna."

Anna knew she should know better, but she bit anyway. "How?"

"You can sell some of your things at my garage sale."

Anna couldn't believe she was actually considering this. "What kind of things?"

"Like anything you have that someone might want to buy." Kendall pointed to her money box. "It's easy."

"Maybe for you. I don't think—"

"Hey, how about if I make a deal with you." Kendall got a sly look now.

"What kind of deal?"

"If you'll work the garage sale for me, I'll give you a piece of the action."

"What action?"

"You know, I'll give you a cut. Like, how about 10 percent?"

Anna frowned. "That probably won't add up to much."

"Okay." Kendall's mouth twisted like she was thinking. "The truth is I'm not really into the selling part of this garage sale. I mean it's no fun bickering with people over my stuff. Everyone keeps wanting me to lower the prices and I think they're getting some serious bargains. I mean when was the last time you saw a pair of barely worn Prada boots for ninety bucks?"

Anna shrugged. Really, why was she even having this conversation?

"Okay, I'll give you 20 percent to work the sale for me, Anna. But that's my final offer. And if you'd been doing it today, you'd have a nice fat wad of cash right now."

Anna considered this. "Okay. 20 percent."

"But you have to promise to work all day Saturday and Sunday. Okay?"

"Okay." Anna was desperate.

"And you have to be ready to open at 7:30 a.m., like the ad in the paper says. Megan told me we'll lose some of the best customers if we don't open early. And she won't come down to help out until around nine."

Suddenly Anna wasn't so sure. "Seven thirty on a Saturday feels pretty early."

"Take it or leave it."

Anna sighed, but she did agree. And then they shook on it.

"Really, Anna, you should go look through your things. You'd be surprised at the kinds of junk people will buy at a garage sale."

Anna was pretty sure that was an insult, but the idea of possibly earning enough money for her airline ticket without having to go to her parents was good motivation. So she went through her drawers and closet, slowly making a pile that steadily grew, of anything she knew she didn't need and wouldn't miss. In a way it was fun getting rid of some things, kind of like a real spring cleaning. Now if only this stuff could transform itself into a ticket to Maui.

Sixteen

Kendall

Kendall was so relieved to be able to sleep in on Saturday. Unfortunately, Tinkerbell did not get the same memo. She thought it was her job to bark furiously at every single garage-sale shopper that came and went from the house. Finally Kendall gave up and got out of bed, and it wasn't even nine yet. Still, she felt hopeful as she pulled on her sweats. With all that traffic down there, she'd probably made several hundred dollars by now. Maybe even more.

But when Kendall went into the garage to check the progress, Anna glumly informed her that there'd only been three sales. "A chipped teapot that sold for seven dollars. A first edition Clancy book for ten and a pair of sunglasses for three."

"You're sure they weren't the real Christian Dior ones that are marked thirty?" demanded Kendall as she glanced nervously at the designer section right next to the money table. "You're keeping a close eye on those things, aren't you? I saw a teen girl who looked like she was going to steal something from there yesterday."

"Yeah, yeah," said Anna. "So you told me last night. And I was watching it. Trust me, the lady bought the counterfeit shades, the ones with the rhinestone CC on the sides, right?"

"Yeah. Those were the Coco Chanel fakes."

"Three sales for a grand total of twenty dollars."

Kendall frowned. "With Tinker barking her head off upstairs, I was certain that you were down here raking it in. All I've made is a measly twenty bucks?"

Anna glared at her. "Don't you mean a measly *sixteen* bucks? Don't forget that I'm getting my 20 percent commission, which means I've made a whopping four dollars for almost two hours out here. At this rate, I might be able to buy a ticket—for the bus!"

"Maybe you should try harder." Kendall noticed an older Mercedes parking in front of the house now. "Here come some customers. Make some money, Anna!"

Then Kendall slipped back into the house, where Tinkerbell was barking like a crazed dog again. This was looking to be a long weekend. If only there was someplace where she could go to escape the madness. After all, she had "hired" Anna to take over for her.

Kendall went back to her room and dug in her closet until she finally found a clean set of pale pink sweats. Then she showered and dressed and even put on makeup. She put a matching pink hoodie on Tinkerbell.

"We're going shopping," she informed Tinker as she slipped the little dog into her carrying case. "Mama needs some new clothes." And the truth was, she did need some new clothes, because there was no way she could go through this pregnancy looking like a bag lady in dirty old sweats. If she was really going to have this baby, which after her talk with Megan's mom seemed to be the only thing to do, she was going to do it in style!

But first she stopped by the garage sale, where Megan had finally joined Anna and was just selling the brass spittoon, and a few other items, to an older woman who said she planned to use it as a container for silk flowers. Kendall waited for Megan to make change from the woman's two twenties.

"It's about time you came down to help," said Megan as she put the cash in the money box.

"Didn't Anna tell you that I hired her to help? She's getting a commission."

"Yes, she told me that. But does that mean you don't plan to work at all today?"

"Not today or tomorrow." Kendall reached under the table to the place where they were keeping the money tin.

"What are you doing with that?" Megan watched suspiciously as Kendall opened the box.

"I don't think it's safe to leave all this money out here at the garage sale," Kendall whispered. "Your mom said that sometimes people try to steal the money box."

"Oh, that's right." Megan nodded. "I forgot."

"Anyway, I'll leave enough cash to keep making change and put the rest in a safe place," Kendall assured her. But Megan was already heading over to help a customer who wanted to know if he could try out Kendall's old treadmill.

Kendall removed most of the cash as well as the checks, leaving plenty for change. Then, feeling slightly like a thief, she slipped the thick wad of bills into her purse and headed straight for her car, which was parked down the street. She knew that Megan might get irritated at her for spending some of the garage-sale money, but after all, it was Kendall's money. And besides she really did need some maternity clothes. Not only that, but she planned to be frugal about it. She'd gotten a Macy's flyer last week, and they were having a big sale in their new maternity department. And some of the clothes weren't that bad looking. In fact, a lot of them didn't even look like maternity clothes. Who knew? Maybe this would actually be fun.

In a way, it was fun. Other pregnant women were shopping and happily discussing which clothes looked best and which trimester expanded waistlines the most and what they were going to name their babies and when they were due.

"You don't look too far along," the sales woman said to Kendall. "When are you due?"

Kendall blinked and tried to remember when her obstetrician had said. "Uh, in the summer."

"Must be late summer."

"Oh, yeah." Kendall remembered now. "Not until the end of August."

"You poor thing," said a woman who looked fairly far along. "I had to go through summer with my first baby. Let me tell you, that was one long, hot summer too."

"When are you due?" Kendall asked her.

"May 14. Right around Mother's Day." The woman put her hand on top of her rounded tummy. "But I've already outgrown some of my old maternity clothes that I wore to full term last time. They say that happens with your second pregnancy."

Kendall nodded like she knew all about this, although it was news to her.

"Is this your first?"

Kendall nodded again. "How did you know?"

The woman chuckled as she pointed at Tinker in the dog carrier. "Once you have a baby, you won't be dressing up your little dog anymore."

The sales woman helped Kendall to find the right sizes and showed her how some of the garments would adjust to the growing size of her stomach. Kendall found it hard to believe she'd ever need all that room.

"I can't imagine my belly ever getting that big," said Kendall as the woman expanded the waist so that it looked like it might fit around a midsized cow.

"You'll be surprised," the sales woman told her. "Your body will change drastically before you give birth."

Kendall pushed those kinds of thoughts from her mind as she tried on clothes, finally settling on an assortment of things. Her favorites were the mix-and-match stretchy knit pieces, including yoga pants, a wrap skirt, several expandable camisoles, a hoodie. But she also picked a little black dress and even a pair of jeans. She was tempted to get some summer pieces in case she went to Maui but decided that was pretty unlikely.

"Did you know they're having a sale in the baby department too?" asked the woman who was due on Mother's Day.

"Really?" Kendall tried to feign interest.

"Come on," urged the woman, "everything is at least 20 percent off, and some of the markdown racks are an additional 60 percent off. I swear they're practically giving some things away."

And so Kendall tagged along with this woman, whose name she learned was Beth. She taught at the same middle school that Kendall had attended ten years ago.

"I was a cheerleader in eighth grade," Kendall proudly told her. "If you looked up an old journal, you'd see me in it."

But Beth wasn't interested in Kendall's illustrious history as a Madison Middle School Pirate. All Beth could think about was baby things, and since her next baby was going to be a girl (the first one, now three years old, was a boy) everything she picked out was pink-pink-pink. Not that Kendall didn't like pink. And not that Kendall couldn't imagine a sweet little infant swaddled in pale pink ruffles, but she just couldn't imagine herself with a baby, period. Buying maternity clothes (which didn't really look like maternity clothes) was one thing. But envisioning herself walking around with a Cadillac stroller was something else.

Despite all that, and to Kendall's own surprise, she got slightly caught up in the baby craze too. And, before she left that busy baby department, she had purchased a khaki diaper bag that could almost pass for a D&G; a soft robin's-egg blue chenille baby blanket that she wished were big enough for her own bed; and what Beth told her was a "newborn layette"—something the baby (either for a boy or girl since it was a buttery yellow) would wear home from the hospital. Now that was an event that Kendall could not even begin to imagine.

Kendall put her out-of-character purchases and Tinkerbell into the car and, since she could now afford it, went to get gas. Finally, she stopped at Quiznos for a late lunch—because she was, after all, eating for two. After that she wasn't sure where to go or what to do to kill a few more hours, but she knew she should probably avoid any more shopping. Especially if she didn't want Megan freaking out and yelling at her.

Kendall hadn't kept really close track, but she suspected she'd spent around three hundred dollars, and what had once been a thick wad of cash had definitely dwindled. Not that Megan had to be privy to that. Still, Kendall did not want to go home and be tortured by that bothersome garage sale. And so it was she found herself pulling into the parking lot of Nana's nursing home.

"Kendall!" Nana looked pleasantly surprised when she opened the door. But then she frowned. "What are you doing here? You didn't come here to get money from me, did you?"

"No, of course, not," Kendall assured her. She held out Tinkerbell's carrying case. "We just stopped in to say hello."

"Well, hello." Nana still looked concerned. "What are you doing here?" she asked again.

Kendall thought for a moment. "Hey, do you want to go get ice cream?"

Nana brightened up and went immediately to get her favorite old handbag—it used to be cream colored, but now looked more like tan, although Kendall suspected it would clean up nicely, since it was vinyl. She used to make fun of that old purse, but then she realized it was a Gucci from the sixties and actually quite valuable, not to mention rather chic in that Jackie-O sort of way. Anyway, Kendall had told Nana more than once that if she ever wanted to get rid of it, she should toss it Kendall's way. Of course, Kendall knew there was no money in Nana's bag. Sticky fingers in the nursing home had taught Nana to hide her cash in smarter places. Sometimes Nana forgot where she'd hidden her money, and at times when Kendall was desperate, she would go hunting. Not today.

"Ice cream," said Nana as they walked through the parking lot. "You scream, I scream, everyone scream for ice cream."

Kendall laughed. "I can't believe you remember that."

"Isn't that what you kids used to say?"

"Pretty close anyway." Kendall opened the door and helped Nana into the car.

As they drove to a nearby ice-cream shop, Nana pointed to a sign. "Garage sale!" she cried so loudly that Kendall hit the brakes. "Stop, Kendall. Stop!"

The last thing Kendall wanted to do was go to a garage sale, but Nana would not give up. And so she parked and helped Nana out of the car, and together they walked past the tables loaded with junk. Real junk too. It actually made Kendall's garage sale look good. And Kendall even mentioned to the other shoppers about how there was a really good garage sale over on Bloomberg Place.

"Oh, that's a nice neighborhood," said one woman.

"And they have nice stuff too," Kendall quietly told her. "Even designer clothes. And some antiques and collectibles."

The woman nudged her friend. "Hey, let's head over to Bloomberg Place."

That's when it hit Kendall. "Nana," she said. "Do you want to go to more garage sales?"

Naturally Nana was game. So, every time Kendall spotted a sale, she stopped and helped her grandmother out of the car. Then, while Nana browsed, Kendall informed the other shoppers about the fantastic sale she'd been to over on Bloomberg Place.

"I think I'll have to go back over there," she told a girl about her age. "I keep thinking about these really gorgeous black Prada boots that I could've gotten for a fraction of their original price. And they looked like new."

"Seriously?" the girl looked surprised. "Do you think they're still there?"

"I don't know, but there were lots of other cool things." Kendall checked her watch. "Maybe I'll head back there now."

And so it went. At the rate that Kendall was advertising her own garage sale, the girls should be swamped in no time. Perhaps they'd be sold out by closing time, six o'clock. And then Kendall wouldn't have to put up with it for another whole day!

Nana eventually wore out and, to Kendall's surprise, remembered that they were supposed to be getting ice cream. Since Nana was tired, Kendall got their ice cream to go and they ate in the car as she drove back to the nursing home. Then she helped Nana out, did her best to wipe the spilt droplets of orange sherbet off Nana's favorite white sweater, and walked her back to her room. Along the way, Nana bragged to all her friends about where she'd been.

"My granddaughter took me for ice cream," she told them.

"And to a bunch of garage sales too," Kendall would add. Naturally, the other inmates all got jealous. And that just made Nana cackle and grin like she'd won the lottery. Kendall thought it might be nice if life were so simple. Not that she wanted to be old and live in a place like this. But sometimes it had its appeal.

After she got Nana safely to her room and settled into her comfy recliner, where she immediately went to sleep, Kendall walked back through the home via the activities room, which, as usual, was not very active. But she spied Walt, a friendly old coot she'd met the time she hid out at Nana's for a day or two. He was sitting by himself in his wheelchair.

"Hey, Walt," she called out. "What's up?"

"Well, if it ain't my best girl." He grinned. "What's your name again?"

"Kendall."

"Yes, yes, Kendall. You're Gert Weis's granddaughter."

She held up the doggy carrier. "And this is Tinkerbell."

"Glad to meet you, Tinkerbell." He chuckled. "Don't recall you having a dog last time you were here, Kendall."

"I got her a few months ago."

"Where's your grandmother? Is she okay?"

So Kendall explained about the garage sales and ice cream and how it had all worn her grandmother out.

"What a good girl you are to come take your grandmother out like that."

She just smiled. It wasn't every day that someone called her a good girl. It felt strange but nice. Maybe now that she was going to become a mommy—someday—she would turn into a nicer, better person. It seemed possible somehow ... at least something she might aspire to.

"How's about a little game of checkers?" Walt asked hopefully.

Since she still had time to kill, plus because she liked the idea of being a nice girl, she agreed. But, after two games, the dinner bell rang and Walt, worried that he'd miss out on his favorite meal of corned beef and cabbage and scalloped potatoes, excused himself.

"Thanks for the games, honey," he called out as he wheeled himself across the room. "Next time, I'll let you win."

Kendall considered joining Nana for dinner, but the smell of cooked cabbage made her want to hurl, and it wasn't even morning. So she hurried on out to her car. It was only five, but Kendall decided that it might be interesting to get home in time to see if any of her free advertising was paying off. To her delight, there were cars parked along both sides of the street and the garage sale seemed to be hopping.

"I'm back," she cheerfully told her friends after she'd put Tinker in the house.

"It's about time." Megan scowled. "It's been a zoo here."

"Yeah," said Anna. "Make yourself useful."

For the next hour, Kendall worked the garage sale, and when someone recognized her from one of the other sales, she just laughed. "Well, I told you the truth, didn't I?" she said to a frumpy middle-aged woman. "This garage sale is way better than all the other ones I saw today."

"You've been going to garage sales today?" asked Anna as they started packing things up.

"Just to advertise this one," Kendall told her as she counted out change to a girl who finally decided to purchase her old rollerblades for eighteen dollars.

"Well, maybe your marketing plan worked," admitted Lelani, "because we've sure been busy. I had to come out and help when it got too crazy out here."

"Thanks," said Kendall.

"Well, you're going to pay her for helping," said Anna. "We all agreed to that."

Kendall just shrugged. "That's okay."

"We promised Lelani ten bucks an hour," Megan told her. "And so far she's put in five hours."

"You can just deduct it from next month's rent for me," Lelani told Kendall.

"Just remind me when the time comes," Kendall said.

"Don't worry," said Megan. "We'll both be reminding you. Don't forget you promised me a break on the rent too."

She had, and though now she was regretting having to spread out her profits, she supposed a break on rent later was better than cash out of hand now.

Finally the last customer left and the girls finished putting stuff away and closed the garage doors.

"I'm exhausted," declared Anna.

"And I'm starving," said Megan.

"I'll call out for pizza," offered Lelani.

"And Kendall is buying." Megan handed Kendall the cash box.

"That's fair." Kendall shook the heavy box. "This feels full."

"And there's more in the house," said Anna. "I stashed it in the top drawer of the china hutch. I was trying to keep track of how much we took in, except it got too busy. But I've been keeping the money from my garage sale things separate from yours." Anna kind of laughed. "Not that I'm getting rich. Unlike you, I've only made a little more than thirty dollars so far. But I'm curious to hear your total."

"I'll count it all out very carefully," Kendall assured them. Then she took the cash box to her room and dumped it on her bed and started to count the bills. To her amazement, it was nearly eight hundred dollars. Combined with what she'd spent today, she'd earned more than a thousand total. And that didn't even include the checks! Who knew you could make that much from a garage sale? Then she remembered that she needed to give Anna her cut. But she also knew that part of the money had been from the previous day, since she'd left some to be used for change. Why hadn't she thought to count it earlier?

So she did a quick estimate and figured it had to be less than a hundred, which she set aside. She added in today's checks for a total of $978.50, then set aside money for pizza. Finally, she had to use pen and paper to figure Anna's portion, which was about $190. Not bad for a day's work. But now Kendall was rethinking her deal with Anna. Lelani had worked for ten dollars an hour. Why shouldn't Anna do the same? But when she suggested as much to Anna, it was as if she'd suggested that Anna should cut off her arm.

"You promised me," Anna yelled at her. "And now you're backing out?"

"It's just not fair that—"

"It's not fair that you don't honor your word."

"I'll pay you ten bucks an—"

"Keep your money," snapped Anna. "I've had it." Then she stomped off to her room.

Kendall felt a twinge of guilt, but it was her garage sale. It didn't seem fair that everyone else was profiting from it. Who needed them anyway? So far Kendall had made around a thousand bucks—and without paying for their help she stood to make more.

Seventeen

Megan

Sunday's garage sale didn't open until ten, and Megan told Kendall that she wouldn't be able to help until she and Marcus returned from church around noon. Just the same, Kendall had already left two messages asking where Megan was and why wasn't she there to help? As Marcus drove her back to the house, Megan held the phone to his ear so he could hear it too.

"Kendall is such a nut case." He laughed. "How do you put up with her?"

"Well, according to this morning's sermon, I put up with her because Jesus in me is able to put up with her. Right?"

"I remind myself that Kendall can be her own worst enemy," Megan admitted. "And then I remember that she needs real friends. Even though I know I fall short most of the time, I figure I better keep working at it. I know that Anna has just about given up on her." Then she told Marcus about how Kendall had cut Anna out of the working-for-20-percent deal. "And Anna would have made around two hundred dollars yesterday. With another day like that, she could've gone to Maui. Now she can't afford a ticket, which has Lelani worried. She'd been counting on having Anna along."

"But Kendall pulled the plug?"

"Pretty much. Anna thinks it's because Kendall wants to go to Maui, and she thinks if no one else can go her chances will improve."

"What does Lelani think?"

"It's hard to say. She's been kind of quiet. I think the whole trip, plus not knowing who is going with her—besides Gil and Edmond—is getting to her."

"So Anna's pretty mad at Kendall today?"

"She's not helping her with the garage sale. And Lelani had plans to have brunch with Gil this morning."

"So that's why Kendall's calling you?"

Megan nodded. "And I know this sounds mean, but it's the truth: I think she deserves to be a little stressed. She brought it on herself."

"In other words, don't hurry to get home."

"Don't get any speeding tickets. Honestly, if I hadn't promised to help her, and if she wasn't giving me a break on next month's rent, I would probably just say forget it." Megan leaned back and sighed. "Man, I'll be glad when that stupid sale is over with. And I will definitely think twice before coming up with any more brilliant ideas for getting Kendall out of debt." She laughed. "I actually thought that a little garage sale would motivate her to want to go out and find a real job. But then she turned the little sale into this great big production."

"Which reminds me, some of her things are doing pretty well on eBay."

"Great. Kendall will probably never want to get a real job now."

"Speaking of real jobs, have you decided not to quit yours?"

"Yeah. I mean I still toy with the idea of walking into Cynthia's office and telling her to take this job and shove it. But then I realize how immature that would be. And, like my mom said, if you want to get another job, it's better to look while you're still employed."

"That makes sense."

"And I've been trying to surrender the whole Maui thing to God. I figure if I was supposed to go, things would've gone differently. Maybe there's a reason I'm staying home."

He reached over and patted her head. "I'm glad to see you're not still bummed."

"Oh, I'm still bummed. I'm just trying to act like I'm not bummed in the hopes that it will rub off into reality."

He laughed as he turned onto Bloomberg Place. "Hey, looks like Kendall's sale is still going great guns."

Now Megan sat up straight and looked to see there were quite a few cars in front of the house. Apparently Kendall hadn't been exaggerating about being busy.

"You better just drop me off," Megan told him. "It looks like she really does need help."

"Want me to stick around and lend a hand?"

"If you really want to. I'm sure Kendall would appreciate it."

"I'll go find a place to park," he called as she got out of the car.

"Business appears to be good," said Megan as she joined Kendall.

"It's about time you got here."

Megan was tempted to remind her about church but decided to help an elderly woman add up her purchases instead. Then Marcus joined them and the threesome worked steadily until Lelani showed up.

"You don't have to keep working now," Megan told Marcus.

"I don't mind," he said as he straightened a pile of books. "It's kind of fun."

She rolled her eyes.

But by midafternoon the wind blew up and the sales slowed down and Marcus decided to make a break for it. Megan didn't blame him. If she hadn't promised Kendall she'd stay until they shut the thing down, she would've gladly gone with him.

"If you guys don't mind, I'll call it a day," Lelani told them. "Anna and I have this family dinner to go to at the Mendez's restaurant tonight."

"Meet the grandparents again?" asked Megan.

"This time it's saying good-bye to the grandparents." Lelani sighed. "Gil promised that if things get ugly, we'll leave."

"Let the good times roll," teased Kendall.

"We might as well start packing it up anyway," Megan told Kendall as a few raindrops started to splat down.

Kendall frowned. "It might stop."

"We don't even have any shoppers," pointed out Megan.

"But there's still another hour until we were supposed to close."

"I don't think it really matters." Megan was already putting old books into a box. "Besides, if someone comes, we can always let them poke around."

Kendall reluctantly began to put things away.

As they quietly worked together, Megan began to feel guilty about the way she'd talked about Kendall to Marcus. Megan knew that it wasn't the way Jesus would act. And yet she wasn't even sure how to turn it off. Perhaps she just needed to apologize. Megan set down the box that she'd just filled and turned to Kendall.

"Kendall," she began, "I need to tell you I'm sorry."

"Huh?" Kendall looked up from where she was folding a pair of jeans. "For what?"

"For being kind of mean spirited toward you. I mean about the garage sale and everything."

"But you've been helping me with it." Kendall looked confused.

"I know. But I haven't been very cheerful about it."

"Well, garage sales are kind of disgusting."

"I know, but I was the one who encouraged you to have it in the first place. And I actually think it's really great that you went through with this whole thing. You put a lot of work into it. I'm sorry I wasn't more supportive."

"Oh, well, that's okay."

"Not really. But I hope you'll forgive me."

"Sure." Kendall smiled brightly.

Megan considered explaining to Kendall that she'd probably been overly stressed at work, that she'd been disappointed by the way Vera was treating her and hurt by the way Cynthia was ignoring her. But those would just be excuses. And this was supposed to be an apology. "Thanks," she told Kendall.

"I'm just glad we're done with the garage sale now," Kendall admitted. "I was getting kind of sick of it myself." Kendall was still working on packing up her designer section, handling each item with special care.

"Oh, I remember when I got this." Kendall sighed as she held up a little white denim jacket with rhinestones. Megan thought it looked small enough to fit a child, but then Kendall had been pretty slender before she'd gotten pregnant.

"It looks like new," observed Megan.

"I was in Vegas with some friends," Kendall continued. "We thought it was going to be hot down there, but it was chilly. I stopped into a Gucci shop and this little darling was on the sale rack." She hugged the jacket close to her. "I wonder if rhinestones will ever be hot again."

Megan walked over and looked at the tag inside. "Gucci? I wonder how much you paid for this."

Kendall sighed. "Well, it was originally around five hundred, but I think it was like 20 or 30 percent off."

Megan did some quick mental math. "So, let's say it was 30 percent off and you paid three-fifty for it, Kendall."

Kendall sort of shrugged. "Okay, what's your point?"

Megan reached for the cash box now. She pulled out enough twenties and tens and fives to equal three-hundred-fifty dollars and held the bills out to Kendall. "So, which would you rather have right now, Kendall? A jacket that's too small and out of style, or *this*?"

Kendall tossed the jacket down and eagerly snatched the money. "Duh."

Megan smiled as she picked up the jacket and held it up. "But you paid three-fifty for this jacket, Kendall. And now it's worth maybe twenty bucks. Can't you see how that's not terribly wise?"

"But I used my credit card when I bought it," Kendall said as she shaped the bills into a fan and waved them. "It wasn't like real money."

"That's true," said Megan. "But the credit card must be paid with real money, plus it has interest added to it. I'll bet by the time you paid for that jacket, if it's even paid for, it probably cost even more than five hundred bucks."

"Huh?" Kendall looked confused now.

So Megan, who had always been good at math, got out the pad and pen and showed Kendall how interest would accumulate until even Megan was stunned to see the figure. "Wow, that is one really expensive jacket, Kendall!"

Kendall picked up the jacket again. "Maybe I should keep it."

"No." Megan took the jacket from her. "The jacket itself is really kind of worthless to you now, Kendall. I mean look, it doesn't even fit. And like you said, rhinestones aren't in style."

Kendall looked like she was on the verge of tears.

"I'm sorry to be so blunt," Megan said gently. "And I'm not trying to hurt you, Kendall. I just want you to realize how much money you've spent on things that aren't really worth that much."

Kendall sat down in a camp chair and shook her head. "I'll bet you think I'm a total idiot."

Megan sat down in the other camp chair and silently prayed, asking God to guide her words. "No. I don't think you're an idiot, Kendall. I just think you've been a little confused."

Kendall just nodded.

"I think you've thought that things were valuable because of their price tags."

She nodded again.

"And I think that magazines and movies and whatever … well, they made you believe that you needed to buy overpriced items so that you would feel valuable too."

Kendall looked at Megan in surprise. "That's true."

"And I think there are a whole lot of girls like you, Kendall. Girls who are being sold a bill of goods and getting into debt, and none of it makes them happy."

Kendall was crying now. "Yes, you're absolutely right. I mean I'll go shopping and pay way too much for something and it feels so great. But then, like a week later, and sometimes just a day later, I feel lousy again. And then I don't even like the thing I bought. I don't even care about it."

"Because you thought that thing would fix your life?"

"Yeah!" Kendall nodded firmly. "And then it didn't."

"In fact, it probably made your life worse, because then the bills start to come."

Kendall wiped her tears with the backs of her hands. "Yeah. And they come and come and come until you feel like you're drowning in them."

"That's why you have to stop living like this, Kendall."

"But how?" Kendall sniffed loudly.

Megan considered this. "I wonder if there's some kind of debtors anonymous group."

"Very funny."

"I'm serious. But besides that, Kendall, I really think you need God in your life—big time."

"I believe in God."

"And that's a great start. But you need to let God *into* your life, Kendall. So he can lead you and guide you and help you to make better decisions."

"So that I'll be more like you?"

"No, Kendall. You know that I don't have it all together. I just admitted to you that I've been pretty mean. You need God so you'll be more like you. I mean the way God wants you to be, the way he designed you to be. And that does *not* mean being driven by a compulsion to purchase things you can't afford just to make yourself feel valuable. Or being up to your eyeballs in debt." Megan went on to tell Kendall that God already valued her, that he'd sent Jesus as the purchase price for her. "It's like you're a designer original," Megan said finally. "God designed you perfectly and paid top dollar for you. But until you get that, you'll keep going about everything all wrong."

Kendall was starting to look confused now, and Megan decided that maybe she should take things more slowly. "How about if you come to church with Marcus and me sometimes?"

Kendall nodded. "Yeah, I think that would be good."

"Next Sunday?" asked Megan. "Since we obviously won't be in Maui then."

"Okay." Kendall's brow creased. "You know, I'm starting to feel guilty about Anna not going with Lelani. I mean if I'd paid her and let her work the garage sale like I promised, she'd have enough money to go to Maui now."

"Yeah, that would've been nice." Megan had actually been thinking about loaning Anna some money to help her to go. "For Lelani's sake, I'd really been hoping that Anna would be able to go."

Kendall looked down at the wad of cash still in her hand, staring at it like she was mesmerized. "I'll be right back," she said. Then she took off into the house and Megan went back to gathering things up, sorting what could go to consignment and what should be given away and what should be tossed.

"I don't believe it," said Lelani as she joined Megan in the garage.

"Believe what?"

"Kendall just gave Anna three hundred fifty dollars."

"Seriously?"

Lelani nodded with a confused expression. "Well, part of it was a gift. Part was a loan. Now Anna can afford to go to Maui with me. She's booking her flight online right now. Hopefully she can get on the same one that I'm on. Can you believe it?"

"That's fantastic!" Megan hugged Lelani. "I'm so relieved."

"Yeah." Lelani still looked shocked. "I can't believe that Kendall would do something like that. My head is still spinning."

Soon Kendall and Anna came back out to the garage, and everyone was talking at once, and Lelani hugged Kendall. "That was so sweet of you, Kendall. I wish you could come with us too!"

Kendall's eyes lit up. "Really?"

Lelani nodded. "Really. I wish all four of us could go."

Kendall looked hopefully at Megan now. "If I paid something on all my bills, like you wanted, and if I had enough money left over, would it be okay if I went to Maui too?"

Megan frowned. "Sure, it would be great, Kendall. But I don't think you can afford it. I already figured out what minimum payments would be and, after what you've given to Anna, you'll barely be able to make them."

"But that's not counting eBay." Kendall smiled slyly.

"eBay?" questioned Anna.

"Yes. Marcus told me how much I've already made. It's more than enough for a ticket to Maui."

"Seriously?" Megan was stunned.

"And I'll still have consignment money," said Kendall as she pointed to what was left in her designer section. "I'll take those to the shop tomorrow."

"For a girl who's not working, you seem to be raking in the dough," said Anna.

"What do you mean *not* working?" Kendall frowned. "This was a lot of hard work."

"And it's not finished yet," Megan reminded her.

Anna hugged Kendall now. "Thanks again, Kendall. That was really nice of you."

"It seemed only fair."

Then Anna and Lelani left for their dinner, and Kendall and Megan continued to sort and box things up. It took a couple hours, but they finally loaded all the consignment clothes into Kendall's car, made a big pile of things for Salvation Army to pick up, and set aside a few more items that Kendall thought might do well on eBay.

"Marcus said he'd show me how to do eBay myself," Kendall said as they closed the garage door.

"Maybe I'll sit in on that lesson," Megan told her. "I wouldn't mind making some extra money myself."

Soon they were scavenging leftovers in the kitchen. And then they sat down at the dining room table to eat.

"Aren't you going to pray first?" asked Kendall as she waited.

This seemed a little odd, since Megan didn't pray before every meal, but she bowed her head and said a quick blessing for their food. "And bless all my friends in this house too. Amen."

Kendall sighed. "I don't think I've ever had such good friends before."

"Really?" For some reason Megan never thought that Kendall considered her housemates very close friends. Oh, they'd had their moments, but Kendall usually kept her distance. Apparently that was changing. Maybe Kendall was changing. She certainly seemed cheerful as they finished up their makeshift dinner, then cleaned the kitchen together.

"I just wish you were going to Maui too," Kendall told Megan.

"You and me both."

"Are you certain that you can't go?"

Megan shrugged as she gave the countertop one last swipe. "Pretty sure."

"That's too bad."

"I'm going to go clean up," Megan told her. "I think I'll call it an early night tonight."

As Megan showered and got into her pajamas, she tried not to feel sorry for herself. It was hard to believe that she, the only one who Lelani had initially invited to go to Maui, would be the only one staying home. But, like she'd told Marcus, she was trying to give it to God. Really, what was the point of having a pity party?

Megan was about to climb into bed with a book when she heard a tapping on her door, followed by Kendall's voice quietly asking if she was asleep yet.

"Not yet." Megan got up and opened the door.

Kendall had what looked like baby things in her arms. Some kind of clothes and a blanket and diaper bag. "I wanted to show these to you."

"Oh?" Megan didn't know what to say, or what to think.

"I know it seems silly. But I was buying maternity clothes and this pregnant lady dragged me over to the baby department and—" She pushed the blanket toward Megan. "Isn't it soft?"

Megan sat down onto her bed as she felt the blanket. "Does this mean you're keeping the baby?"

Kendall sat in the chair across from her and nodded. "I mean I'm keeping the baby until the end of the pregnancy."

"But the baby things you bought?"

"Don't worry, they were on sale. And … I don't know what will happen after the baby's born. I guess I just was caught up in the moment."

"Right."

"But here's what I wanted to tell you, okay?"

"Okay?"

"Your mom really helped me to decide that I didn't want an abortion."

"Really? My mom?"

"Well, you all had something to do with it. But her story pushed me over the edge."

"Her story?"

"You know, about the miscarriage."

Megan felt confused. "Miscarriage?"

"You know, after you were born."

Megan vaguely remembered hearing something. "But then she had a hysterectomy."

"That was a year later. But the miscarriage story was what got me."

"I guess I don't really know that story." Once again, Megan felt left out.

"Well, that's because you were like a toddler. Your mom was pregnant, about six months along, and she was really excited about it. She was home alone with you and you were having a nap and she had felt kind of crampy so she took a bath. And then, for whatever reason, she just had a miscarriage. It happened so fast she didn't make it to the hospital until later. But she said she saw the baby, all his fingers and toes, and it just broke her heart."

"Really?" Megan was still trying to wrap her mind around this. "Mom never talked about it."

"She said she didn't like to talk about it, but that she thought about the baby for years afterward. She said she would imagine you being a big sister to him, helping him with things, holding his hand. And later on she imagined him as a boy playing baseball and climbing trees and playing with frogs and stuff like that. She said she never fully got over it."

"I never knew that." Megan just shook her head. "I mean I sort of remember hearing something, but she never talked about it."

"Well, she told me about it. And that's what helped me to decide. I just thought you should know." Now Kendall gathered up her baby things. "And I wanted to say thank you for helping with the garage sale and everything. And, oh yeah, there was something else I wanted to tell you. I was online booking my flight to Maui, and I did a little Google search and found out that there really is a group called Debtors Anonymous—DA. I just sent them an e-mail and they're supposed to get back to tell me where and when the chapter meets around here. Cool, huh?"

Megan nodded. "Cool." But she was still thinking about her mom and the baby she'd lost and how she'd shared that story with Kendall. Though Megan was glad for Kendall's sake, she felt slightly lost and forgotten.

Kendall said good night and Megan got back into bed and opened her book. Then she stopped. She set her book aside and actually got out of bed and down on her knees.

"Dear God," she prayed in a husky voice that was on the verge of tears. "I want to give all of this to you. I give you my loneliness, my self pity, my feeling so out of things. I lay it all at your feet and I trust you to take care of me and to give me what I need and to direct my life. I give it all to you. I trust you. Thank you for loving me. Amen."

Eighteen

Lelani

Lelani was tired of pretending she was happy to make this trip. When her coworker friends, like Margot, Abby, or Mr. Green said things like, "Are you counting the days until Maui?" or, "Sure wish I was going with you," or, "Aren't you lucky to be escaping this horrible rainy weather?" She'd just smile and feel like a hypocrite.

She longed to yell out, "I'm only going to Maui to decide whether the baby I abandoned needs her mother or not!" That would sure quiet everyone down. At least for a few minutes anyway. After her words sank in, the store would be abuzz with the latest hot tidbits of gossip. Like, "Have you heard that Lelani has a child?" and, "Did you know she abandoned her baby?" and, "What kind of a person would do something like that?" Who knew what else they might say? Some of the girls could get pretty catty.

Finally, it was time to go home. Lelani buttoned up her coat against the cold, damp wind. Would winter never end? She'd heard that it was unseasonably cold for March, but she felt like it had been cold ever since she came to Oregon last summer. She wondered what it would be like to go home and never come back here. But then there was Gil. Lelani sighed. How could she possibly give up Gil? Not that she knew where their relationship was headed. Most of the time she was trying to slow it down, to keep things calm and friendly. Lately, it seemed that Gil respected that. Or maybe he was simply losing interest.

If he was, who could blame him? She shook her head to remember what Abuela Castillo had said as Gil and Lelani told her good-bye last night.

"You're a pretty girl," she'd whispered in Lelani's ear, "but looks are not everything. I question a woman who can give up a child so easily."

Lelani had not responded. And when Gil asked what his grand-mother had said, she had actually lied, or at least partially lied. "She told me I was pretty."

"That's all?"

"That and some sage words of wisdom."

Gil had frowned then. But he had also let it go, something Lelani had been unable to do. And, really, wasn't Abuela Castillo right? What kind of a woman gives up her child? What kind of a woman was Lelani?

"Hey," called Megan as she ran to catch up with Lelani. They had both just started to walk down Bloomberg Place. "I have some really good news!"

"What's that?" Lelani forced yet another smile.

"Cynthia called me into her office this morning," Megan said breathlessly. "I thought she was mad, because she told me to close the door and sit down. I was almost ready to give her a piece of my mind for taking me for granted and for letting Vera walk all over me and everything. But I controlled myself."

"And?"

"And that was a good thing, because she had called me in to tell me that she was giving me spring break off!"

Lelani turned to face Megan. "Really?"

"Yeah. I couldn't believe it. And get this: She told me that she knew I was doing a good job and she *gave me a raise.*"

"A raise?"

Megan shrugged and grinned. "Not a very big one. Still, it was a nice vote of approval."

"That's wonderful news." Lelani hugged Megan. "I'm so glad you're coming too! I was really sad to think you'd be home alone."

"And I called Mom's travel agent, and she got me on the same flight as you."

"That's fantastic." Now Lelani was smiling for real, and it was the first genuine smile she'd worn all day.

"And that's not all," Megan told her.

"What?"

"Well, Marcus took me to lunch, which is why I forgot to call you, but he's going to see if he can get time off and come too. He already called Gil, and if the guys split the hotel three ways, they can upgrade to a nicer room."

"That's great." Lelani wondered how her parents would react to this news, but she knew she'd better give her mom a heads-up or suffer later. So as soon as she got to her room, she called. To her stunned surprise, her mother seemed to approve the idea of Lelani bringing her room-mates to Maui. Either that or someone else was listening to her phone conversation and she was merely pretending to be polite.

"I'll tell Meri to have the guesthouse ready for the four of you," she told Lelani in a businesslike manner. "When will you arrive?"

"We're not all on the same flight," she explained. "Megan and I are flying out Saturday morning, we arrive at Kahului at 2:00 p.m."

"Shall I send a car?"

"No," Lelani said quickly. "We'll do a rental car."

"A rental?" Her mother's voice was suspicious. "Why a rental? You know we have extra cars, Lelani."

"Because some of our friends are on the same flight," Lelani explained. "They're staying at a hotel in Kahana and they'll need a car to get around the island. They can drop us on their way."

"Oh?"

Lelani knew that her mother was curious, but that was all Lelani planned to tell her for the time being.

"Well, I have guests here just now," she said. The explanation for her good behavior. "And I need to attend to the baby. So I'll have to go, Lelani. You take care."

Lelani told her mother good-bye and hung up. She had wanted to ask where the nanny was and why she couldn't "attend to the baby." But that would have been pointless. Perhaps her mother had let the nanny have the day off, or even let her go altogether, though Lelani doubted it. She couldn't imagine her mother devoting her energy to caring for a child 24/7, giving up her precious beauty sleep, her morning shopping, her lunches with friends, her afternoon mai tai by the pool, or her leisurely evening swim or walk on the beach. No, Alana Porter was accustomed to the good life and, as much as she enjoyed spending time with baby Emma, she had probably kept the nanny.

Lelani lay back on her bed and closed her eyes. She didn't want to remember any of this, but images came flying at her as if they had wings. Perhaps it was for the best to begin facing these memories now. And if she needed to cry, why not cry now? Maybe it would make whatever happened next week seem easier.

So Lelani allowed herself to remember the day she had learned of the nanny. She even remembered the nanny's name. Ginger. She was about the same age as Lelani, but she was from Great Britain, Wales if memory served.

Lelani's dad had picked her and Emma up at the hospital, and when they got home, he informed Lelani that they'd decided she should stay in the guesthouse. When Lelani asked why, he said because that's what her mother thought would be best, explaining that it would be quieter.

But when Lelani carried Emma out to the guesthouse, she was met by her mother and introduced to the nanny.

"Why do we need a nanny?" Lelani had asked as she set her bag in the guesthouse.

"For baby Emma." Her mother had cooed softly as she swayed the sleeping infant gently in her arms and then handed her over to Ginger.

"But I can take care of Emma myself," Lelani had protested.

"No, there's no need for that. You get your rest, Lelani. Recover from your ordeal and get strong again."

"I am strong."

"Don't argue with me, Lelani." Her mother locked eyes with her, giving her that warning look that Lelani knew so well, then nodded at Ginger as if to give her some kind of a clue, which Ginger seemed to get, since she took the baby out of the guesthouse. Lelani thought that was wise, since she was determined to stand up to her mother. Already, she had started to bond with little Emma. Despite her mother's warning that breast-feeding would ruin her figure, Lelani had begun nursing the baby. "I took care of her in the hospital," Lelani stated, "and I can take care of her now."

Her mother's brow creased, a warning that this wasn't going to go well. "Tell me, Lelani, how do you intend to care for your baby? You have no job, no money to buy diapers or formula or anything, you have no college degree, no place to live, you don't even have your own car."

Lelani just stared at her mother, too stunned to answer.

"Tell me, do you plan to take your baby out to beg on the streets? Or perhaps you will camp on the beach?"

"What are you saying?" Lelani asked quietly.

"That you need your rest. That Ginger will care for the baby."

"Where?" demanded Lelani.

"In the house. Emma's things are all set up in your old room. Ginger will be in the spare room next to it. It's a perfect arrangement."

"Perfect for whom?"

"Don't make this any more difficult than it already is, Lelani. If you don't appreciate our help, you can take your baby and leave. No one is stopping you."

The implication was crystal clear. Unless Lelani complied with her parents' wishes—rather, her mother's wishes—she would be cut off from all help and support. As wealthy as her parents were, it was their wealth, not hers. And they had every right to withhold as they wished.

Her mother had smiled. "Take my advice, Lelani, get some rest. Get strong. Emma will be in good hands. Don't worry." And then she had left.

Lelani began to slip into what she later recognized as a combination of postpartum depression and an actual broken heart. She was not brokenhearted over Ben, Emma's father, since she'd been well over him by then, but brokenhearted that her mother had cast her aside, and even more brokenhearted that she was not allowed to care for and love her own baby. Her departure came fairly easily after that. What did she have to stay for? It wasn't as if her parents had given her any options. She had agreed to a year's absence, and her mother had probably figured that Lelani would've moved on with her life by then. And it might've happened. But now, nine months later, Lelani was going back.

><◆><

The week was a whirlwind of activity at 86 Bloomberg Place. Lelani felt like she was a spectator as she watched her housemates get ready, buying last-minute clothes and sunscreen and sunglasses, digging out their favorite summer things, packing and repacking bags and making phone calls, making arrangements for Kendall's dog, and coordinating things with the boyfriends—including Marcus, who found out Wednesday that his travel agent had finally found him a seat on the flight with Lelani, Megan, and Gil. Edmond, Anna, and Kendall would fly out later in the day, make one stop in Oahu, and arrive about five hours later. As all this went on around her, Lelani felt detached and almost unemotional, but maybe that was just her imagination.

Saturday morning, when the four of them hopped on the metro to save some parking fees at the airport, she still felt like she wasn't really there, kind of like she was hovering over them in some surreal sort of way, as they joked and laughed in anticipation of this big adventure.

"I can't believe that's all you're taking," Gil told her for what had to be the seventh time.

She just smiled as she looked down at her wheeled carry-on. "And I can't believe that you're taking all of that." She nodded at his large duffle bag and backpack.

"Lelani probably has a closet full of clothes at her parents' house," Edmond suggested.

Lelani just smiled again. She had left a lot of things in the guesthouse, but she doubted they were still there. "You don't need much in Maui," she told them. "And if you don't have what you need, there are plenty of stores."

"But aren't things expensive?" asked Megan.

Lelani shook her head. The buildings and signs and light Saturday-morning traffic swirled past in a foggy blur as the tram zipped out toward the airport. "Not really. Oh, I guess it depends on where you shop. The resort shops are always outrageous. But only tourists—and wealthy islanders—shop there." She thought of her mother then. Alana liked the resort shops sometimes. And sometimes she would take an interisland flight to Oahu.

Sometimes, back when Lelani was a girl, her mother had taken her along too. They would dress up and fly to Honolulu for a mother-daughter day of shopping, lunch, and sometimes a concert or theater, then they'd spend the night in a big hotel. Lelani wondered if her mother planned on doing the same thing with Emma someday.

Thanks to spring break, the terminal was crowded and crazy, but Lelani checked in electronically, and since she didn't have a checked bag, she soon found herself waiting for the others to join her at security. The lines were long and it took forever to pass through the security gates. Then they walked back to the Hawaiian Airlines gate, where it seemed the travelers were already in a festive party mood.

Once again Lelani felt detached, like she wasn't really there, like none of this was really happening, and for a while she pretended it was only a dream. Even as they boarded the plane, she felt like she was in heavy fog, not unlike what had surrounded Portland this morning. As she sat in her seat, she felt like she'd soon wake up and discover that none of this was real. Or maybe she was just in shock.

Her mind got even fuzzier after Gil insisted on buying them all a glass of champagne to celebrate the beginning of their vacation. She dozed off, and when she woke up, it was to the announcement that they were about to land in Kahului, Maui. And everyone was saying "aloha," and "mahalo" like they'd been natives forever.

"Here we go," said Gil as he took her hand to walk through the open-air terminal. Despite all her fears and misgivings, Lelani couldn't help but sigh in relief as she took a deep breath of the warm air. She was home!

Nineteen

Anna

Anna was afraid of flying. Okay, it was a well-kept secret, but it was true just the same. Now that she was sitting in the terminal, at their gate, with their jet outside in full view, she watched every move the mechanics and service people made and felt certain that flying over the vast Pacific Ocean was a huge mistake.

"Are you okay?" Edmond asked her for the third time.

"I'm fine," she snapped at him.

"Sorry."

"No, I'm sorry." Anna took in a deep breath. "I guess I just get a little nervous about flying."

"Why?" He adjusted his glasses and peered curiously at her.

"Why?" She looked at him like he was nuts. "Because planes crash. People die. Why not?"

He kind of laughed, then looked sorry when he saw her glaring at him. "Anna, Anna," he said, patting her hand. "Don't you know that plane travel is statistically the safest transportation out there?"

"Yes, yes," she snapped back at him. "I've heard the old it's-safer-than-bicycles line before."

"And?"

"And it's one thing to blow a tire on a bike, but something altogether different when you blow an engine on a jet."

"Jets can land with one engine."

"Okay, what if they lose a wing?"

Just then Kendall returned from the news store with an armful of magazines. "Isn't this exciting?" she gushed. "The others are out there over the ocean somewhere and tonight we'll all be together in Maui."

"Excuse me," said Anna as she stood. "I'm going to get some coffee."

"Like she needs coffee," Edmond said quietly.

Anna turned and narrowed her eyes at him.

"But if you want coffee, well, by golly, you should have some coffee." He smiled nervously.

The truth was, Anna *didn't* want coffee. She just wanted to use her phone. In private. She wanted to call her mother. Okay, she wasn't calling her mother so that her mother could lovingly soothe her and tell her that all would be well. After all, it was *her* mother she was about to call. No, Anna wanted to call her mother to apologize for their recent arguments.

"Hello?" her mother said in a weary tone.

"Hi, Mama."

"Anna?" her mother's voice grew anxious. "Where are you? Are you okay? Has there been an accident? Have you heard from Gil?"

Anna thought about the old adage of the apple not falling far from the tree and almost laughed. "Everything is fine, Mama." Anna was fully aware that she called her mother *Mama* when she was being nice and *Mom* when she was not. It was an old habit.

"Oh." Her mother almost sounded disappointed.

"Did you want something to be wrong?"

"No, no, of course not."

"Well, good."

"So did Gil get off okay?"

"I assume that he did, Mama. I haven't heard otherwise." She looked at the clock in the center of the terminal. "In fact, they should land in a couple of hours."

"A couple of hours? Didn't they only fly out at nine?"

"They land at two." Then Anna realized her mistake. "Oh, that's two o'clock Maui time. Sorry. I guess it'll be a while still."

"Gil promised to call me when they get there. Unlike some other thoughtless child that I will not mention."

"Mom, I'm calling you now."

"Well …"

"And I'm calling for a reason."

"Yes?"

"I want to apologize for the way I've spoken to you lately."

"Yes?"

"What? You want more than that?"

"Do you call that an apology, Anna? You say, 'I want to apologize,' but I did not hear you say, 'I am sorry, Mama.'"

"Okay, I'm sorry I've been disagreeable lately, Mama." Anna bit her lip. She wanted to remind her mother that she'd been equally disagreeable. Not just about the credit-card business, but about Edmond and Lelani and lots of things.

"What about what you said at the going-away dinner?" persisted her mom.

"I'm sorry." Anna couldn't help but smile to remember the shocked reactions of Abuela and the other relatives when she'd made her silly announcement. "I shouldn't have told everyone that Edmond and I were eloping and honeymooning in Maui."

"It was very immature, Anna. Not something I expected from you."

"It's just that Abuela was so aggravating."

"She is who she is, Anna."

"Yes." Anna sighed.

"And?"

"You want more?"

"You're my daughter, Anna. What you said to the family reflected on me."

"Okay. I'm sorry if I embarrassed you."

"You *did* embarrass me, mi'ja. And your grandmother, well, I thought she was going to have a stroke."

Anna thought that was unlikely. If anything, Abuela enjoyed the attention she got for her dramatic reaction. "Well, she'd been asking for it. I don't know what Abuela said to Lelani at the party, but I could tell it wasn't nice."

"Are you saying that Lelani didn't tell you?"

"Lelani is a lady."

Mama didn't have anything to say to that.

"Anyway, before I get on the plane, I just wanted to clear things up between us, Mama. I'm sorry I embarrassed you. But I'm sure everyone knew I was only joking."

"They did after I straightened them out."

"I also wanted to say I love you, Mama. Tell Papa I love him too."

"And we love you too, mi'ja. I know we are a little old-fashioned. But we only want what's best for our children."

"Unfortunately you can't dictate that."

"Dictate?"

"You know, you can't force us to live the life you think is best."

"Isn't that the truth?"

"But I don't think we're doing too badly," Anna pointed out. "We haven't been arrested, we don't do drugs, we finished college, and are gainfully employed … you know, some parents would be proud."

"We are proud, Anna."

"Thanks."

"And you really aren't eloping with Edmond, are you?"

Anna laughed. "No, Mama, I'm not. I will be staying with Lelani's parents, with my housemates, all girls, in the guesthouse."

"And when you get home, mi'ja, you'll tell me all about Lelani's family, won't you?"

"Why?"

"Why?" Her mother sighed. "Because I think that girl might be in our family someday. I see it in your brother's eyes, Anna."

"Well, I can't imagine Gil doing any better," Anna admitted. "Lelani is one of the kindest, nicest, sweetest, most caring persons I know."

"I know. And she's very beautiful."

"Yes."

"And she has a baby—a baby she left behind."

"Mama." Anna took in a big breath. "We don't know the full story yet."

"No, we don't."

"Okay. I love you, Mama, but I see they're starting to load the plane now."

"Are you scared, mi'ja?"

"What?"

"Are you frightened?"

"Of?"

"I know that flying terrifies you, Anna. You've always been like that."

"Okay, yes," Anna told her as she walked back to the gate. "I'm a little scared."

"Order a Bloody Mary."

Anna laughed. "Are you kidding?"

"No, it will calm you down."

Anna wasn't so sure about that, but she knew that the laughing that came with the idea had a soothing effect. "Adiós, Mama."

"Be safe, mi'ja. I love you."

"I love you too." Then Anna hung up.

"Everything okay?" asked Edmond as she joined him and Kendall in the line.

"I think so." She took his hand.

"And you're going to be all right?"

Anna smiled. "Yes. I'm going to be just fine."

Twenty

Kendall

Because the guys were sharing a rental car, Gil picked the late arrivals up at the airport. He was driving a little yellow Jeep Wrangler with the top down—cute but tight. They stuffed in their luggage and barely had room for the four of them. But at least Kendall got to ride shotgun. Nice, since she'd felt a little queasy on the last couple hours of the flight. But with the fresh warm air washing over her face and tousling her hair, she started to feel much better.

"Woo-hoo!" she shouted as Gil pulled out of the airport area and onto the busy street.

"So how's it going?" yelled Anna from the backseat.

"Great!" Kendall yelled back at her.

"No, I was talking to Gil. How's it going for *Lelani*?"

Gil stopped for a traffic light, then glanced back and kind of frowned. "I'm not sure."

"Poor Lelani," said Kendall. "It must be hard seeing your baby. I mean after such a long time."

"That's not really the problem," said Gil.

"What's wrong?" asked Kendall.

"Lelani's mother." Gil shook his head.

"What's she doing?" asked Anna.

"She's making it very difficult for Lelani."

"How so?" asked Kendall.

"For starters, she wouldn't let Lelani go into the nursery to see Emma until after her nap."

"That seems understandable," said Anna.

"Maybe, but when Lelani finally went into the house, Emma was gone."

"Gone?" Kendall felt alarmed. "Like kidnapped gone?"

"Not exactly. Mrs. Porter claimed that Emma needed to be at a playgroup. The nanny had taken her there."

"So Lelani hasn't even seen Emma yet?" Kendall frowned. "That's sad."

"Yeah. Lelani is pretty bummed." Gil pulled quickly into the intersection now, causing Kendall's head to jerk back.

"Hey, take it easy, cowboy!" she yelled.

Soon they were on the open highway. Kendall wanted to enjoy herself, but something about the smell was making her feel sick. Plus, there didn't seem to be any ocean anywhere nearby. "What *is* that smell?" she finally demanded.

"The sugar-cane plantations," Gil told her.

"Ugh!" she made a face. "And *where* is the beach?"

"We just cut through the center of the island," he told her. "We'll be driving along the coastline in a few minutes."

"Oh, good."

But by the time they reached the coastline, the sun was already going down. As Gil drove them down a very curvy road, it became dark and Kendall started to feel like she was carsick again. At least if she had to hurl, she could lean out the open window. Or maybe she should ask him to pull over. But the road seemed so narrow. And so busy. Where were all these crazy cars going anyway?

"How far is it?" she asked after they went through a tunnel.

"About twenty minutes."

"You're kidding," she groaned. "I thought Maui was a small island."

"It is."

"Are we there yet?" teased Anna from the backseat. "Just relax, Kendall, feel that warm night air—isn't it wonderful?"

"Wonderful," she muttered.

For some reason this was not how she had imagined Maui. This dark, curvy road never seemed to end, the weird smells seemed to come and go, and she feared that she was going to hurl around the next corner, or that Gil was going to get them into a head-on collision with one of these other cars that seemed to be driving way too fast. Or maybe he was going to take a curve wrong and plunge them off a cliff and straight into the ocean, where their remains would probably be devoured by sharks. She thought she'd heard there were sharks in Maui. Oh, why had she wanted to come so bad?

Gil hit the brakes and she felt certain they were doomed for a wreck. But then nothing happened and he just kept driving, a little slower now. What if they did get into a wreck? Kendall's hand went protectively down to her midsection and she realized that, maybe for the first time in her life, she felt more concerned for someone else than she did for herself. She didn't want anything to hurt her baby.

"That's Lahaina," Gil told them. "Lelani's house is on the other side of town."

"Thank goodness," said Kendall. She sighed as Gil slowed down even more, but the traffic thickened. "Lelani said it's busier than usual here, thanks to spring break."

"I'm starving," announced Edmond from the back.

"Me too," echoed Anna.

Kendall didn't feel hungry yet, but she knew as soon as this horrible car trip ended, she'd probably be famished.

"Lelani made reservations for us in town."

"Why don't we just meet there?" suggested Kendall.

"Your bags," he said as he slowed for a traffic light. "They might not be safe in an open car."

"Oh, yeah."

Soon he was turning toward what Kendall suspected was the ocean, then they went through some gates. He parked in a circular driveway and hopped out. "Here you go, ladies."

The guys helped Kendall and Anna unload their bags, then hopped back into the Jeep. "I'll run Edmond to the hotel to dump his stuff, and we'll meet up with you girls at the restaurant."

"What do we drive?" asked Anna.

"Lelani's parents are letting her use a car." He lowered his voice. "It used to be her car, but they took it back."

"Oh." Kendall nodded. Maybe Lelani's parents were kind of like her parents. They give and then they take it back. At least Lelani's parents were giving them a place to stay, and this didn't look too shabby.

"The guesthouse is around back," Gil told them, nodding to where a well-lit path led around the side of the house. "You need to go directly back there—not through the main house."

So Kendall and Anna lugged their bags along the pathway alongside the sprawling house and past a pretty nice pool and on back until they finally found a smaller house. "This must be it," said Kendall in relief.

"You're here," said Lelani as she burst out the door to greet them. "Aloha!" Then she put real flower leis around their necks. "Mahalo," she said, kissing them both on the cheek. *Mi casa es su casa.*

Anna laughed. "Hey, that's not Hawaiian."

"No, but Gil's been teaching me some Spanish."

"Come in, come in," called Megan from inside. "Check out our digs."

"This is nice," said Anna as they entered the spacious room with polished wood floors and bamboo furnishings. "Pretty."

"This couch makes into a queen bed," Lelani told them. "And there's a small bedroom that Megan and I already dumped our stuff in, but if you like I'm happy to—"

"No," said Anna. "Kendall and I will be fine out here, won't we, Kendall?"

Kendall wanted to protest but thought it might sound selfish.

"Actually, it's a lot roomier in here," said Lelani. "And those doors open right out to the beach." She pointed to sliding glass doors.

"Cool."

"There's a closet for your stuff here," said Lelani. "And those end tables are really dressers." She glanced at the clock on the wall. "But we should head out to meet the guys."

"Not until I have a potty break," announced Kendall. "I'm not only eating for two, but I'm peeing for two as well." Lelani showed them the bathroom that all four of them would be sharing, but at least it was fairly roomy and the shower was nice.

Soon they were back in the car. Lelani's car, unlike the Jeep, was pretty comfy and a convertible too. "What kind of car is this?" asked Kendall, who had asked to ride in front again, explaining about her carsick feeling on the way from the airport.

"It's a Chrysler Sebring," Lelani told her. "My dad gets good deals on cars from the rental car places. The year he got me this one was the big Sebring convertible year."

"I like it better than the Jeep," admitted Kendall.

"But the Jeep is good for the beach," Lelani pointed out.

Soon they were back in town, which appeared to be right on the ocean and filled with lots of cars and people. Kendall almost felt dizzy as they pressed through the crowds of people—the music, lights, the smell of good food, and activities on every corner—toward the restaurant, which overlooked the water. Finally, what Kendall had hoped Maui would feel like.

"This is nice," she told Lelani after they were seated at a table that overlooked the ocean. Kendall knew it was the ocean because lights were spotted out over it, and she guessed boats were bobbing out there.

"Welcome to my Maui." Lelani smiled, but her eyes seemed unhappy. "The guys should be here soon."

"So you're glad to be back?" asked Anna tentatively.

"Oh, yes, definitely." Lelani nodded. "I really do love it here. It feels so good to me." She sighed. "I mean things aren't going too smoothly on the home front." She glanced at Megan now. "You got to see that firsthand today."

Megan made an uncomfortable face.

"My mom sent the housekeeper out to greet us," said Lelani. "By telling us to go directly to the guesthouse."

"The baby was sleeping," Megan explained.

"Yes." Lelani fiddled with her napkin. "And then Emma had her playdate."

"Which took all afternoon." Megan looked skeptical.

"And then Emma was *so worn out* that Ginger, the nanny, fed her supper and put her down for the night."

"So you haven't even seen her yet?" asked Anna.

"No." Lelani forced a brave smile. "But tomorrow is a brand-new day."

Kendall nodded. But still she wondered. How would it feel to be the mother of a child you couldn't even see? Then she realized that could actually be her. Would that be her?

The guys arrived. They took seats next to their girlfriends and Kendall was aware that she was the only one without a date. Her hand reached down to touch her midsection again, and for some reason that was reassuring, like she wasn't totally alone. Still, it felt odd being the dateless girl. Even the waitress gave her a slightly sympathetic glance as she took her order. But Kendall just smiled. No big deal.

Still, she didn't talk much. Not that there was room to get a word in edgewise. It seemed everyone was talking at the same time, sharing their travel experiences, talking about what they wanted to do tomorrow, where the best surfing beaches were, how to book snorkeling trips, and whether it was a good time to go whale watching. Kendall felt like telling them all to put a lid on it. If they'd shut up, maybe they could hear the ocean.

At least the food was good. Kendall ate everything on her plate and wished that the others wanted to order dessert. But they were eager to walk around the town before the shops started to close. So she trailed behind the couples, since she didn't really fit in, though she also was careful not to lose them, since she didn't want to be left behind.

Twenty-one

Megan

"If I told anyone that I spent my first morning in Maui inside a church, they would think I'd lost my mind or that I was lying," said Kendall from the front seat. The sun wasn't even up yet, and Lelani was driving the four of them to a place that Marcus had told Megan about last night.

"We're not going to be *inside* a church building," Megan said from the backseat. "It's church on the beach. A sunrise service. The guy told Marcus that it was something everyone should do at least once in their lifetime."

"I don't think I've ever been up this early in my lifetime." Kendall yawned and stretched sleepily.

"All I can say is it's a good thing our bodies are still on home time," said Anna, "or else I wouldn't have been able to get up this early."

"Everyone can sleep in tomorrow," Megan assured them. "And every day until we go home."

"This is the place." Lelani pulled off the road to a beachside area where a number of other cars were parked. The wind was blowing and the sky was a dusky dark-gray color. The ocean seemed to match.

"This sure doesn't look like the Maui that I imagined," said Kendall as they walked through the sand.

"There are the guys," Megan whispered, pointing at the Jeep just pulling into the parking area. For some reason she felt she needed to be quiet now—as if there were a hush over the still-sleeping world.

The girls waited for the guys, then they quietly joined the small crowd gathered right on the beach. Megan estimated there were about fifty in the group, and from all walks of life. In front, three musicians (with a guitar, ukulele, and some kind of flute) were playing what sounded like a Hawaiian-style hymn. Everyone was singing. Even though Megan didn't know the words she felt the peacefulness of the beat and the melody seeping into her. And she felt at home.

The singing continued in this quiet and reverent way until the first rays of the sunrise began to break through, coming from behind them and spilling over the mountain and into the sea. As if following the lead of the sun, the songs grew more joyful, until they were singing a full-blown praise song that Megan and Marcus actually knew. Tambourines and drums came out, and everyone was clapping and singing wholeheartedly.

The group sang a few more similar songs, then the musicians joined the other worshippers, and a man in a Hawaiian shirt stepped forward and introduced himself as Rick. "Some people call me Pastor Rick, some just call me Rick, and some call me names I shouldn't use here in church." Everyone laughed, and then he prayed for a blessing on their time together. After that he opened his Bible and read a simple parable (the one about the shepherd who went looking for one of his hundred sheep), then shared briefly about what that meant to him.

"I was a lost sheep once," he told them. "I had gone my own way and made a mess of my life ..." He explained how he'd started smoking marijuana and got caught up in some crazy money-making scheme, and how it all crashed down on him. His own family would have nothing to do with him. "I felt hopeless and lost and ready to give up. I was at rock bottom." He smiled and held out his hands. "And that's when my shepherd found me."

He talked more about how he felt called to be the one who goes out looking for lost and lonely sheep, and how finding one was better than having a big flock that didn't appreciate what they had. "Not that I'm saying our church is like that." He chuckled. "I guess what I'm saying is that I see my friends here more like the shepherds who will be out there looking for lost sheep." Everyone said amen, and then they sang more songs. Pastor Rick asked for prayer requests and they prayed again, and then the service was over.

"As usual, we'll have a picnic here in the park," Rick called out, "and everyone is welcome. Mahalo!"

The man who had told Marcus about the beachside church came over and greeted them now, extending the invitation to have lunch with their group of seven.

"I'll check with the others," Marcus told him, but Megan suggested they were getting antsy to leave. "This is our first day in Maui and I think our friends want to have some fun," Marcus explained.

The guy slapped Marcus on the back and grinned. "Tell them they came to the right place! Aloha!"

"That was a cool service," Marcus told Megan as they went to join their friends.

"I actually got goose bumps when the sun came up," Megan admitted, "and not because I was cold either."

"Yeah, me too."

But the others were ready to begin their day, already making plans about who was going where. Edmond and Anna wanted to be dropped in town, where they could make arrangements to take a whale ride on a raft. Kendall just wanted to find a nice beach.

"There's a great beach right outside the guesthouse," Lelani told her.

"That'll be perfect." Kendall smiled as she looked out toward the turquoise blue ocean, framed by gently swaying palm trees. "Now, this looks more like the Maui I imagined."

"I think I'd like to stick around my parents' house today," said Lelani. "But if anyone wants to, feel free to borrow my car."

"I want to go surfing," said Marcus.

"I'm with you there," said Gil. "We could drop Anna and Edmond in town, then check out the rental store."

Megan was unsure as to what she should do. Part of her wanted to tag along with Marcus and Gil and try surfing, but she sensed that Lelani might need her today. "Do you mind if I stick around the guest-house today?" she asked Lelani.

"Not at all." Lelani looked relieved. "I would appreciate it."

⋈

"Would you like to meet my parents?" Lelani asked Megan after Kendall had gotten her beach stuff together and headed outside.

"Sure." Megan smiled nervously.

"And hopefully we'll get to see Emma too."

"Hopefully." Megan wasn't so sure.

"I'll warn you," said Lelani, "this probably won't be much fun."

"I didn't expect it to be." Megan patted Lelani on the back. "But I'm here for you, okay?"

"Thanks."

Megan followed Lelani through a beautifully landscaped courtyard that led to an immaculate pool area and finally up to the backside of the larger house. "This place is so gorgeous," Megan whispered. "The plants and flowers and everything—it's like an oasis in here."

"Thanks to Sam's and Meri's handiwork." Lelani's expression grew serious as she pushed what looked like a doorbell by the back door. "They take care of the house and grounds."

Megan wanted to question why Lelani didn't just walk into her parents' home, but she knew that things were different in Lelani's life.

"Lelani," said a short heavyset woman. "Aloha!"

"Aloha, Meri," Lelani said politely. Then she introduced Megan. "Is my mother home?"

"She is still in her room."

Lelani nodded. "Is Ginger with the baby?"

"Yes." Meri nodded. "They are in the nursery."

"Do you mind if I go and see them?"

Meri looked uncomfortable, standing in the doorway as if she was contemplating blocking their entrance.

"It's okay, Meri," Lelani assured her in a gentle voice. "If Mrs. Porter complains, I will take all the blame."

Meri just sighed and slowly stepped aside.

"This way," Lelani whispered to Megan.

Just like the exterior, everything inside this house was perfect. Polished dark hardwood floors, oriental rugs, bamboo furnishings, large vases of stunning fresh flowers. Megan knew enough about interior design and expensive homes to know this one had to be worth a bundle.

"Here we are," said Lelani as she quietly knocked on a door.

A young woman with her brown hair pulled back in a tight ponytail opened the door, but when she saw Lelani, her eyes grew wide.

"It's okay, Ginger." Lelani spoke quietly as she pushed her way past. "I just want to see my baby."

"But Mrs. Porter said—"

"I don't know what my mother has told you—" Lelani stopped speaking when she saw the small, dark-haired baby sitting on the butter-colored carpet. She wore a blue-and-white flowered sundress and held a pink ball in her hands. She was as pretty as a picture. "Hello, Emma," cooed Lelani as she dropped to the floor next to her daughter.

"Her name is Kala now," said Ginger in a chilly voice.

Lelani frowned up at her. "*Kala?*"

"Yes. For princess."

"I know what Kala means." Lelani looked back at the baby, who was looking curiously at Lelani. "Do you want to play ball?" She gently took the ball from the baby and rolled it back to her. The baby picked it up and smiled. Then Lelani did it again and again.

"Does your mother know you're here?" asked Ginger.

"Yes." Lelani didn't even look up, just continued playing with the baby.

"I'm Megan," she extended her hand to Ginger. "Lelani brought some of her friends here for spring break. We're staying in the guesthouse."

"I *know* that you're staying in the guesthouse." Ginger eyed Megan with suspicion. "But does Mrs. Porter know that you are *in* her house?"

Lelani picked up her baby now, still cooing and talking, and Emma (or whatever her name was) seemed to be enjoying the attention.

"Are you saying that we're not supposed to be in the house?" Megan asked Ginger.

Lelani nodded at Megan. "Probably not. How about if we take Emma back to the guesthouse?"

"But you're not supposed to—"

"It's okay, Ginger," Lelani spoke gently but firmly. "Why don't you just take a little break? Emma is fine with me. After all, *I am her mother.*"

That seemed to shut Ginger up. Then, as quietly as they came in, Lelani and Megan left with the baby. Back in the guesthouse, Lelani put Emma on the floor and continued to play with her, talking to her like she'd been doing this forever. Megan just sat back and watched. She was surprised at how comfortable Lelani seemed with the child. And Emma seemed perfectly happy as well.

"You seem to know what you're doing," Megan observed.

"How's that?" Lelani looked up from the peek-a-boo game she was playing.

"I mean you seem like a natural." Megan smiled as Emma giggled. "I've never been that good around kids. You look like you've been doing it your whole life."

"I love kids."

The door to the guesthouse opened and a tall slender woman who looked like a slightly older version of Lelani walked in without knocking. She wore a white silky dressing gown and her long dark hair was mussed as if she'd just gotten out of bed.

"Lelani!" she said loudly. "What do you think you are doing?"

Lelani looked up calmly. "Playing with Emma."

"I have not given you permission to—"

"I didn't think I needed permission to play with my own daughter." Lelani's voice continued to be sweet and calm as she gathered Emma into her arms and stood. Megan went to stand by her, preparing herself for what she suspected might be a showdown.

"The baby is *not* to leave the house." Lelani's mother scowled at both Megan and Lelani. "I thought I had made that clear."

"It may be clear to you." Lelani smoothed Emma's hair. "But those are your rules, Mother, not mine."

"You will play by my rules, or you will leave my premises."

"Fine." Lelani nodded. "Then we will go." Now she looked directly at her mother. "But Emma is going with us."

"Lelani!" Her mother looked stunned.

"It's not the way I had planned this," continued Lelani. "But if you want to act like this, I suppose I'll—"

"You have no right to—"

"Emma is my daughter. I have never signed her over to you or anyone else, Mother. I have every right to take her with me if I wish."

"I will call the police."

"Go ahead, Mother. And when they come I will tell them the truth and I will ask you to produce the paperwork that proves Emma belongs to you."

"Why are you doing this?"

Lelani didn't answer, but Megan saw her eyes glistening with tears, and she knew how hard this must be. Lelani, more than anyone Megan knew, loved peace. She hated confrontations of any kind. Megan knew it was time to intervene. And she was ready!

"Listen, Mrs. Porter, there must be a—"

"Who are you, anyway?"

"I'm Lelani's friend. Megan Abernathy. And I think there should be some way for everyone to sit down and discuss this whole thing calmly and rationally."

Mrs. Porter just blinked.

"Yes," agreed Lelani. "That's what I want, Mother."

"Then why did you steal Kala from the nursery?"

"I didn't steal her, Mother. And her name is Emma, not Kala."

"Ginger told me that you stole the baby!"

Now Emma was starting to fuss. She probably sensed the bad vibes in the room. Lelani took her aside to soothe her and Megan decided to step in again. "Ginger got it wrong," she calmly told Mrs. Porter. "Lelani simply said she was taking Emma to the guesthouse so that Ginger could have a break."

Mrs. Porter's eyes narrowed at Megan. "But I explicitly told Ginger that—"

"Don't you think that if Lelani wanted to kidnap her own child, she wouldn't come back here to the guesthouse with her?" continued Megan. "If she was trying to steal her away, we would've gotten in the car and just taken off. Lelani obviously only wants to spend some time with her daughter." Megan stepped closer to Mrs. Porter now, peering into her face, taking in her flawless features, so similar to Lelani's—except for the coldness. "I have to be honest with you, Mrs. Porter. I do not understand the way you treat your own daughter. Are you saying she's not welcome in your house? It feels as if you're holding Emma hostage. Why is that?"

"You do not know what you are talking about."

"Feel free to enlighten me." Megan waited.

"My daughter was given every privilege. Everything was handed to her. She could've done anything she wanted with her life. And yet she brought shame onto our house."

"By getting pregnant?"

Mrs. Porter took in a sharp breath and narrowed her eyes.

"Everyone makes mistakes." Megan softened her voice. "I'm sure that even you have made mistakes. That's what being human is about. But we have to forgive each other."

"I don't have to forgive anyone if I don't want to."

Megan blinked. "That must be a miserable way to live."

"It is," said Lelani as she rejoined them. She looked directly at her mother. "Aren't you tired of being miserable?"

Mrs. Porter laughed. "I am not the least bit miserable, Lelani. If anyone has been miserable, I'd say that it's been you."

Lelani nodded. "Yes, I have been somewhat miserable, Mother. Because of the way you've shunned me, the way you sent me away, the threats and accusations … all that has made me miserable. But I'm ready to move on now. I'm ready for it all to end."

Mrs. Porter looked slightly hopeful. "Good. I hoped you'd come to your senses."

"I have, Mother. And that means I'm ready to take responsibility for myself and for my daughter."

Mrs. Porter's brows shot up. "So, I was right. You are planning on taking her."

"That's not what I said, Mother. I said I want to take responsibility for my role in her life. To be honest, I'm not even sure what that means."

Her mother laughed again. "Of course. You march in here, acting all high and mighty, and when it comes right down to it, you are completely clueless. Oh, yes, it just figures."

"Maybe I am clueless," admitted Lelani. "But I do know this: I am committed to finding out what is best for my daughter. And then I will do everything within my power to see that she gets it."

"She already has it." Mrs. Porter's voice became more condescending. "She has everything she needs right here. She's had it all for the past nine months, and she's been perfectly happy, perfectly cared for. Really, what could you possibly give her that we have not?"

Lelani's chin quivered slightly, but she didn't answer.

"I know what Lelani could give her," said Megan. "She could give her love."

Mrs. Porter laughed again. "How cliché. Well, for your misinformed little mind, she does get love here. Everyone in the house loves her. They adore her. She is our princess. Our little Kala." She reached out her hands to Emma now. "Come to Mommy, my little princess."

And to Megan's irritation, the baby reached out her chubby arms and Lelani allowed her mother to take Emma away from her. But first she leaned down and kissed Emma's forehead and then she locked eyes with her mother. "This isn't over."

"Oh, I didn't think that it was, dear."

Then Mrs. Porter left and Lelani closed the door, then crumbled onto the couch and sobbed. And the cries that came from her reminded Megan of a wounded animal, deep and guttural and totally broken-hearted. Megan didn't know what to do. And so she just sat by her, stroking Lelani's sleek black hair with her hand and saying, "It's going to be okay. It's going to be okay ..." again and again.

"What happened?" asked Kendall as she emerged from the beach looking pink and flushed.

"Her mother," whispered Megan.

And to Megan's total surprise, Kendall sat on the edge of the coffee table opposite Lelani and put her hand on her shoulder. "Don't you worry, Lelani, your friends are here to take care of you."

Twenty-two

Lelani

Lelani woke up wondering where she was, then remembered she was in Maui, in her parents' guesthouse, on the couch. She'd just been through round one with her mother. And now she heard female voices in the kitchen area. It sounded like Megan and Kendall.

"I'm awake," called Lelani as she stood and stretched. "I hope my mother and I haven't been too upsetting."

"Not at all," said Megan as she handed Lelani a glass of iced tea.

"And don't worry about me," said Kendall. "I'm used to family fights."

"Unfortunately, that was just the beginning," said Lelani.

"I was wondering," began Megan, "if you maybe need a lawyer."

Lelani nodded. "Yes. I've thought of that. And there's a family friend that I—"

"A family friend?" Megan looked concerned. "But your mother might—"

"Clara isn't terribly fond of my mother," Lelani explained.

"Maybe you should give her a call," suggested Kendall.

"I might do that. But first I want to talk to my dad. Without my mom around." Lelani shook her head. "That won't be easy."

"Why not?" asked Megan.

"Because he will try to avoid it."

"Why?" asked Kendall.

"Because he knows my mom will get mad." Lelani sighed. "And if there's one thing my dad cannot stand, it's to have Alana Porter mad at him. He will do almost anything to avoid it."

"Even turn his back on his own daughter?" Megan frowned. "I'd think he'd be glad to see you."

"You think that because you have a normal family," Lelani pointed out. "Your parents both loved you."

Megan shrugged. "Even so, maybe you should give your dad a chance."

"I agree with Megan." Kendall smiled coyly. "Dads usually have a soft spot for their little girls."

"Except that Emma—rather, Kala—is his little girl now."

Kendall frowned. "Oh, that is tricky."

"Is your dad home?" asked Megan.

"It's hard to say." Lelani opened a sliding door to let the breeze into the guesthouse. "But if he is home, there won't be a chance of getting to him without my mom finding out."

"Maybe we can run interference for you," offered Kendall.

Lelani considered this. "Maybe."

"I've been keeping an eye on your house," Kendall told her. "Spying to see if any cars are leaving the driveway."

"Seriously?" Lelani was shocked.

"She has," confirmed Megan. "I told her what happened and—"

"And I was worried your mom might take off with your baby."

"Oh, I don't think she'd—"

"No," said Kendall, "I've seen it happen time and again on Lifetime TV."

"But that's not really real—"

"It is real," protested Kendall as she peeked out the window. "Those are true stories."

"Dramatized true stories," Megan corrected.

"Anyway, I've been watching, and no cars have come or gone."

"Don't worry," Lelani assured them, "my mother won't sneak around to get her way. She'll come right out in the open. It usually works for her."

"But what about your dad?" Megan persisted. "I'm sure he'd at least want to see you, wouldn't he?"

Lelani considered this. "Yes, you're right. He would." She looked at Kendall and Megan. "And I think he'd like to meet my friends too."

For the second time, Lelani went through the backyard to the main house. But this time, instead of ringing the bell and waiting for Meri, she went around to the family room wing off the pool. It was her dad's favorite place to watch TV. She hoped her mother was at the other end of the house with Emma.

"Hi, Daddy," said Lelani as she walked through the open door off the pool.

His face lit up but then quickly turned somber. "Hello, Lelani." He pushed himself up from his leather recliner, smoothed his hair, which was even sparser than the last time she'd seen him, and then gave her a tentative hug. She could tell he was watching the doorway to see if his wife was about to pop in and catch him in an open display of affection. Then he stepped back and she introduced her friends.

He was polite but cool. And suspicious.

"I'm guessing that my mother told you I tried to kidnap Emma."

He nodded. "Something like that."

"Well, I wasn't trying to steal her. I just wanted to see her." Lelani smiled. "Can you blame me for that, Daddy? She's such a sweetie. I can't believe how she's grown."

He softened now. "Yes. She's trying to take steps now. Did you see her walk?"

"No, I didn't have a chance before—"

"Lelani," her mother's voice cut through the room like a sword. "And you've brought your friends."

So Lelani turned and introduced Kendall. Her mother was dressed now, looking sleek and sophisticated in a pale yellow sheath dress and matching sandal flats. And pearls. Lelani wondered what the special occasion was. Her mother usually reserved her pearls for going out or entertaining.

"It's a pleasure to meet you, Kendall," her mother said politely. "And nice to see you again, Megan. Are you girls enjoying your stay?"

"Yes," said Kendall. "You have a beautiful place, Mrs. Porter. And Maui, or what I've seen of it, is absolutely gorgeous."

"We like our little island." Her mother smiled—perfectly—and motioned to the pale blue sectional. "Won't you girls sit down? Can I get you anything? Meri makes a lovely papaya smoothie."

Megan glanced at Lelani and Lelani said, "Sure, smoothies sound great." She knew this would distract her mother for a couple of minutes. And as soon as she was out of earshot, Lelani turned to her dad. "I need to talk to you, Daddy, in private."

"Well … your mother won't like—"

But Lelani was already grabbing his hand and tugging him. "Come on, Daddy. You can't let that woman boss you around forever."

Kendall giggled, and that seemed to trigger something in Lelani's dad, because he simply nodded and said, "Fine. Let's go."

Before her mother returned, Lelani and her dad slipped out the back, and she led him past the guesthouse directly to the beach.

"You know that you're going to get me into trouble, don't you?" he warned.

"You're already in trouble," she pointed out as she hurried down the beach and away from the house. "The trouble began when you sided with Mom to keep my child."

"What?" He stopped walking and turned and looked at her like she was crazy. "You're the one who took off, Lelani. You're the one who left her baby for her parents to raise."

She looked into his eyes. "Is that what she told you?"

"It's what I know."

"No, it's what my mother has brainwashed you to believe."

"You were miserable here, Lelani. Everyone could see it. You were unable to care for your child. You didn't even want to. Your mother took over your responsibilities because you refused to—"

"That is not true!"

"Oh, you can call it the baby blues or whatever you like, but I saw you, Lelani. You hid out in the guesthouse with dirty hair and ratty clothes. You wouldn't speak to anyone. You were a mess." He shook his head. "And I kind of understood. But to leave everything just hanging the way you did, well, I don't—"

"My mother *forced* me to go. You don't know that?"

"She thought it might help you to get away."

Lelani felt like screaming. How could her dad be so gullible? Or maybe he didn't care. Maybe he just wanted to believe his wife's spin. Maybe it was just easier.

"I agreed with her, Lelani, I thought you needed a year in the mainland to clear your head and figure out whether you wanted to return to med school."

"I didn't know what I wanted, Dad. When mother refused to let me be with my baby and—"

"Alana didn't refuse to let you be with Kala—"

"Emma! Her name is Emma."

"Fine. Emma. Kala. Whatever. Your mother did not—"

"She hired a nanny, Dad. Even before I came home from the hospital, she hired Ginger to care for Emma."

"Because she thought you needed help."

"NO!" Lelani shook her fist at him. "Because she wanted Emma for herself."

"Don't be ridiculous, Lelani. What parents, at our age, want to start a family over again? Your mother was simply trying to help you. And then you fell apart and—"

"No, Daddy." Lelani's voice grew calm now. "My mother hired Ginger to take over the baby, and before I could do a thing, she moved Emma to my old room, and then she moved me out to the guesthouse. When I said I was going to care for Emma myself, she told me that I couldn't."

"Well, you couldn't."

"Sure, I didn't have a job or money, but I wanted to care for my own baby. I wanted to be a mother. I just needed a little help."

"We helped you, Lelani." Her dad wiped the sweat from his brow, then shook his head. "And you were nothing but ungrateful. That's probably why I agreed with your mother. I thought you might learn to appreciate all that you have, all that I've worked so hard to give you, if you didn't have it to take for granted anymore. I thought it might knock some sense into that stubborn head of yours and maybe you'd come—"

"It's useless!" Lelani closed her eyes and shook her head to keep herself from screaming.

"We should go back to the house," her father said quietly.

Lelani opened her eyes and willed herself to be calm. "Yes, Daddy, you should go back. It's clear that Alana Porter has you under her thumb and there is nothing I can do to make you see the truth. Nothing I can do to change the fact that you are controlled by your wife and probably always will be. But at least I tried." She smiled sadly at him and, despite all the emotions raging within her, she felt sorry for her father. "But I still love you, Daddy. And no matter what happens, I'll always be your little girl."

Then she turned away from him and ran as fast as she could go down the beach in the opposite direction of the house. She ran and ran and ran. She thought she could run forever, but the beach finally came to an end, and she was forced to stop.

Out of breath, she turned and looked back. Her father was nowhere to be seen. He'd probably returned to the house to report that Lelani had lost her mind and gone screaming down the beach. Well, fine. Maybe she had lost her mind.

She walked out into the surf and let the ocean swallow her. The water felt chilly against her hot skin at first, and then delicious as she adjusted to it. She went under, allowing the coolness to seep into her scalp before she swam out a ways and just relaxed. She had always felt comforted by the ocean, and sometimes the gentle waves reminded her of a loving parent holding a child, rocking it gently. She stretched out her arms and legs, allowing the rolling surf to sway her back and forth. Her sundress swirled about, sometimes twisting around her body and sometimes floating free like a jellyfish. When she finally tired, she slowly swam back to shore.

With her dripping dress clinging to her, she walked a few feet from the ocean's edge and collapsed on the wet sand. She closed her eyes and sighed deeply. Somehow, this was going to turn out all right. She couldn't explain why, or even wrap her mind around the way she felt, but out there in the waves she had imagined herself resting in the hands of God. She had let go of some things and entrusted them to him. And she knew that everything was going to be okay.

Maybe not for her parents. But for Emma and Lelani, it was going to turn out all right. Because Lelani knew, the instant she laid eyes on Emma this morning, that they belonged together, and that neither of them could ever be really happy unless they were together.

Because of that, Lelani knew that she would do whatever it took to care for Emma. She would work hard, maybe go back to school, whatever. Emma would have the best that life could give. Oh, she might not have the expensive luxuries that her grandparents offered, but she would have enough. More than enough. And she would have love—the kind of love that would allow Emma to grow up to be whatever it was she wanted to be, and the kind of love that would forgive, again and again. This is what Lelani knew in her heart.

Twenty-three

Anna

Edmond and Anna were just coming back from an exciting whale-watching trip, where they'd seen humpbacks breaching and slapping their tails and all sorts of things, when her cell phone rang.

"Whale-watchers anonymous," she joked into the phone. "I'm officially an addict now."

"Hey, Anna," said Megan's voice. "A little emergency here."

"What?" Anna imagined her brother being attacked by a shark. "Is it Gil? Is he okay?"

"No, it's not Gil. But I've tried to call both him and Marcus, and I'm guessing they're on the water and that their phones are on the beach."

"What is it?" Anna's heart was still pounding and now Edmond was looking on with concern. "What happened?"

Then Megan told Anna that Lelani had gone missing. "She was talking with her dad, which we assume didn't go well. And, man, you should meet her mom. She makes my boss Vera look good."

"Oh, no."

"Anyway, Kendall and I looked up and down the beach for Lelani but didn't see her anywhere. Of course, she doesn't have her phone with her. I thought maybe Gil could help look, but I don't even know where they went. Maybe you or Edmond might—"

"We'll get right on it, Megan. I'll start calling Gil."

Anna quickly explained to Edmond and they both tried to call the guys. "Poor Lelani," said Anna as she closed her phone. "Her mother sounds horrible."

"Even worse than yours," teased Edmond.

Anna smacked him in the arm.

"Sorry." He smiled sheepishly. "How about I get us a taxi?"

"How about it." She gave him a warning look. It was one thing to make fun of your own mother, but Anna had to draw the line somewhere.

Just as they were getting into a taxi, Anna's phone rang.

"It's Gil," he said. "What's up?"

She quickly filled him in.

"Where did they last see Lelani?"

"On the beach behind her house."

She could hear Gil talking to Marcus now. "We're on our way," he assured her.

So as they drove, Anna called Megan back. "Gil and Marcus are on it. We're coming home."

"Poor Lelani," said Anna as she leaned back into the taxi.

"Do you think she's okay?"

Anna considered this. "Well, Lelani is a pretty levelheaded girl. I doubt that she'd do anything stupid."

"Maybe she was abducted."

"Oh, Edmond."

"I'm just saying. A lone girl in Maui—"

"Maui is Lelani's home. I'm sure she's knows how to be careful."

He nodded. "Yeah, sure."

Still, Anna wondered. She also wondered how devastated her brother would be if anything happened to Lelani. Not that Anna wouldn't be crushed as well. They all would be. Good grief, everyone loved Lelani. Who couldn't?

Apparently her parents.

The yellow Jeep was in the driveway when they pulled up. Marcus came to meet them. "Everything's under control," he assured them. "Gil and I found Lelani on the beach."

"Is she okay?" demanded Anna.

"She just took a swim—probably she was out there when the girls searched for her—and then she fell asleep."

"Where is she now?" asked Anna as they got out of the taxi.

"With Gil." Marcus shook his head. "Her mother sounds like a monster."

"So I've heard."

"Megan said she tried to have a private conversation with her dad, hoping that he would understand."

"But he didn't?"

"Apparently not."

"Poor Lelani."

"She actually seemed in pretty good spirits," Marcus said as the three of them went around to the guesthouse. "She keeps saying that everything is going to be okay."

"That's a relief."

Everyone gathered in the guesthouse. Lelani apologized for worrying them. "I just needed some space," she said as she handed out sodas and water to everyone. "I needed to clear my head. It seemed like no big deal. But I'm sorry I worried you guys."

"Guess we should know that the local girl can take care of herself," said Gil.

She smiled at him. "Not completely. I do appreciate the moral support."

"So what are you going to do now?" asked Kendall. "I mean about your baby?"

"There's not much I can do right now," said Lelani. "Except maybe get a late lunch. Is anyone else starving?"

All hands went up. So Lelani told them about a nearby barbecue place with pulled-pork sandwiches. "It's only take out, and only the locals know about this place," she assured them as they headed for their cars. "There's a great beach nearby where we can eat."

It was close to four by the time they had everything they needed and were settled on a private and pretty strip of beach. It seemed like everyone was tired and hungry. After the food was gone, and after a brief argument about whether swimming too close to eating caused cramps or not, the boys and Lelani went to play in the water and Kendall took a nap.

Anna and Megan (both still unsure about the cramp thing) cleaned up their picnic area. Megan filled Anna in on how the day had gone so far with Lelani and her parents.

"It was so sad to see Lelani trying to reason with her mother," said Megan as she crushed a paper cup. "I finally couldn't stand it and stepped in and went a few rounds with her myself."

"Who won?"

Megan just shook her head. "Mrs. Porter acts like she wins every time. She's so smug and sure of herself, like everyone else is a complete fool. Really, it's like she's delusional."

"Sad."

Megan frowned. "I probably shouldn't have said that about Mrs. Porter. I mean it wasn't very Christian of me. But seriously, I've never met anyone like her—or anyone so polar opposite of Lelani. And yet Mrs. Porter acts like Lelani is some kind of evil, devil girl."

"Our Lelani?"

"For a minute, I wondered if maybe we don't really know Lelani. But then I realized we've been living with her for months. She couldn't hide her real self."

"Sounds like her mother didn't hide her real self very well."

"Except that she did sometimes," Megan admitted. "Like when Mr. Porter and Kendall were there, Mrs. Porter was very polite to everyone. Okay, she was like the Ice Queen too. But she smiled and offered us drinks and was Mrs. Congeniality. Even when she realized that Lelani took off with her dad, which I know really made her mad, she covered it fairly well. Kendall almost bought into it. But then Mr. Porter came back, and Kendall and I excused ourselves, but before we were out of earshot, we heard Mrs. Porter laying into the poor guy." Megan squinted out to where the swimmers were playing. "Do you think it's been twenty minutes yet?"

Anna checked her cell phone's clock and nodded.

"You coming?"

"Not yet. I need to call my mom."

"Yeah, I should do that too," said Megan. "Maybe you can remind me later."

Anna nodded as she hit number three on her speed dial. Edmond had moved to the number-one spot and Gil to second.

"Anna!" her mother said. "Is something wrong?"

"No, Mama. Just calling to say hi."

"My, my," her mother sounded pleased. "Do you know, mi'ja, this is the third time you've called me in two days? I think you should go on vacation more often."

"Very funny." Anna sighed. "Mama?"

"Yes, mi'ja? Are you sure you're okay?"

"Yes, I'm—"

"And Gil, he's okay?"

"Yes. He's swimming right now."

"Not with the sharks?"

"No, he's swimming with his friends, Mama."

"What is it then? I can hear something's wrong in your voice, mi'ja. Aren't you having a good time? Did you and Edmond have a fight?" She gasped. "Oh, no! Tell me you didn't really get married, Anna?"

"No, I did not get married. Good grief!"

"What then? I am dying of suspense."

"It's Lelani, Mama."

"Something has happened to Lelani?"

"Not exactly. But her parents, particularly her mother—she's a beast, Mama. And poor Lelani. No wonder she's been so sad since she moved to Oregon. I think her own mother has broken her heart." And then Anna spilled out the whole story, at least all that she knew. "I just feel so sad for her, Mama. And I wanted to talk to someone."

"Poor Lelani." Her mother made a *tsk-tsk* sound. "I never knew."

"No one did."

"Maybe Gil?"

"Maybe."

"But what can you do about it, mi'ja?"

"I don't know. I just needed to talk."

"Well, you just keep being her good friend, Anna. I know she has several good friends, but someone whose mother is—well, you know. She needs all the good friends she can get."

"I know."

"Give Gil my love, mi'ja."

"I will."

"And Lelani too."

"Really, Mama? Do you mean that?"

"Of course. What do you think I am? Some horrible witch?"

"No, not at all. I think you're my mama." Anna smiled and told her adiós, then hung up. Really, her mother seemed to be getting nicer by the day. Or maybe it was just that old distance-makes-the-heart-grow-fonder thing.

Twenty-four

Kendall

"You guys go and have a good time," Lelani told Anna and Megan and Kendall. "You can take my car too, so there'll be plenty of room."

"No," Megan said. "If you're not going, I'm not going. I heard the Road to Hana is highly overrated anyway."

"I heard it's something you shouldn't miss seeing," said Anna.

"Well, I'm going to miss it." Megan sat down on the couch.

Lelani smiled at all of them. "Look, I appreciate the moral support, but really, I'll be fine here on my own."

Megan shook her head stubbornly. "I refuse to leave you alone."

"But Marcus really wants you to go," said Lelani. "And this is your vacation. You can't spend the whole thing babysitting me."

"It's just a silly curvy road," said Megan. "I'll probably end up getting carsick anyway."

"Carsick?" Kendall stepped in now. "No one mentioned anything about getting carsick."

"It's supposed to be one of the windiest roads in the world," Anna held up a brochure so Kendall could see the map.

"In that case," said Kendall, "you guys go and I'll stay here with Lelani."

"You don't have to—"

"Look," said Kendall firmly. "I want to. Okay? And you all know how selfish I am. I wouldn't say I wanted to stay if I didn't want to stay, would I?" She grinned. "Seriously, there are worse places to stay than in this little corner of paradise." She glanced out toward the pool. "Are we allowed to use that, Lelani?" she asked quietly.

Lelani just laughed. "Have at it."

Kendall pointed to the door. "You guys are like so outta here."

As it turned out, Gil decided not to go either, so the foursome just took the Jeep. Then Gil called to see if Lelani wanted to do something.

"Do you want to come with us?" Lelani asked Kendall while Gil was still on the phone.

Kendall considered this. "Not really," she said.

"But I feel badly leaving you here alone."

Kendall just laughed. "Are you kidding? Between the pool and the beach, what more could I want? Really, this is perfect. I feel like a princess."

Lelani frowned. "And I feel like a prisoner."

"I guess it's all a matter of perspective."

"I guess."

Kendall meant what she said. She was perfectly happy to have this lovely place to herself. And she did feel like a princess. If she hadn't witnessed some of Lelani's mother's tantrums herself, she would probably go over to the big house right now and beg them to adopt her. But then Kendall remembered that she, like Lelani had been, was pregnant and unmarried. So she'd have to nix the adoption plan. Still, what they didn't know wouldn't hurt them, would it? For today, she planned to enjoy that gorgeous pool. And if Meri wanted to give her another papaya smoothie, well, Kendall wouldn't say no.

First, she did her toenails. This was a little save-money trick that Megan had talked her into. According to Megan, Kendall would save around three thousand dollars a year if she did her own nails. Manicures weren't such a big deal, although Kendall wondered if the pedicures might get tricky when she got bigger with the baby. Already, she could feel the pinch when she bent over too far.

When her toenails, pretty in pink, were dry enough, she gathered up her pool things and headed to what seemed like a sorely underused pool. She laid claim to a padded lounge chair and then went over to dip her feet into the water. It was lukewarm but refreshing, so she got in. The water, compared to the ocean, felt silky and clean against her skin, and although she hadn't wanted to get her hair wet (chlorine on bleach, not good) she couldn't help but stretch back and just relax, still keeping her head above water. Ah, yes, this was the life.

She heard the sound of a baby squealing. She looked up in time to see a young woman in a very bad bikini, carrying what must be Emma, in an adorable pink skirted swimsuit, and approaching the pool.

"Oh." The young woman frowned. "I didn't expect anyone to be out here."

Kendall stood up and smiled. "I'm Kendall, a friend of Lelani's."

"Uh, right. I'm Ginger. Kala's nanny."

"Don't you mean *Emma's* nanny?"

"Yes, whatever. We usually have our morning swim about now." She stepped back as if rethinking this routine.

"And?"

"We seem to be disturbing you."

"The pool seems big enough for all of us." Kendall felt like giving poor Ginger some fashion tips about bikinis, but then the nanny sounded British and everyone knew that British girls—well, besides the Spice Girls—were all fashion challenged.

"All right then." Ginger stepped into the shallow end of the pool.

Suddenly Kendall was worried. "That is unless, well, does Emma ever go potty in the pool?"

"She has on her Little Swimmers."

Kendall frowned. "Huh?"

"It's a swimming nappie, a diaper. She wears it beneath her suit to keep excretions contained."

Kendall wasn't crazy about the word *excretions*. So, just in case, she kept a safe distance, watching warily as Ginger eased the baby into the water. First she sat Emma on the top step. The baby happily splashed her hands in the tepid water, laughing in glee and causing Kendall to smile. Really, had there ever been a cuter baby? Well, maybe there would be someday. Kendall patted her tummy.

"One, two, three," said Ginger. Then, to Kendall's shocked amazement, Ginger actually splashed the baby in the face, picked her up, and dropped her right into the water! The baby sank!

"What the—?" Kendall dived into the water and, ruined hair or not, swam to the other end of the pool to rescue poor Emma, grabbing up the slippery baby and pulling her out of the water.

"What are you doing?" demanded Ginger.

"What are *you* doing?" cried Kendall as she cuddled the frightened baby to her and stepped away from the evil Ginger. "You murderer, you!"

"Have you lost your mind?" Ginger was coming toward Kendall now.

But Kendall was taller and, she felt certain, madder. "You just keep your distance, you horrible thing!"

"What is *wrong* with you?" Ginger's cheeks were flushed now.

"Stay away from me, or I'll scream."

"Give me the baby!"

"I mean it," Kendall glared at her. "I'll scream and then I'll call the police and I'll have you arrested for child abuse."

Ginger's anger turned to worry at that. She stepped back and folded her arms across her front.

"That's right," said Kendall. "I saw it with my own eyes. You tried to drown my friend's baby." She shook her head. "You are a monster!"

"Who is a monster?" asked a female voice from on the deck.

Kendall looked up to see Mrs. Porter standing in the shadows. "I saw Ginger trying to drown Emma. She dropped her right in the water and—"

"Emma knows how to swim," Mrs. Porter said calmly.

"But she dropped her in, and the baby went under, just like a rock, she was sinking."

"That's how she swims."

"But I—"

"Return Kala to Ginger, Kendra."

"It's Kendall, and the baby's name is Emma," snapped Kendall.

"Give the baby to Ginger, *Kendall*." Mrs. Porter's eyes looked lethal.

"She'll drown her again," pleaded Kendall.

Now the maid and the man who looked after the yard were standing in the shadows too. Everyone was watching.

"She'll show you that Kala knows how to swim."

"That's right," said Ginger as she stepped forward and took Emma, who seemed happy to get away from Kendall. Then she sat Emma on the step again. But this time Emma didn't look quite so sure.

"It's okay, Kala," said Ginger. Then she did something that Kendall couldn't see that seemed to make Emma smile. Emma did the happy splashing again. Ginger counted to three again, then picked up Emma and dropped her into the water.

Kendall's eyes grew wide and she was about to make another rescue, but she noticed that little Emma was indeed swimming, moving
her arms and legs like a little tadpole. Kendall couldn't believe it. Emma
was swimming. Then she bobbed up and Ginger picked her up and
everyone on the deck clapped.

Naturally, Kendall felt like a fool.

"You see," said Mrs. Porter.

Kendall just shook her head. "I didn't know that babies could
swim."

"They can if they're taught," snapped Ginger. "By someone who
knows what they're doing."

Kendall nodded. "I'm sorry. I just thought she was drowning."

"Maybe next time you'll ask first."

"Oh, Ginger," said Mrs. Porter. "You shouldn't fault our guest for
trying to rescue our baby. She didn't know."

"I suppose."

"Don't let it spoil your swim, Kendall."

But Kendall was already getting out of the pool. She went over and
wrapped her towel around her waist, gathered her things, and headed
back to the guesthouse.

"Sorry we gave you such a fright," called Mrs. Porter.

Kendall didn't look back, but she could hear the snootiness in the
apology. And she knew that Lelani's mom was smiling in a snide way.

Kendall went inside and showered and scrubbed the chlorine out
of her hair. To think she'd risked her hair over nothing. But then again,
it hadn't felt like nothing. All of her motherly instincts (and who knew
she had them?) had kicked into gear when she'd seen that sweet baby go
under the water, and again when she held Emma close to her.

Well, not only was Kendall thankful that she hadn't "terminated" her pregnancy, she felt more certain than ever that she wanted to keep her baby, she wanted to be a mother to her baby, and she didn't care whether Matthew was involved or not. Oh, it would be nice if he would send money. But that was it. She didn't need his help to do this! And neither did Lelani. In fact, Kendall was of a mind to encourage Lelani to bring the beautiful little Emma home with them. She was welcome in Kendall's house. She and Lelani could raise their poor fatherless children together.

As Kendall dried off, she imagined herself and Lelani with their children and sharing the house at Bloomberg Place. Perhaps Lelani would be the one to go out and work and Kendall would stay home and care for their children. Okay, Kendall realized that she didn't have the slightest inclination of what one did to care for children, but it seemed to her that if someone like Ginger (of the bad bikini) could learn these things, certainly Kendall could as well.

Or perhaps both she and Lelani would have jobs, and together they would hire a nanny (a good one who didn't try to drown the children!) to take care of their babies. Why not?

Twenty-five

Megan

"I wonder what it would feel like to have grown up in a place like Maui," Megan mused as she and Marcus took a break on a beach in Hana. It felt good to have the solid ground beneath her and the warmth of the sun above. The Road to Hana, about fifty winding miles of thick jungle vegetation and numerous beautiful waterfalls along the way, had taken more than three hours to travel. And Megan was not ready to get back in the Jeep yet.

"It's sure a different world here." Marcus picked up a handful of sand, letting the grains trickle like fountains between his fingers. "I think I'm starting to understand the island mentality."

"What mentality?" Megan curled her toes into the sand, digging them down to where it was cooler.

"You know, the why-work-if-you-can-play mentality."

"Oh, right." Megan remembered what Lelani had told them about how most Hawaiians worked to live, not lived to work. They valued an extra day at the beach more than a fatter paycheck at the end of the week. "Well, if I lived here, I'd probably adopt a Hawaiian work ethic myself." She chuckled. "In fact, I wouldn't mind taking work less seriously at home too."

"Really?" Marcus looked curiously at her. "You always seem like such a driven sort of worker."

"I do?" Megan considered this.

"Yeah, I'm not saying you're a workaholic, but you really do work hard."

She nodded. "I get that from my dad."

"And I'm not saying it's bad"—Marcus leaned back and looked at the sky—"but do you ever wonder what your dad thinks about all that work now?"

"You mean … like he's probably not up there in heaven going, 'Man, I wish I'd worked more.'" She sighed. "At least he enjoyed his work. He was a great architect, and he loved what he did."

"I guess that would make a difference."

"Do you love what you do?"

"I used to think I loved it, but now I think I really just loved the money." Marcus laughed. "Investment brokers used to make more. But now, even if I made more, I still wouldn't love it. I might not even like it."

"Then why do you do it?"

"To pay the bills, to keep the wolf from the door." He turned and looked at her. "How about you? I haven't heard you saying anything positive about your job these last few weeks."

"Because I pretty much loathe my job."

"Even after Cynthia gave you a raise and a week off?"

"That was nice. And I plan to go back and work hard in return, but …"

"But?"

"I'm going to get more serious about finding a teaching job."

"Do you think you'd love to teach?"

"More than I'd love helping to decorate rich people's houses."

"Teachers don't make much money."

"I don't need much money."

"You know, since we've been going to church, I've been thinking about a lot of things."

"Like what?"

"Like what I want to do with my life."

She turned and looked at him. "What do you want to do with your life?"

"I want to make a difference."

"I know what you mean," admitted Megan. "I want to make a difference too. I've been thinking about that Hawaiian princess that I was reading about at lunchtime."

"The one born in the cave?"

"Yeah. Ka'ahumanu."

"I can't believe you can remember her name, let alone pronounce it right."

"I sort of made a point to remember it. I wanted to ask Lelani if she was related to her. I mean there are some similarities. Ka'ahumanu had a home in Lahaina, and they're both tall, intelligent, beautiful Hawaiian women."

"Except Lelani doesn't have any tattoos."

"Not that you know of anyway."

"Does she?"

Megan laughed. "I don't know. But I haven't seen any."

"Anyway, back to Ka-ah-what's-her-name."

"Ka'ahumanu. She was a woman who made a huge difference. Her influence on this island is really profound."

"Uh-huh?" Marcus leaned back into the sand again. "Tell me more."

Megan leaned back too. "First of all, she married well."

Marcus laughed. "Yes, considering she was born in a cave."

"But after her royal husband died, she did a lot for her people. She made laws to protect their religious practices, which in turn allowed Christianity into the island."

"Which was kind of a mixed blessing, don't you think?"

"I think some of the missionaries took advantage of the wealth of this land—and of the culture. But you have to give credit to some, like the missionaries who taught Princess Ka'ahumanu to read and write and introduced her to Christ. They made a difference too."

"So Princess Ka-ah was a Christian?"

"Yes." Megan punched him in the arm. "I already told you all this at lunch, don't you listen to me?"

"Well, you were reading the back of the menu and I was reading the inside since I was hungry. Sorry."

"Anyway, after she became a Christian, she did a lot of things to help and protect her people. She was an amazing leader—especially for a woman back in the eighteen hundreds."

"So you want to grow up and be like Ka-ah-hoo-ha?"

"Ka'ahumanu." Megan laughed. "Actually you were a little closer that time. But, yes, I wouldn't mind doing something influential in my life. I don't aspire to be a Hawaiian princess. But I'd like to make a difference. I suppose I could be a missionary."

"A missionary?" Marcus sat up and stared at her.

"I know. It sounds crazy, but I've actually thought about it from time to time."

"What would you do?"

"Well, I've heard that there's a need for teachers in a lot of places. And I do have my teaching credentials."

"Wow. That's kind of mind-blowing, Megan."

She nodded. "I've never actually told anyone before. I guess I sort of thought that if you're supposed to be a missionary, well, God would call you to it."

"Like, 'Yoo-hoo, Megan, God on the line. Can you please go teach African children to read and write?'"

Megan laughed, then punched him again. "No, silly. Not like that. And if I'd known you were going to make fun of me, I never would've told you in the first place. Sheesh."

"I'm not making fun of you. Not really. In fact, this interests me … a lot."

"What interests you? That I might hop on a boat and head off to regions unknown and teach orphans and you'd never hear from me again?"

He shook his head. "That's definitely not what interests me."

"What then?"

"Well …" He looked slightly uncomfortable now. "I'm not sure I'm ready to say it just yet."

A tiny alarm went off in Megan, and she wasn't even sure why. She had just teased him about heading to the ends of the earth and he had said he didn't like that idea and that he had something to say, except he wasn't ready to say it yet. Or maybe she wasn't ready to hear it yet. Surely, he wasn't about to pop the question, was he? No, that was crazy.

"Oh, dear!" She picked up her cell phone. "It's after three and we told Anna and Edmond we'd pick—"

"Let's go!" Marcus was on his feet, reaching down to pull her up to him. And then, to her surprise, he pulled her into a hug. "You're one great girl, Megan."

"Well, thanks." She smiled up at him.

"And now we better rock and roll." He chuckled as they hurried to the parking lot. "I guess we're already getting sucked into Maui time."

Fortunately, Edmond and Anna must've been sucked into Maui time too, because they came walking up to the prearranged meeting place only seconds after the Jeep pulled up.

"Sorry to be late," said Anna. She set a shopping bag in the back. "But we found some great-looking fruit to take back to the guesthouse."

"Oh, that's okay." Marcus winked at Megan. "We haven't been waiting too long."

"So," Megan produced a map. "We can either go back the way we came, or we can continue on around the east side of the island."

"Which might be quicker," said Marcus.

"And it might be more interesting," added Edmond, "since we'll see more of the island that way."

So it was decided. But Megan was surprised at the difference in the terrain. "I feel like we've gone to another place," she said as they rode through what actually seemed like a desert. "Look, there's another cactus."

"Are you sure we're still in Maui?" asked Anna.

"Well, since we haven't taken any boats or bridges," teased Marcus.

"Or stepped into the Twilight Zone," added Edmond.

"It says here," Megan read from her brochure, "that this is the dry side of the island. Because of the weather pattern and trade winds, most of the moisture ends up on the west side, which explains why it's so green over where we're staying." Then Megan went on to read other statistics about weather, elevation, and history.

"You're a good travel guide," called out Anna from the back.

"And a great teacher," added Edmond.

Marcus nudged Megan with his elbow. "See, maybe God is calling."

Megan just laughed. But then she wondered. Maybe God was calling. At least he might be calling her to teach. That seemed fairly obvious. As far as being a missionary, well, maybe that was simply Maui calling.

She glanced at Marcus now. He actually looked quite attractive in his aviator sunglasses and worn khaki ball cap. Already he was sporting the beginnings of a pretty nice tan. His profile, the straight nose and strong chin, was just as handsome as always, although it looked like he'd forgotten to shave this morning, which only added to those rugged good looks. He didn't notice her looking, because his attention was tightly focused on navigating the Jeep to avoid potholes in this washboard stretch of road.

She turned away and wondered what it was that he'd been about to tell her on the beach this afternoon. Why had it suddenly felt awkward and quiet between them? Or had she simply imagined that? No, she didn't think so. She couldn't deny feeling hugely relieved when she realized they needed to get Anna and Edmond. Otherwise, what would've happened? Was he really about to ask her to marry him?

Seriously, what would she have told him if he'd made a genuine, honest-to-goodness proposal? Would she have been able to speak at all? She imagined herself with her jaw hanging open, too stunned to respond. Lovely image.

Megan had no doubt that some girls, take Kendall for instance, would think it wildly romantic to receive a proposal in a place like Maui. Perhaps at the right time, it would be wonderful, sweet, and memorable. Unfortunately, Megan didn't feel ready for that kind of commitment. Not just yet. She sure hoped that Marcus didn't either.

But, just in case, she began rehearsing a response in her head. Something honest but kind, direct but open-ended.

Then Megan began to question herself. Why should she tell him no? Didn't she love him? Yes, she thought that she did. She felt like she did. But marriage? She was only twenty-four. Okay, almost twenty-five. He was only a year older. He didn't even like his job. And she didn't like her job. No, she decided, neither of them was ready for a big commitment like marriage. Were they?

Twenty-six

Lelani

"You really don't *have* to go with me," Lelani told Gil as he snagged a parking spot and did a rather commendable job of parallel parking in a pretty tight space.

"Like I've already told you about ten times, I *want* to go with you." He frowned now. "Unless you don't want me there, in that case I can just wait in the—"

"No, I absolutely want you there, Gil." She put her hand on his arm. "I need you there. It's just that this is your vacation. You only have four days left."

"And I would sit in a stuffy lawyer's office for all four of those days as long as I was with you, Lelani. Don't you get that?"

She smiled. "Thanks. Hopefully that won't be necessary."

He handed her the car keys.

"Why don't you keep them," she told him. "In case things get boring and you want to take—"

"I told you already."

"Okay." She took the car keys and dropped them into her purse while he put some coins in the parking meter.

"Are you nervous?" he asked as they walked toward the office building.

"Yes. But I'm also sort of relieved. It's like I should've done this a long time ago."

"No time like the present."

"Right." She took in a deep breath as he opened the door for her. She knew she could do this. She would do this. She glanced at Gil. "Thanks for coming." He smiled. Lelani had considered asking Megan to come. She would've if Gil hadn't volunteered, but she knew that Megan and Marcus planned to drive around the north side of the island today. And Lelani had really wanted them to do that. She was happy that Megan was so taken with Maui's history. The way she'd told Lelani all about Princess Ka'ahumanu had been really sweet. And for Megan to compare Lelani to her was even sweeter.

"You'll be like her today," Megan had assured Lelani this morning. "Strong and wise and doing what's best for your child."

Lelani had thanked her, but as she waited for the receptionist to announce her arrival, she felt unsure. Maybe going to a lawyer would simply make things worse. In fact, maybe her mother had already gone to a lawyer. What if she'd accused Lelani of abandonment? It was entirely possible.

"Lelani." Clara Chan met her at the door, taking both hands in hers and smiling warmly. "It's been too long."

Lelani smiled and introduced Clara to Gil. "He's my moral support."

Clara nodded in a somber way. "Yes, you'll need it. Come into my office. Let's talk."

Lelani had already given Clara most of the facts over the phone. But something about the way Clara was looking at her made Lelani feel worried. "Is something wrong?" she asked as they sat down in the chairs across from Clara's cluttered desk.

"Well, I did some checking, Lelani. And records show that your mother attained custody of Emma in August of last year."

Lelani felt like someone had just jerked the floor out from under her. "What? No one told me. I never signed anything."

Clara nodded. "No, you didn't need to. Because you were out of state and your child was here, your mother had the legal right to file for custody."

Lelani turned and looked at Gil. Tears were filling her eyes and she felt a huge lump wedging itself in her throat. She didn't think she could even speak. Gil took her hand in his and gave it a gentle squeeze.

"Excuse me if I'm butting in," he began. Lelani just nodded. "But shouldn't Lelani's mother have consulted with Lelani about this?"

"Under normal circumstances, a custody arrangement would be discussed with all parties involved and agreed upon together. Or else it would be settled in court."

"But neither of these things happened, right?"

Clara shook her head. "But, in Mrs. Porter's defense, she had the right to file for custody. For instance, if Emma needed medical treatment, she would need to have the authority to get it for her."

"But I did sign a paper to allow Emma to have medical treatment," Lelani said. "And I didn't relinquish my parental rights either. It was the same kind of form that's used for child-care purposes."

Clara made note of this. "So, you assumed that was sufficient before you left."

Lelani nodded. "But I did leave."

"Only because your parents forced you to leave," Gil pointed out.

"That's true."

"That's a valid point," said Clara. "But it might not be terribly valuable in court."

"Do you think this will go to court?" Gil asked.

Clara frowned. "I'd be surprised if it didn't go to court. I, uh, I'm acquainted with Alana Porter. She's not the kind of person to give in to anything without a good fight."

Lelani nodded and looked down at her lap.

"We'll give her a good fight," said Gil.

"If you don't mind, may I ask what your involvement with Lelani is?"

"I'm her friend."

Lelani looked at him and smiled.

"And I'd like to be more than that."

Clara nodded. "I see, but you're not the baby's father?"

"No, he's not," Lelani said quickly.

"And the baby's father? What role does he play in this custody dilemma?"

"No role."

"Because?"

"Because he didn't want anything to do with her." Lelani looked down. "He was already married."

"Married men often have children outside of their marriages. That's no excuse not to take responsibility."

"I don't want him involved with Emma. He doesn't want to be involved. Is there anything wrong with that?"

"No, if it's mutual consent. But you are aware that fathers have custody rights too?"

"I'm aware. But he made it clear he wanted nothing to do with Emma."

"Don't you think," Gil injected, "that this is more about Lelani and her parents and Emma's best interest?"

"I couldn't agree more, but I just like to shake every tree first.

That's for Lelani's and Emma's sakes. We don't want to get surprised on down the line."

"So what do you think I should do?" asked Lelani.

"To start with, we'll file a petition for custody. But then we'll have to build your case."

"Build my case?"

"The court is willing to change a custody arrangement when it's proven to be in the best interest of the child. We must provide evidence to this. We must convince them that it's in Emma's best interest to be with you."

"I thought that courts always showed preference to the mothers," said Gil.

"Generally speaking. But grandparents are highly respected in Hawaii. And it's not unusual for grandparents to raise their grandchildren."

"Even if they steal them from their real parents?" Lelani clenched her fists, still fighting to hold back her tears.

"Where does your father stand in all this, Lelani?"

Lelani just shrugged. She was afraid to speak because she knew she was about to cry.

"He seems to be siding with his wife," Gil told her.

"I'm not surprised," Clara admitted. "However, I've known Will Porter for quite a long time. He's always been an honest businessman with a sound sense of fairness."

"Except when it comes to my mother," muttered Lelani.

"Yes."

"So what kind of evidence does Lelani need to gather so that she can prove that she should have custody of her own child?"

Lelani nodded eagerly, thankful that Gil was on top of things.

"The court looks primarily at three criteria. First being the safety and well-being of the child. Then the court considers the history of the guardians, if they have previously caused physical harm or reasonable fear of physical harm to another person."

"Would that include emotional abuse?" asked Gil.

"Yes. Emotional abuse would be considered."

"What's the third criteria?" asked Lelani.

"If a parent has been absent or has relocated as a result of family violence, the relocation shall not be a factor against the parent in determining custody."

"Bingo!" yelled Gil. "That's it, isn't it? Emotional abuse sent Lelani into a depression. It's what forced her to leave."

"It will be difficult to prove. Lelani already told me that although her mother is verbally abusive, she never physically harmed her. Emotional abuse is a slippery slope."

"And it will be my word against hers," pointed out Lelani.

"But you have witnesses." Gil stood now. "Lelani has been living with three other women, including my sister. They've seen how Lelani has been traumatized by all this. She's had nightmares and panic attacks and all sorts of things."

Clara nodded and wrote something down. "Interesting."

"Some of Lelani's friends actually heard Mrs. Porter verbally attacking Lelani, just this week, right here in Maui. Even in front of Emma." He turned eagerly to Lelani. "Right?"

"That's true. Megan saw it."

"A witness," declared Gil.

Clara actually chuckled as she made note of this. "Gil, have you considered going into law?"

"Not really."

"But he's very intelligent." Lelani reached up and took his hand. "I'm glad you're on my side."

He squeezed it and smiled. "Me too."

"Well, Lelani, I suggest you get affidavits from your friends. Both in regard to your emotional state while living in the mainland, and things they witnessed in your parents' home. Both will be valuable. In the meantime, I will file the petition and began to prepare for your case. By the way, you have the legal right to visitation with your daughter. I will get that started as soon as possible."

"Does this mean I should remain here?" asked Lelani. "Not return to Oregon?"

"That would definitely be in your best interest."

Lelani frowned. "I'll need to find a job and a place to live."

"Yes, you probably won't want to live with your parents, under the circumstances."

Then Lelani told Clara about how her mother postured to get rid of Lelani in the first place. "If I'd been stronger then," said Lelani, "if I hadn't been struggling with post-partum depression, I think I would've gotten a job and found a place to live. I never would've gone to Oregon."

"Why Oregon?" asked Clara.

"My dad's sister lives in Portland with her husband and three kids. I stayed with them at first. But their house was tiny and my aunt and uncle seemed to think I was the nanny and maid and, well, other things." Lelani shook her head at the memory.

"Who decided that you should live with them?"

"My mother." Lelani kind of laughed. "Of course."

"Has your relationship with your mother always been strained, Lelani?"

Lelani considered this. "No, not always. As long as I agreed with her, as long as I lived my life the way she felt was best, as long as I was her adoring daughter, as long as I was perfect"—Lelani swallowed hard—"then things were okay."

"That's a hard act to keep up," said Clara sadly.

"Tell me about it."

Gil put his hand on Lelani's shoulder. "I don't know anyone as close to perfect as Lelani is. I would think any mother would be proud to have her as a daughter."

"Unless that mother saw her daughter as her competition," said Clara. "Do you think that's a possibility, Lelani?"

Lelani thought about it for a minute. "Yes, I suppose so. Especially as I got older and tried to make my own decisions. Like when I wanted to go to medical school, my mother hated the idea, but my dad supported me. That got a little ugly."

Clara nodded, then began summarizing their meeting, rattling off a list of the things that Lelani needed to do. Fortunately, it looked like Gil was listening carefully, because Lelani felt like her head was spinning.

"Okay, then." Clara looked at the clock on her desk. "I think I have enough to go to work on here. I'd like to make some notes about your case, check on some things, before my next client arrives at two."

So Lelani and Gil thanked her, and Clara told Lelani that she would be in touch.

Outside, Lelani couldn't contain the emotions anymore. She put her hands over her face and began to cry. Then Gil took her in his arms and there on the busiest street of downtown Lahaina, Lelani sobbed. Wouldn't her mother be ashamed to see her daughter now?

"I'm so sorry," she told him when she finally pulled away, touching his dampened shirt—a Hawaiian one that he'd just gotten yesterday. "Look, I soaked your new shirt."

He stroked her hair and smiled. "You're welcome to soak my shirt anytime."

Lelani was still trying to remember all that Clara had told her to do, gathering material for affidavits, dates, records, letters … and then she remembered that she'd have to stay in Maui until the custody was resolved.

"Oh, Gil, what am I going to do?" she asked when they reached the car.

"You're going to do whatever Clara thinks will help you to win custody of Emma. I'm starving. Let's go get some lunch and we'll make a list while it's still fresh in our minds."

"But that means staying here in Maui." She turned and looked at him.

He nodded as he dropped some more change in the meter. "If that's what it takes, that's just what you'll do."

"But … what about … *us*?"

He gave her his brightest smile. "Hey, you really do think there's an us!"

"Well, isn't there?"

"I like to tell myself that there is, but sometimes I worry that I'm delusional."

"I will miss you so much if I stay here."

He hugged her again. "It's just temporary. Just until you get custody."

"What if it takes a long time?"

"Then I'll come and visit." He grinned.

"What if I changed my mind about living on the mainland?" She studied him closely, "What if I found out that I couldn't bear to leave Maui again?"

His brow creased. "Do you think that's possible?"

"I don't know. I'm just trying to be honest, Gil. Maui *is* my home. And being here now, despite the unfortunate circumstances, well, I still love it."

"What's not to love?"

"The fact that your family, your job, everything, is back in Oregon."

"Everything but you."

"You couldn't leave all that."

"I could for you, Lelani."

She didn't know what to say. This was too much. It was hard enough trying to figure things out regarding Emma. And now there was Gil to think of.

"Hey, we don't need to resolve everything in one day." He took her hand. "And there's a restaurant around the corner that I've been wanting to try out."

Gil changed the subject as they walked. He talked about the restaurant business and how the skills it took to run a restaurant could be applied to other businesses. "It's not like I specifically wanted to handle the business end of my parents' restaurants," he confessed. "It's more like I fell into it. Still I can't complain. I've learned a lot."

Lelani remembered the questions he'd asked Clara now. "You know, you probably really would make a good lawyer."

He shrugged. "You never know."

They were seated and Gil reached across the table to hold her hand again, looking at her with so much warmth in his eyes that Lelani thought she was melting.

"Lelani, Lelani," he said quietly. "What does your name mean? I know that all Hawaiian names have meanings, right?"

"A lot of them do. But some are just our translations for English names. I had a boyfriend in high school whose name was Mikala, Hawaiian for Michael. In his senior year, he started going by Michael, but his parents didn't like it."

"So what does Lelani mean?"

"When you spell it the right way, it means flowers from heaven. *Lei*, spelled *l-e-i*, means *flowers*, like the lei necklaces. *Lani* means *heaven*."

"But your name is missing an *i*."

It was a story she used to have to tell often when she was in school, but this was the first time she'd explained it in a while. "My mother had a difficult birth with me, and she was sort of out of it when my dad filled in the information for my birth certificate. He knew I was to be called LeiLani, but…"

"He misspelled it."

"Yes. Apparently my mother threw a fit, but my father put his foot down. He said that since I was half Hawaiian and half Porter, I deserved a name that was uniquely my own." She smiled sadly. "That was probably one of the last times he stood up to her."

"And you got stuck with a misspelled name."

"I actually kind of liked it in school. It's a fairly common girls' name, and being an *i* short made me feel unique."

"Well, the name still fits you. Lelani. You are like a flower sent from heaven."

As Lelani considered the legal battle ahead of her, she felt more like a flower about to go through hell. Still, it would be worth it to get Emma back. As much as Lelani loved peace, she knew that she was willing to go to war for her daughter.

After they ordered lunch, Gil got out a notepad and began writing down things that Clara had suggested Lelani do. Somehow, seeing it neatly down on paper made Lelani think maybe she could do this thing.

"I should start looking for a job right away," she said. "As well as a place to live. A cheap place. Some of the resorts have housing available for workers. Maybe I can find something like that to start with."

"I wish you could go back and finish your medical degree," said Gil. "I think you'd be a great doctor."

"I wish I could go back too," she admitted. "In fact, I've been daydreaming about going to Portland State. I did some online checking and thought I might even get enrolled for summer term."

"Well, in due time. First things first, right?"

She nodded. "Right. What matters most to me now is proving to my parents and the court that I can support myself and my daughter. Even if I have to scrub floors and toilets at the Pukahanalakimana Hotel, I am willing to do it."

Gil laughed. "They'd never hire me there, I can't even say the name."

"Most people just call it the Puka."

But Lelani was serious. She would even work at the low-class, sleazy Puka Hotel if that was the best she could do. She just wished that she'd had the strength to do that last year. But then, she realized, she never would've met Gil.

Twenty-seven

Anna

Wednesday, Edmond arranged for everyone to take an all-day snorkeling trip at the island of Lanai. His treat. Anna wasn't sure what she thought about snorkeling, but she was proud of Edmond for setting it all up. According to Lelani, the cove they were going to visit had some of the best snorkeling in the world. And according to Edmond, the gear that Lelani borrowed from her dad's shop was some of the best in the world too.

As they boarded the ferry to take them to the island, Anna knew that this had all the makings of a great day. Except for one thing: Anna was not a good swimmer. The idea of being underwater, even just slightly, was totally unnerving. Still, she didn't want to spoil it for the others. So she played along, imitating them, acting like she planned to have the time of her life even though she was just plain tired.

Last night, Lelani told the girls about her appointment with the attorney and her decision to remain behind in Maui. There had been tears and hugs and everyone felt shocked and saddened that their little "family" was breaking up.

"I don't know what else to do," Lelani had admitted. "I want Emma more than I've wanted anything in my life. And the only way to get her back is to stay."

"What about Gil?" Anna had demanded.

"Nothing will change between us," Lelani reassured her.

"Except that you'll be an ocean apart," pointed out Kendall.

"We'll remain in touch." Lelani's voice sounded positive, but her eyes were sad.

"Absence makes the heart grow fonder." Megan smiled weakly.

"And Gil is 100 percent supportive of this," added Lelani.

Anna just nodded. "Yes, that's not surprising." Still, Anna felt disappointed. Both for Gil and herself. She felt like she was losing a sister. Also, she knew that although Gil would maintain a brave front, he'd be heartbroken when it was time to get on the plane and leave Lelani behind. Despite Megan's trite quote, Anna knew that absence could also pull people apart. And she knew that someone as sweet and beautiful as Lelani would attract all kinds of male attention. Poor Gil!

"Well, I'll be holding your room for you," Kendall had assured her. "For you and Emma when you come back."

"Hopefully, it'll be soon," Megan had added.

But Anna suspected by the look in Lelani's eyes that it might not be that soon.

"Right now I just need to focus," Lelani had told them. "I need to get everything together to fight this battle." Then she'd asked them about writing letters on her behalf, describing observations they'd made about her or her parents. "My attorney needs affidavits that she can use in court."

Naturally they all agreed to do whatever they could to help. Anna knew she'd have plenty to say. She even offered to help the others with the editing of their letters. Then she'd stayed awake until 2:00 a.m. thinking of all the things she wanted to say in her letter. She got up, quietly took out her laptop, which Edmond had teased her for bringing, and took it to the bathroom, where she sat on the john and wrote.

She read it to her housemates over breakfast, and the next thing she knew, Kendall was dictating a letter of her own. When that was finished, Megan asked to borrow the laptop to write her own letter.

"You guys are great," Lelani had told them as they gathered their things for the snorkeling expedition. "My lawyer is going to be surprised at how speedy you are."

"Hey, why don't I e-mail them to her?" offered Anna. Lelani dug out Clara's business card, and Anna wrote a quick e-mail, attached the documents, and hit send.

"I asked if her assistant could print them out," Anna said as they went out to the car. "If they print them in time, we can all go in and sign them."

"They'll probably need to be notarized." Lelani lowered her voice as they got into her car. "Just in case anyone questions their authenticity."

So the day had started out well, but by the time the ferry landed and everyone got off with their snorkeling gear in tow, Anna was having serious second thoughts.

"I better warn you about something," Anna told Edmond as they walked down the trail to the cove together.

"You're really a tiger shark in disguise and I better not get too close to you in the water?"

"Very funny." Anna looked at Edmond. "There aren't sharks around here, are there?"

"Well, it's an ocean, Anna."

"Is Anna freaking over sharks?" teased Gil from behind them.

"Yes." Anna nodded vigorously. "I have a serious fear of sharks."

"The key is to just relax," said Lelani as she came up and walked beside Anna.

"Because some people think that sharks can smell fear," said Edmond.

Anna stopped in her tracks. "Smell fear? Then that makes me, what, shark bait? Because, trust me, I am afraid. Very afraid."

"Oh, Anna, I don't think sharks really smell fear. Although they do smell blood."

"Great," said Anna. "I cut my finger slicing that pineapple this morning. Does that mean I'm shark bait?"

"You're not going to be shark bait," Lelani assured her. "We'll stay together, okay? And close to the shore."

"Maybe you girls will stay close to the shore," said Edmond, "but I plan on seeing everything I can today. I've got an underwater camera and the conditions look perfect."

"Thanks," said Anna. "It's nice to know that my own boyfriend won't even come to my rescue in the likely event of a shark attack."

"No sharks will come near where we'll be." Lelani reached over and punched Edmond in the arm. "And if they do, Edmond, the great white snorkeler, will swim like the dickens to your side."

"Oh, yeah, I'll be holding my breath." Anna shook her head.

"Don't worry," Lelani put a protective arm around her shoulders. "I'll be your buddy." She lowered her voice. "Seriously, no one knows these waters like I do. You're safe with me."

Anna nodded. Actually, of everyone here, she did feel safest with Lelani. "But I don't want to hold you back. I mean it's kind of like making you stay in the kiddie pool."

"I can snorkel anytime I like, Anna."

Anna frowned to remember that Lelani wasn't planning to return with them. Still, Anna did not plan to bring the subject up again today. Today was for fun. Well, fun for some. Maybe not for Anna.

As it turned out, Lelani was the perfect snorkeling buddy. She started by giving Anna lessons on the shore. Everyone else made fun of them. But Anna was truly appreciative. Lelani taught Anna how to put on her mask, how to use her snorkel, then made her practice relaxing and breathing as they sat on the bench of the picnic table. She carefully explained how the surf would practically knock them over when they got in. "So you'll put your flippers on out in the water." She demonstrated, pulling her knee to her chest and slipping it on. "And now for the magic piece of equipment." Lelani tugged an orange vest out of her pack and helped Anna into it. "It doesn't really go with your swimsuit." She smiled at Anna's tropical colored stripes. "But it will help you to stay afloat so you can relax." Anna looked at Lelani, she looked sleek and at ease in her navy tank suit and diving shorts, whereas Anna knew she probably looked ridiculous in comparison. But she didn't care. "Now, just remember to do like I told you," Lelani reminded her as they headed for the water. "And relax."

It took a while for Anna to get her flippers on and readjust her mask, get the snorkel back into place and, finally, to put her face in the water. She tried to just breathe … and relax … and suddenly she saw a yellow fish dart by. Anna lifted her head out of the water and immediately sucked in a gulp of ocean. Lelani was right there though, helping her, calming her, getting her situated again, reminding her to relax and breathe slowly.

This time Anna did better. She started to enjoy spotting fish, and everything seemed to be going fine, but when a fish brushed up against her leg, once again she stuck her head out, sucked in more salt water, and had to be calmed down.

"You're doing great, Anna." Lelani smiled.

Anna wasn't so sure, but she wasn't ready to give up either. She put her face down again. Relax … breathe … slowly kick fins … relax …

breathe. She was seeing more fish, and they were really amazing. Striped ones, spotted ones, turquoise blue and purple ones, and coral along the bottom, and starfish and anemones. Really spectacular. Amazing. She was glad that Edmond was taking photos.

She saw what looked like an eel! Eek, an eel! She was about to poke her head out again, but she felt someone taking her hand. She glanced over to see it was Lelani, and she was smiling and pointing to the eel, like "Look, see, isn't it cool?" Anna nodded and looked and relaxed. Really, it wasn't so bad.

After what felt like an hour but might've only been thirty minutes, Anna was ready to go back to shore. Lelani didn't even complain as she swam back with her.

"That was really amazing," Anna admitted. "I'm really, really glad I went out there. And you're an awesome instructor." She smiled sheepishly. "But …"

"You've had enough?"

Anna nodded. "I think so."

"Well, you did great, Anna."

"You can go back and join the others if you want."

"No, that's okay. The sun feels good. I was getting a little chilled anyway."

Anna figured that wasn't the complete truth but didn't question her as they sat back down on the picnic bench and removed their snorkeling gear.

"You know, Lelani," Anna began carefully. "I couldn't sleep very well last night."

"I'm sorry. Is it the bed?"

"No. I was thinking about you and Emma and the custody suit."

Lelani nodded. "Yeah?"

"And I had this idea."

"What?"

"Oh, it might be a bad idea, but just bear with me."

"I'd love to hear your idea. Any ideas are welcome."

"Okay." Anna set her snorkel and mask on the table. "Well, you know how I have problems with my mother, right?"

Lelani smiled. "Yes. Although they seem tame compared to mine."

"Oh, trust me, it can get pretty wild. But I called my mom right before we left the Portland airport. I'm sure Gil told you that my mom and I had another little blowout after you and Gil left the grandparents' farewell dinner."

"He mentioned something."

"Anyway, I should probably admit that besides being afraid of sharks and open-water snorkeling"—Anna smiled—"I also have a fear of flying. I was kind of panicking and thinking maybe the plane will go down, so I called my mom to make things right. And even though I thought the fight we had was mostly her fault, I went ahead and apologized for my part in it."

"And?"

"And she seemed touched. And we had this really nice conversation. Well, nice for my mom anyway. We made headway. I've called her a couple of times since we've been here." Anna shook her head in amazement. "It's like she's changing. Or maybe I'm changing. But we're not fighting." Anna shrugged. "I suppose that could all change once I get back home. Anyway, for what it's worth."

"You think I should apologize to my mother?"

Anna frowned. "Well, I realize that she's done a lot wrong. A *lot* wrong. And she should really apologize to you. But I doubt that's going to happen."

"Probably not."

"You've said yourself that you made some mistakes in the relationship."

"That's true. I don't claim to be innocent. I pretty much wimped out. And then I got angry at my mom for hiring the nanny. It's possible that she really only hired Ginger to help me out ... although I don't think so. But, let's say that was the case. Let's give her the benefit of the doubt." Lelani nodded as if taking this in as she continued to talk to herself. "Let's say that she never intended to send me away, but she was just so frustrated and she saw me moping about. Maybe we just totally misunderstood each other. And maybe my mother really thought she was helping me by sending me to Portland!" Lelani stood up now. "That really could be possible, couldn't it?"

Anna nodded eagerly. "Then you assumed she wanted your baby more than she wanted you. But what if she was just too proud to say the truth?"

"That sounds like my mom."

Anna grinned. "Mine too."

"Wow." Lelani sat down again. "Do you think?"

"I think you'll never know unless you make the first move, Lelani."

"And apologize to her!" Lelani threw her arms around Anna now. "I think you're a genius. Maybe you should get a job on the *Dr. Phil* show. Or start your own show. Let's see. We could call it *Ask Anna*."

Anna laughed. "Well, don't go selling ad space just yet. We still need to see if this plan works."

"Oh, I really hope it does. I would give anything to keep this thing from going to court, Anna. It's not like I hate my parents. I don't. I don't understand them either. But if they could just see my side ... if they could let me have Emma and give me some space to raise her … well, I think it could be fun having them as grandparents."

"Who knows? Maybe they'd like it too." Anna wanted to add that she'd enjoy playing Aunt Anna to Emma too. But she knew that was pushing things. Despite her mother's claim that Gil was in love, which Anna didn't doubt, no commitments had been made. And Anna never felt totally sure that Lelani's feelings for Gil were as strong as his for her. Still, Anna knew that Lelani had a lot on her plate. Perhaps there just wasn't room for falling in love too. At least not yet.

Twenty-eight

Kendall

Kendall really hadn't meant to eavesdrop Thursday morning. She was only trying to find Lelani to let her know that her cell phone was ringing in the guesthouse. In case the attorney was trying to reach her. At first she thought maybe Lelani had taken a morning swim in the pool. She'd done it a couple of times, getting up early enough to avoid her mother. But it was a little late for that. So then Kendall assumed that Lelani had snuck into the nursery to spend time with Emma again. She'd done that several times too. But their visits were usually cut short because Ginger, the tattletale nanny, always ran off to tell Lelani's mom.

The back door to the main house was open, so Kendall let herself in, thinking she'd find Lelani in the nursery and get to spend some time with that adorable Emma herself. But, although the nursery door was cracked open, only Ginger and Emma were there, and it appeared she was getting Emma ready for her morning swimming—or drowning—session. So Kendall continued to prowl through the quiet house. Okay, maybe she was snooping, but then why shouldn't she snoop? They were, after all, guests in the Porter home, shouldn't they be allowed to look around? And this house was worth looking at too.

Besides, Kendall reminded herself as she tiptoed down a hallway at the other end of the house, she had opted to stay behind today so that the two couples (Anna and Edmond, Megan and Marcus) could do some more sightseeing. Before she left, Megan specifically told Kendall to keep an eye on Lelani. If anyone asked, that was simply what she was trying to do. For all she knew, Lelani's witch of a mother could be poisoning Lelani—she could be slipping a teaspoon of arsenic into the coffee, smiling as she handed her daughter a cup of the finest Kona.

Just when Kendall imagined that scene, she heard their voices. Rather, it was Lelani's voice. She was speaking calmly, rationally, just the way Lelani normally spoke.

"So you see, Mother, I've been giving it a lot of thought, and I can understand that you might have thought you were helping me by hiring a nanny. When I rejected the idea, I might've sounded ungrateful. I might've even said some mean things that hurt your feelings. To be honest, I can't remember my exact words, but I do remember being angry. And so I think I owe you an apology."

Kendall gasped. What was going on here? Why was Lelani caving like this? Had her evil mother cast some sort of spell on her, slipped her drugs, turned her into a Stepford daughter? What was going on?

"Well, Lelani, have you started to come to your senses?"

Kendall clenched a fist. Then she just waited.

"All I'm saying, Mother, is that I didn't handle things well. I didn't appreciate that you were trying to help me."

"That's all I was doing, Lelani. I could see you were unhappy. I just wanted you to get on with your life."

"But I didn't see it like that. I thought you were trying to take my baby."

"Oh, dear, why would I want to do that? You're my daughter."

There was a pause, and Kendall imagined Lelani's mother as a spider, spinning her web, reeling in her prize.

"I just wanted you to know that I really do appreciate you. And I'm thankful for what you've done for Emma. For taking care of her these past nine months."

"We're family, Lelani. Why wouldn't we care for our own?"

"So you accept my apology?" Lelani's voice was hopeful and vulnerable. "Do you understand that I really never meant to hurt you?"

"I had always hoped that you'd come to your senses, Lelani."

"So I'll be taking Emma back with me when I leave."

The silence grew so thick that Kendall thought she might gag on it. With her hand pressed over her mouth, she waited.

"My poor Lelani." Her mother actually laughed now. "It's rather sweet that you're suddenly experiencing all these maternal urges and motherly emotions. But you must understand that it's too little too late. You must be able to accept that time has come and gone."

"No. I cannot see that." Lelani's words came slowly now, almost as if each one caused her real physical pain. Maybe they did. Kendall certainly ached inside. "I cannot accept that. I *can* accept that I was confused after Emma's birth. I *can* see that I didn't make good choices. I can even admit that I said some harsh things to you. But I cannot understand why you should hold that against me now. I am apologizing to you, Mother. Can you forgive me?"

"If you are speaking of the kind of forgiveness that sweeps all that's been done under the rug, no, I cannot forgive you. If you think your pretty words are all it takes for you to waltz in here and take Kala—"

"Emma!"

"No, Lelani, her name *is* Kala. The sooner you accept that, the easier it will be for everyone."

"*Her name is Emma, Mother.* And she is *my* child. Not yours. I am sorry for the pain I've caused you. And I am sorry that I will be forced to fight you in court, but apparently you give me no—"

"What?"

"I spoke to an attorney this week. She is ready to file petitions and take this to court. I have sworn affidavits attesting to the emotional abuse I suffered from you."

"You are bluffing, Lelani."

"I am not bluffing."

Alana laughed again. And this time Kendall couldn't take it. She burst into the room, causing both Lelani and her mother to jump. "She is *not* bluffing, Mrs. Porter," declared Kendall. "We've been living with Lelani for months now. We all know what you've put her through. We all know that you are trying to steal her baby. We've seen you treating her like—like this!" Kendall flung out her arms for drama. "I heard every word you just said and I am willing to write another sworn statement." Kendall pointed her finger at Mrs. Porter now. "And another thing—I think we should take this to the news. I mean, you seem like a pretty respected woman in the town. And your husband's businesses are popular. How would you look if everyone on this island knew what you were really like?" Kendall took a step toward Lelani's mother. "Huh? How would you like to see this story all over the newspapers and—"

"That's enough, Kendall." This came from Lelani. "I appreciate your trying to help, but I would never subject Emma to that kind of publicity."

Mrs. Porter stood and faced Lelani now. "You object for the sake of your daughter, but not for your own parents? Your parents who have given you everything and—"

"Everything?" Lelani took a step closer to her mother now. "I don't want *everything*. I never did. All I ever wanted from you, Mother, was to be loved and accepted. But, as you say, maybe it's too late for that. For now, the only thing I want from you is my daughter. I will not leave this island without her."

"That's right!" Kendall stepped next to Lelani, standing tall. "And she has all her friends to back her on this too."

"I'm sure it will take all her friends. And a lot more." Mrs. Porter pointed to the door. "I do believe you have trespassed into my house. I may be forced to call the police."

"Are you kicking us out?" asked Lelani.

Her mother's eyes narrowed. "Yes. I am kicking you out of this part of the house. You and your friends have until Saturday to evacuate the guesthouse."

⨯◌⨯

"I'm sorry." Kendall wished that Lelani would stop crying. "I shouldn't have butted in."

"No, that's not it. I actually appreciated it."

Kendall handed her another tissue. "Then can you *please* stop crying. You are seriously bumming me out."

"I'm sorry." Lelani blew her nose. "I had just hoped that it would go differently."

"I don't understand why you were in there apologizing to her. She should apologize to you, Lelani. That was nuts."

"Maybe." Lelani sighed. "It seemed to make sense at the time."

"Yeah, well, that's what I said about sleeping with Matthew Harmon and look where that got me." She patted her ever so slightly rounded tummy.

Lelani actually laughed. "That is so outrageously off the mark, Kendall. Only you would think what you just said made any sense."

"At least it made you laugh." Kendall sat down next to Lelani. "Okay, like it or not, you are stuck with me for the day. What is something you like to do to take your mind off of something, well, nasty like this? If it were me, I'd say shopping. But then I promised Megan that I wouldn't and so far I've only cheated once. Well, twice. But enough about me. What do you want to do to forget all that—"

"Surfing."

"Yeah!" Kendall gave her a high five. "Let's do it. I was really getting the hang of it last time. Where do you want to go?"

"Right in my own backyard." Lelani stood. "Well, what used to be my own backyard. Although my parents don't own the beach."

Soon they were paddling out to where about a dozen other surfers were already enjoying the surf action and attempting to catch what looked like some pretty decent waves. Kendall couldn't believe how good Lelani was at this. If Kendall was just one tenth as good, she'd be happy. But she wasn't about to give up. She was, after all, in Maui. And this was her vacation. She was going to enjoy it and give it her best shot.

Just then a big wave came up from behind them, and Kendall was ready. She got her board in place and she was riding. She pulled her feet under, just like she'd seen Lelani do again and again. Then she was up on her board, arms spread for balance, and moving through what felt like a good wave—she was flying! Then—*smack!* She was tackled from behind and knocked off her feet. She and the board went into the air, then tumbled into the water. It felt like she was in the spin cycle, whirling round and round until she couldn't tell up from down and then, just when she thought her lungs were bursting, something smacked her in the forehead and the lights went out.

The next thing Kendall remembered was a pair of big strong hands—was it God?—lifting her out of the water and laying her out on something hard and smooth.

"Can you hear me?" said a deep voice. Again, Kendall wondered—was it God? Because she had been praying, or at least she thought she had.

"You're going to be okay," the voice told her.

She slowly opened her eyes to see a dark, kind face smiling down at her—the most dazzling smile she had ever seen—framed in blue sky.

"You're awake," he said. "Now, don't move. Help is on the way. You took quite a tumble. Your friend ran ahead to call for help." He smiled. "Hey, did anyone ever tell you how beautiful you are?" He shook his head like he was dazzled. "Seriously, when I pulled you out, I thought I had rescued a mermaid."

She attempted a smile and then the world grew dark again.

When Kendall woke up the second time, she was in a bed. And her handsome rescuer was nowhere to be seen. But a concerned Lelani was standing by. "Oh, Kendall," she said. "How are you?"

Kendall blinked at the bright lights overhead. "I've been better."

"You took a pretty severe bump on the head, which caused a concussion and rendered you unconscious. And your left wrist is fractured. But that seems to be about all. And at least you didn't drown."

Kendall closed her eyes again. Her head was throbbing.

"Are you in pain?"

"Uh-huh."

"Let me run for a doctor. You can have some pain meds now that you're awake."

"Thanks." Kendall had meant to ask about her handsome rescuer—that is, if he was real and not just an incredibly well-built figment of her imagination.

Lelani returned with a doctor who looked into Kendall's eyes and ears and asked her some questions and finally told her that they'd keep her overnight for observation.

"Overnight?" she complained. "But I'm on vacation. Tomorrow is our last full day."

"Sorry about that. But that was quite a hit you took to your head, Kendall," he said. "And if you're traveling home on Saturday, we want to make sure there are no complications before we release you."

Kendall frowned.

"They'll release you in the morning," Lelani assured her. "That will give you almost a whole day."

"But I wanted to go to the luau with you guys," she protested.

"Tell you what, you'll come back to Maui and I'll take you to the luau, okay?"

"Yeah, even if I do come back to Maui, which seems unlikely considering my financial affairs, where will we stay? It's not like your mom's going to be rolling out the red carpet."

Lelani smiled and patted Kendall's good arm. "At least you still have your sense of humor."

"And my good looks?"

"Yes. Definitely."

"Hey, speaking of that, what about that surfer dude who rescued me?" Kendall paused. "Please, tell me he was real."

"Killiki?"

"Killiki?" Kendall smiled. "Seriously, is that his real name?"

"It is. I've known him for years."

"Killiki … I like it. Anyway, what happened to him?"

"He had to go do some work. He's a plumber."

Kendall frowned. "A plumber?"

"Hey, plumbers make good money." Lelani nodded. "And they get to keep their own hours. Plumbing is an admirable profession on the island."

"Oh. Is he married?"

Lelani threw her head back and laughed. "Only you, who has nearly drowned and suffered a concussion, would think to ask something like that."

"Well, is he?"

"As a matter of fact, Killiki is single."

Kendall smiled. "Do you have his phone number?"

Lelani laughed even harder now. "No. But it's probably in the yellow pages. And, no, I'm not going to get you a phone book. I can tell the pain meds are starting to work. So why don't you be a good girl and get some rest? That's probably the best treatment for a head injury anyway. And, while you're sleeping, you can dream of Killiki."

Kendall closed her eyes. "It's a deal."

But when Kendall woke up, several hours later, she was not dreaming or even thinking about her gorgeous Maui man. The only thing she could think about was her baby. She had totally forgotten about her baby! And Lelani, Dr. Lelani, had not said a word about it. Kendall's hands were on her stomach, which actually felt flatter than usual, and she began to cry. What if she had lost her baby? They had said she almost drowned. And then she'd been unconscious. Wasn't it possible that all that trauma had caused a miscarriage?

If that was the case, she had only herself to blame. What an idiot. She didn't deserve to have a baby! Tears were streaking down the sides of her face, cool wet tracks going straight into her ears.

"Hey, beautiful," said a familiar voice.

She opened her eyes to see Killiki—he was for real!

"Hey, are you crying?" he asked in a gentle voice.

"Yeah."

"What's wrong, Kendall? I thought you'd be happy to be alive."

"I am. Well, sort of. But I'm really worried."

"About your arm?"

"No. Did Lelani tell you that I'm …" Kendall bit her lip.

"What?"

"That I am pregnant." Now she was crying even harder. "Or maybe I was pregnant. I forgot to ask about the baby. And they gave me pain meds—and I'll bet they wouldn't do that if I was still pregnant because you're not supposed to do drugs and—" Now she was crying like a baby.

"Hang on," he said, but then he disappeared. Who could blame him for running away? Not only had he rescued a blithering idiot, she was a baby killer too!

Kendall was still crying, only not so loudly, when Killiki returned with the doctor in tow. "Tell her, doc."

"I'm sorry, Kendall—"

"No! No! I don't want to hear—"

"No, I mean I'm sorry that I forgot to reassure you that your baby is just fine. It was the first thing Lelani told me when you were brought in. Everything checked out just fine. I'm just sorry I didn't tell you. I assumed she had."

"Really?" Kendall blinked. "You're not just saying that to make me feel better?"

"I use medicine to make people feel better … not lies."

"Thank you."

The doctor waved and left the room. Kendall thanked Killiki for helping her, both for rescuing her and for getting the doctor just now.

"I'm happy to be of help," he said as he pulled a chair next to her bed. "It's not every day I pull a beautiful mermaid out of the sea."

Kendall put her good hand on her face. "I'm sure I look like a mess."

"Not at all."

"Well, then, as usual, looks are deceiving, because, let me tell you, I am a mess. I may be the worst mess you've ever laid eyes on."

"Really?" He leaned over with interest. "How messy are you?"

And so she told him. Without sparing any details, she told him about all the ugly messes she had made in her life. About being a shopaholic, about being in debt, about sleeping with a married man. "Well, I thought they were getting divorced," she said. "But he was a movie star, so the truth is I might've done it anyway just to say that I did it." She thought for a moment. "But I wouldn't do it again."

"See, you must be learning something."

"But I got pregnant with his baby. And now he hates me. He's trying to work things out with his wife. He actually accused me of stalking him. Maybe I was. But it didn't really seem like it then. Still, it probably was. And then I come to Maui and I messed up again."

Killiki frowned. "Getting hit by a wave wasn't really your fault."

"But you see, I am pregnant. What kind of a woman goes out surfing when she's carrying a baby?"

"A Maui woman."

"Really?"

"Oh, yeah. My own mother surfed when she was pregnant with me."

"Really?"

"Totally. That's why I'm such a good surfer now."

Kendall smiled. "Okay, so maybe I'm not so messed up about the surfing part. But everything else. Really, I am a mess. Just ask my friends."

"That's a good point. You see, I happen to know Lelani. And there aren't too many women I respect as much as I do her."

Kendall's eyes grew wide. "Are you in love with her?"

He laughed. "No, not really. I probably thought I was at one time. Not now."

"Oh."

"Anyway, as I was saying, you're friends with Lelani, right?"

"Yeah. Totally."

"So, I'm thinking you can't be too messed up and have a friend like her."

"Maybe not." Kendall thought about this. "I actually have two other good friends too."

"So, see, that tells me you're not that messed up."

Kendall considered confessing that she had sort of tricked them into being her friends by renting rooms to them, but decided she should save something for later. If there was a later. And she hoped there would be.

"I see my mermaid is getting sleepy." He gently pushed some hair away from her face. "Sweet dreams, pretty mermaid." Then he knelt over and kissed her on the cheek and she felt tingly all over. She intended to have sweet dreams!

Instead, she had a restless night. She was thinking about all the things she had confessed to Killiki. Besides the fact that she'd been dumb-dumb-dumb—although what was new with that?—and had possibly driven away a totally cool guy, she was now painfully aware that she really was a mess. A pathetic, mixed-up, certifiable mess.

Then, for no particular reason, she remembered what that pastor dude on the beach had said about how he liked to go out looking for messed-up people because they were like God's lost sheep. And, really, wasn't that her? Wasn't she more lost than anyone? Was it possible that God was out looking for her?

For the first time since she'd been a little girl, Kendall attempted a prayer. Oh, it wasn't much of a prayer, and she realized as she was drifting off to sleep that she hadn't even said amen, although she wasn't really sure what was up with amen in the first place. But really, what could God expect from a messed-up girl like her? She just hoped he was listening.

To Kendall's surprised delight, Killiki showed up the next morning. A nurse had just helped Kendall to dress in the yoga sweats and hoodie that one of her friends must've dropped by last night, since they'd also left flowers and balloons, probably on their way to the luau, which she had missed. The nurse wheeled her to the entrance, where Lelani was due to pick her up any minute now. But then in walked Killiki, wearing a pale blue shirt and that dazzling smile. And in his hands was a perfect white lei that he tenderly placed around her neck.

"Ooh, that smells yummy," she told him. "Thanks."

"I was afraid I wouldn't get here in time before you left."

"Yeah, that was close." Kendall glanced to where Lelani's silver convertible was pulling up. Gil was driving and Lelani was waving from the passenger side. Apparently her witch mother hadn't taken away her car privileges yet. "There's my ride."

She stood and he gave her his arm. "I know you're leaving tomorrow," he said, "but I cannot stop thinking about you."

"Really?"

He nodded. "There's an old folktale that says when you rescue a maiden from the sea, she belongs to you." He kind of laughed. "Okay, I'm not into slavery or anything kinky. But I sort of feel like part of you belongs to me now, Kendall."

She felt her eyes growing wide. "Really?"

"Did you know your eyes are the color of the ocean on a sunny day?"
She just shook her head.

"Hey, Killiki," said Lelani as she came over to join them. "What's up?"

"I'm claiming your friend as my prize," he grinned.

Kendall laughed. "Yeah, to the winner go the spoils."

Lelani looked curiously at both of them.

"I feel kind of silly acting like this," Killiki continued. "In fact, it's a little out of my comfort zone—I'm not really a nutcase. At least I wasn't *before* I rescued you." He looked nervously at Lelani. "I think Lelani can vouch for my character."

"That's true," said Lelani. "I can vouch for Killiki. He's a good guy."

"So, I guess what I'm saying is"—he turned back to Kendall and continued awkwardly—"would you spend some time with me today, before you fly away to the mainland tomorrow? So that we can get to know each other better?" He smiled hopefully. "But I will understand if you think I'm crazy and tell me to go take a hike."

"No," said Kendall.

He frowned.

"I mean, no, *don't* go take a hike. I *do* want to get to know you better." She turned to Lelani. "Do you mind if—"

"Not at all. That is, if you feel up to it. How's your head doing?" Lelani studied Kendall carefully. "And your arm?"

"I feel fine. And this is my last whole day in Maui. You and the doctor said I'd be able to do stuff."

Lelani grinned, then turned to Killiki. "Just take it easy, okay? And tell me you're not on your Harley today."

He held up his hand like a pledge. "No, of course not."

"You have a Harley?" Kendall was beaming now.

"Yes. And she's a beauty, but we won't be riding her today."

"You two have fun. And, Killiki, you know where to bring her home, right?"

"You know it."

Lelani hugged Kendall and whispered in her ear. "Killiki is a really good guy. And by the way, you may have put the fear of God—or maybe the media—into my mother."

"Really?" Kendall blinked.

Lelani crossed her fingers. "My dad wants to talk to me when I get back home."

Now Kendall crossed her fingers. Then she waved at Gil and Lelani as they drove off. She wished she knew how to pray better.

"Something wrong?" asked Killiki.

She frowned. "I was just wishing I knew how to pray better. I mean I gave it a try last night, but I'm such a beginner. I wonder how you get really good at something like that."

His eyes lit up. "You just keep doing it."

"Do you pray?"

"Oh, yeah. But I never read a book about it. Besides the Bible. Mostly I try to keep it simple. I imagine God as a regular guy like me and I just talk to him normal-like, the same way I'm talking to you."

"Really?"

"Absolutely."

Kendall smiled. "You're an interesting guy, Killiki."

"So, my mermaid, are you ready to roll?"

"You know what they say: Today is the first day of the rest of your life."

Killiki nodded, then looked serious. "Did Lelani tell you that I'm a plumber?"

"She did."

"And you're okay with that?"

"I hear that plumbers are highly respected in Maui."

"You know what they say: When your toilet's overflowing, there's no one you'd rather come to your rescue than a plumber."

Kendall laughed. Wasn't that the truth!

Twenty-nine

Megan

The Jeep, with Marcus, Megan, Anna, and Edmond, pulled into the driveway right behind the Sebring convertible. Lelani and Gil were just getting out.

"Where's Kendall?" asked Anna. "I don't see her in the car."

"Oh, dear," said Megan. "I hope her injuries weren't more serious than they thought."

"Is Kendall okay?" called Anna as they joined the others.

"Yes." Lelani actually laughed. "Kendall is even better than okay."

"Huh?" Megan was confused.

"Her Maui man was there," said Gil.

"Her Maui man?" Anna frowned.

"The guy who rescued her." Lelani reached into the car for her bag.

"That still doesn't explain why she's not here." Megan was getting irritated.

"Are you saying Kendall ran off with her Maui Man?" asked Marcus.

"First of all, quit calling him the Maui man." Lelani poked Gil. "His name is Killiki and he's a friend of mine."

"And Killiki took Kendall away somewhere?" Megan was determined to get to the bottom of this.

"Actually, he did take Kendall, for the whole day."

"Why?" asked Edmond.

"Because he wanted to," said Lelani. "I think he's in love with her."

"They just met," pointed out Megan.

"Maybe it was love at first sight," suggested Gil. Then he winked at Lelani like he knew something about this.

"So do we know anything about this guy?" asked Edmond.

Lelani laughed. "You guys! Suddenly you're all protective of Kendall."

"Well, she looked like she needed some protection," said Megan.

"Yeah," Anna agreed. "Last night she looked kind of pathetic and wiped out. And now you let her run off with some stranger."

"Killiki is not a stranger." Lelani held up her hands. "Like I said, he's my friend. We've surfed together for years."

"A surfing buddy?" Megan frowned. "Is that all you know about him?"

"No. I know that he's a plumber and—"

"The Maui man's a plumber?" Marcus started to laugh. "Are you telling us that Kendall has run off with Killiki the plumber?"

Lelani frowned at all of them. "Trust me, Kendall is in good hands. Now, if you'll excuse me, I'm going inside."

"Uh-oh," said Marcus. "Do you think we offended her?"

"I just think she's nervous," explained Gil. "Her dad wants to talk with her this morning."

"Do you think he's mad about the things that Kendall said to Mrs. Porter?" asked Megan. Lelani had told them the whole story last night.

"I think he's pretty concerned. The good news is that he wants to speak to Lelani in private—without her mom there."

"That is good news," said Megan.

"Unless he plans to read her the riot act and send her packing," said Edmond.

"She's already been told to leave," Megan reminded him.

"So how was the volcano ride?" asked Gil.

"The sunrise was amazing," Marcus said. "You should've seen it."

"Totally epic," added Edmond. "Did you know Haleakalā is more than ten thousand feet high? One of the older dudes on the ride actually fainted."

"I was a little lightheaded myself," admitted Megan.

"And it was freezing up there," said Anna. "I mean actually freezing."

"So are you guys exhausted?" Gil asked.

"It was downhill," Anna reminded him. "All we had to do, for the most part, was stay on our bikes and coast."

"So what's everyone doing today?" Gil glanced back toward the guesthouse as if he was concerned about Lelani.

"We were talking about driving down to Kihei," Marcus told him. "Want to come?"

"There's supposed to be an awesome beach down there," Edmond said.

"Thanks, but I think I should stick with Lelani today." He frowned. "Especially since we won't be seeing each other for a while after tomorrow."

"Maybe we should all stick around," said Megan.

"I don't know." Gil seemed to be weighing this. "I actually think Lelani would feel badly if you gave up your last day to mope around with her. Why don't you go on down to Kihei and maybe Lelani and I can catch up with you later this afternoon."

So they agreed that was a good plan, and the girls went inside to get changed out of their biking clothes and gather some things for the beach.

"Did you talk to your dad already?" asked Megan when she found Lelani sitting in the bedroom, staring out the window with an unreadable expression.

"Not yet."

"Are you okay?"

"Just thinking."

"About?"

"I guess I'm questioning myself."

Megan sat down by her. "In what way?"

"You know. About Emma. I'm wondering if it's wrong for me to take her away from here. I mean she's got everything she needs. She has a beautiful nursery. A nanny who actually seems fond of her. Private swimming lessons. A lovely yard. Beach within walking distance. How selfish is it for me to take her away from all that?"

Megan considered this. "What do you think is best for Emma?"

"That's it." Lelani was actually wringing her hands. "I don't know for sure."

"But you do love her?"

"With my whole heart. I know I would do anything for her."

"But?"

"But I'm just not sure that's enough."

Megan didn't know what to say. So she actually sent up a quick help-me prayer and just waited.

"I work at a department store," continued Lelani glumly, "and I rent a room in a house. I don't even own a car. I haven't finished college. Seriously, am I mad to think I can do this? Am I even thinking of Emma? Or is it just all about me?"

"Okay." Megan took in a deep breath. "Think about this, Lelani: If you were Emma, which would you choose? Would you want to be raised like a princess with, well, your mother as a mother? Or would you rather be raised by someone like you?"

Lelani didn't answer.

"Okay, let me say what I would want. And I can say this with confidence because I have a wonderful mother who loves me and forgives me and I would be lost without her. I have to say, if I were Emma, I would pick you for my mommy—hands down."

Lelani's eyes were glistening. "Really, you would?"

"Absolutely. Because here's the deal, Lelani. You are looking at where your life is right now. Sure, it's not that impressive to work at Nordstrom, rent a room, and all that. But you could finish your degree. You could be a doctor or whatever. You could buy your own home and car if you wanted. Not that those things are going to make Emma any happier than having a devoted, kind, caring mother—one who truly loves her. Honestly, Lelani, what could possibly be better than that?"

She shrugged. "I don't know."

"So don't sit here doubting yourself. Emma deserves a mother like you."

"Thanks, Megan." Lelani sighed. "I needed that."

"Do you want us to stick around for moral support, because we don't have—"

"No. I think it would just complicate things. And I'll have Gil."

"He said maybe you guys could catch up with us later in the day."

"That sounds great."

"I'll be praying for you," promised Megan. Then she hugged Lelani. "Somehow this is all going to come out right."

Lelani nodded, but her eyes were still sad.

The beach in Kihei was nice, but crowded. Even so, the four eventually found a quiet spot, which they claimed. But before long, they all fell asleep. When Megan woke up, she realized that she'd forgotten to put on a new coat of sunscreen, which she'd been wearing religiously since they got here, and now her fair skin was turning pink. She grabbed her bag, noisily dumping it onto her towel, then located the sunscreen and began lathering it on.

"Need some help with that?" asked Marcus quietly.

"Sorry, did I wake you?"

He grinned. "If you haven't noticed, this is a pretty noisy beach."

"Want to get my shoulders and back?" She handed him the bottle. Maybe it was prudish, but she usually asked one of the girls to help with this task. For two reasons—one, she didn't want Marcus to see the freckles on her shoulders. And two, she wasn't sure she wanted him rubbing her with his hands. She was only human! But just then, she didn't care. He didn't seem to mind either.

"Thanks," she told him when it seemed he had applied more than enough.

"You know, you have beautiful skin."

She felt her cheeks getting warmer. "And it's turning a beautiful shade of pink too, isn't it?"

"That's not what I meant."

Megan shoved her things back into her bag and slid her feet into her flip-flops. "I think I need to get some shade," she said as she stood up.

"And something to drink?" he offered.

She nodded. "That sounds like a good plan."

They walked over to the nearby hotel kiosk and got pineapple smoothies, then found a shady spot to drink them.

"Are you okay?" Marcus asked as he wiped the cool drink over his brow. "You seem kind of agitated or something."

"Sorry." Megan frowned. The truth was, she was still thinking about the conversation that they almost had in Hana. But she wasn't about to bring that up again. "Actually, I'm concerned about Lelani." Then she told Marcus about how Lelani had been doubting her ability to adequately care for her own daughter. "And I encouraged her."

"What's wrong with that?"

"Well, it's easy for me to sit there and say, hey, no big deal. Sure, you can do that, Lelani. Go ahead, be a single mom, even though you work at Nordstrom and rent a room. I mean babies are expensive, Marcus. You have to buy diapers and baby food and there are doctor bills, and what about day care? I've heard it's really expensive."

"All good points."

"So where do I get off telling her that it's best for Emma to be with her?"

"Because you know Lelani loves her. And because you've seen Lelani's mother in action."

Megan nodded. "I know we're supposed to love everyone, Marcus. But that woman makes it hard."

"She's a little on the cold side." He grinned. "Like *ice* cold."

"But even so, how is Lelani going to do all that? I mean she's already looking for jobs here, and a cheap place to live. But Maui is expensive. And then there's the whole court battle." Megan shook her head. "Lelani is a strong person in some ways, but not when it comes to confrontation. She's a peacemaker at heart."

"Maybe she'll toughen up."

"Or maybe they'll crush her." Megan thought of another thing. "And she won't have us around—or Gil—to help her. She'll be all alone."

"It does sound kind of dismal."

"Maybe I should call her and take it back. I mean what if she was having second thoughts for a legitimate reason? What if her instincts are telling her that Emma is better off here?"

"Maybe we should just pray for her."

Megan was surprised. She knew that Marcus had been chang-ing, that he'd been drawing closer to God and taking his faith more seriously. But he had never said anything quite like that before. "You mean, you and me? Praying together?"

He gave her a half smile. "Why not?"

And so right there, amid all the tourists and busyness of a popular resort during spring break, Marcus and Megan bowed their heads and prayed for Lelani. They prayed for her to have wise discernment, for God to lead her, and finally for Emma's best interests. Then Marcus said amen and grinned. "See, what was wrong with that?"

"Nothing. That was great. Thanks!"

They sat quietly, watching the tourists going to and from the beach, children throwing tantrums, couples holding hands—and the whole while Megan kept wondering what it was that Marcus had been going to tell her in Hana. Still, she was determined not to bring it up.

"This has been a great week," she said finally.

"Yeah. Who knew Maui was this cool?"

"Or how fun it would be to vacation with all your friends?" She sighed happily. "I mean despite the drama with Lelani's parents. But we knew what we were getting into before we came."

"It's been cool having time to think." Marcus turned to her now. "To really examine my life, to consider who I am and where I'm going, and how that compares to who I want to be, where I'd rather go. Those are things I don't usually take the time to reflect on."

"I guess we get caught up in the daily grind." Megan studied him as he looked out toward the ocean with a thoughtful expression. "So ... who do you want to be, Marcus. Where do you want to go?"

He frowned now. "Well, I know this much. I don't want to be an investment broker anymore."

"Really?"

He nodded.

"What then?"

"I was going to tell you something in Hana."

She took in a quick breath. "In Hana?"

"You know when you were talking about being a missionary?"

"Well, I was kind of rambling, Marcus. I mean it's not that I really plan on being a missionary, although I must admit I admire people who give up everything to go serve others. I do think I want to be a teacher. Maybe not just an art teacher, even though it was my focus in college. Mostly I just want to be involved in young people's lives—and to make a difference."

"Yes, that's it. I want to make a difference too."

"That's great."

"I'm just not sure how to go about it."

"Maybe you just need to ask God to lead you." She felt relieved to know that what had been on his mind had not been marriage after all. And then she felt slightly disappointed, which left her feeling rather confused. Didn't she even know her own mind? Or her own heart?

"I know that some people wouldn't think this was such a big deal," he told her. "I mean to want to make a difference. But before, like when I was in college and just starting out in business, I was always so certain that I wanted a successful career more than anything. I wanted to be a millionaire by the time I hit thirty." He laughed. "Now that seems so stupid and shallow. What was I thinking?"

She shrugged.

"Anyway, I just wanted to tell you. I haven't told anyone else."

"Thanks." She smiled at him, wondering what more she could or should say. But just then her cell rang. "Maybe that's Lelani," she said as she fished it out of her beach bag. "Nope, it's Kendall."

"Maybe her Maui man has proposed and she's inviting you to be in the wedding."

Megan shushed him and answered. "Hey, Kendall, how are you doing?"

"Great. I just remembered something I wanted to tell you."

"What's that?"

"Have you considered becoming a pirate?"

"Huh?" Megan was confused. "Did you say pirate?"

"Yeah." Now Kendall giggled.

"You had a blow to your head, right?"

"Yeah, I'm just joking with you. But didn't you say you wanted to find a teaching job?"

"Yes." Megan waited to see what that had to do with being a pirate.

"Well, when I was in the hospital and my mind was kind of wandering, I remembered this woman I met in the maternity department."

"Kendall, are you okay?"

"Come on, Megan, hear me out. We were at Macy's. She was a teacher at the same middle school that I went to. The Madison Middle School Pirates."

"And?"

"And this lady was pregnant, like really pregnant. I meant to tell you before we left for Maui that you should go there and apply for her job, but I forgot."

"Oh."

"If it'll help, you can use me as a recommendation. I used to be a cheerleader there."

"Are you drinking?"

"No, of course not. I'm pregnant, remember?"

"Yeah." Megan used her finger to do the crazy gesture on the side of her head, and Marcus just laughed.

"I was afraid if I didn't tell you now, I'd forget again."

"Okay." Megan smiled. "How is your arm? Lelani was concerned that they hadn't put a cast on it last night, when we stopped in. Did they do that yet?"

"Oh, yeah. I've got this ugly green plastic thing around it, and it aches some, but the doctor gave me some pain medication. Do you know where I am right now?"

"Uh, are you still on the island?"

"Sure. I am sitting here in the shade, drinking a virgin piña colada on one of the most beautiful beaches I have ever seen."

"And, uh, your friend?" Megan refrained from saying *Maui man.*

"Killiki."

"He's with you now?"

"Oh, yeah."

Megan wanted to ask if Kendall was aware that Killiki was a plumber but controlled herself. Why spoil Kendall's last full day in Maui? "Well, thanks for the teaching tip. I guess I'll see you—"

"Don't hang up yet. I was wondering how Lelani's doing. I tried her cell, but it's off. Did you hear how her chat with her dad went?"

"I haven't heard from her."

"Oh. I just hope she's all right." Kendall sounded genuinely concerned. It was touching to see her caring about someone else for a change.

"Marcus and I prayed for her." Megan had no idea why she told Kendall that, not that it mattered one way or the other.

"Wow, so did we!"

"Huh?" Megan tossed Marcus a puzzled look.

"We prayed for her too, Megan."

"Really? You prayed for Lelani? You and, uh, Klikity?"

"Keel-lee-kee," Kendall said slowly. "Killiki."

"Right. Killiki. You guys prayed together?" Now Marcus was looking at Megan with a puzzled expression and she just shrugged.

"We certainly did."

"Well, that's very cool, Kendall."

"So, Megan, if you hear from her, could you give me a call?"

"Absolutely."

"And, oh yeah, in case anyone wonders, Killiki is taking me to a luau tonight."

"That's great!"

"Yeah. I was so bummed about missing out on last night, and Killiki has this good friend who's having an authentic luau—not the kind you buy tickets for—but the real deal where they bury the pig in the sand and everything."

"Very cool. Have fun!"

"Thanks."

After Megan hung up, she turned and looked at Marcus.

"Did Kendall tell you that she and Killiki were praying together?"

"That's what she said." Megan giggled. "I wanted to ask her what kind of pain meds she was taking, but I managed to control myself."

Marcus just shook his head. "Well, that is pretty mind-blowing."

"Makes me think that God is really up to something."

Thirty

Lelani

It was close to noon by the time Lelani's dad showed up at the appointed spot on the beach not far from their home. It was a place that she and her dad had claimed as their own when Lelani first began surfing. They had even constructed a palm-branch shelter that her dad reinforced at regular intervals. Naturally, it was gone now. But the memories still lingered, and Lelani marveled at how much her dad had changed over the past few years, how he had hardened. He didn't even surf anymore.

Lelani had been waiting on the beach long enough to get extremely anxious, which eventually reminded her to pray. But all she could pray was for God to have his way, and for Emma to end up in the place that was best for her. Even if that wasn't with Lelani.

"Sorry to make you wait," he said when he joined her. "Something came up."

The way he said *something* told Lelani it was her mother that had come up. Had she figured out where he was sneaking off to? Did she suspect he was talking to his daughter? Lelani glanced nervously down the beach toward the house.

"I think it'll be okay."

"I'm sorry to put you in this position, Dad," she began carefully. "And before we get into this, I want to say to you what I said to Mother yesterday. I am really appreciative of how you've cared for Emma. I'm sorry that I was unable to do more for her after she was born. So much was happening then. And when Mother hired a nanny and separated me from Emma, well, I did get pretty depressed."

"I know."

Lelani took a deep breath. "I wish I'd had the strength to have taken Emma then, but I was confused and, like Mother said, I had no way to care for a child. I could barely care for myself. And I knew that I would be cut off if I didn't leave and so—"

"Cut off?" His voice was tinged in anger.

"Just financially," Lelani added. "I knew that I didn't deserve to go back to college and, in the state that I was in, I didn't even think I was capable of going back. I felt guilty and sad, and I knew that I'd squandered your money—"

"I never said anything like that!"

"Maybe not in words, but Mother did. I could see the disappointment in your eyes."

"Sure, I was disappointed. And I was sad. But I never planned to cut you off, Lelani. Not financially or any other way." He looked directly into her eyes now. "You must know that."

She bit her lip.

"You do know that, don't you?"

"All I know is what my mother told me. You weren't really around much at the time, Daddy."

"I know. It was a pretty uncomfortable time. Your mother was very unhappy."

"And ashamed. I know she was terribly ashamed. And so were you."

"At first. But good grief, you're not the first girl to have a baby outside of marriage, and you won't be the last. I got over it."

"Really?"

"It wasn't so easy for your mother. You know how she is. She puts such great stock in … you know, certain things."

"Like appearances."

He nodded.

"Anyway, Daddy, I just want you to know that I'm sorry. I never really told you that before. But I want you to know that I am. And I hope you can forgive me someday."

"I already do forgive you, Lelani."

"Thank you."

"But, as you know, your mother hasn't."

"I know."

"So where does this leave us?"

"Well, as you know, I am not willing to give up my daughter. I love her dearly, Daddy, and I will fight for her. I have an attorney. I am gathering what I'll need to go to court."

He looked shocked now.

"Didn't Mother tell you this?"

He shook his head. "She said that you're crazy and that you planned to bring more shame on us and that you'd probably be out camping on the beach."

"She said that?" Lelani rubbed a hand over her forehead and then wondered why that should surprise her.

"Words to that effect."

"Well, I'm not crazy. But I am driven. I love Emma and I know that I can be a good mother to her. I know that I need to remain in Maui until the court date."

"Court date?"

"For Emma's custody. Clara Chan is handling my case."

"Clara?"

"Yes. She's wonderful."

"She's a good woman."

"She said you were a good man. In fact, she encouraged me to speak to you."

"But why do you need to do this? Why do you need to go to court? Why make this into such an ugly thing when all we've done is to care for your child until you were able—"

"Until I was able?" Lelani stared at him. "Is that what you truly believe?"

"That's what I agreed to."

"Until I was able …" Lelani considered this. "And who is supposed to determine if I am able, Daddy?"

He shrugged. "Well, you, I suppose."

"I am able."

He looked at her and nodded. "I believe you."

"So why can't I have my child?"

He shrugged again.

"Because of my mother."

He said nothing, just drew a line in the sand, making it deeper and deeper.

"Because my mother has turned this into a power game, and she plans to win."

"She is a strong woman."

"But is she motivated by love, Daddy? Does she really love Emma?"

"Yes, of course she does."

"But I've been here a week. I've sneaked into Emma's nursery over and over again. I've played with her and aggravated Ginger. But is Mother ever with Emma?"

"She spends some time with Emma."

"When? Do you see her?"

"No, but I go to work. And then there's Ginger. Emma is well cared for, Lelani. You can see that, can't you?"

"But I love her, Daddy. She's my baby. And I really love her."

"I know you do. I can see that. But, think about this, Lelani. If you have Emma, you'll be forced to work to support her. Who will care for her then? Not you."

Lelani pondered this.

"So, really, what difference would it make? At least Emma has stability here. She's not going to some dirty day-care center, staying among strangers."

"Do you think I'd let anyone watch her that I didn't know and trust?"

"I'm just saying."

"And I'm saying that I can take care of her. She is my daughter. If you and Mother stand in my way, we will let the court decide. I can't promise that it won't get ugly."

"Is that a threat?"

"No, of course not." Lelani looked into his eyes again. "You know what would make me happier than anything, Daddy?"

"To have your daughter."

"No. To have my family. I love you, Daddy. I have missed you severely. Not just in the last year, but for years now."

He smiled faintly. "I've missed you too."

"I would love to be able to bring Emma here to visit her grandparents. I would love it if you and I could teach her to surf together."

"I would love that too."

"Because Emma will need a grandfather."

He nodded. "I'd like to be a grandfather."

"More than a father?"

He ran his fingers through his graying hair. "To be honest, yes. I had never dreamed that at this stage of life, your mother and I would be parenting a young child. It wasn't anything I wanted, Lelani. I'm too old to go through this again. Once was enough for me. But for Emma to come visit, well, that's different."

"So, do we agree?"

He shrugged. "Not that it matters."

"Because of my mother."

"You know how she can be."

"But what if we both stood up to her—together—and we convinced her that this is not only in Emma's best interest, but everyone's. Wouldn't she get that?"

He sighed. "You know your mother as well as I do."

"Yes. But does that mean that she must always get her way? I know you love her, Daddy. And I'm sure you'd do anything for her. Right?"

"Of course."

"How about me? Do you love me too?"

"You know I do."

"And Emma?"

"Yes, of course."

"But you're willing to hurt me—and Emma—just to placate your wife."

He didn't say anything, but he slowly stood and Lelani wondered if she had crossed the line. What she said was true—there were certain truths that her dad refused to face. Especially those related to his wife.

Lelani continued to sit on the beach, watching as her father walked away. For the first time since coming back, she noticed how old he looked. Not only was his hair thinning and gray, but his shoulders were slumped and his step was slower. He was aging fast. Perhaps that was just one more reason he didn't have much fight in him. Or maybe it was just that old habits were hard to break.

Lelani sat there until her dad was out of sight. He had probably sneaked back into the house, slumped into his favorite recliner, and turned on his big-screen TV, which was always tuned to ESPN. Really, why had she expected anything more? At least she had tried. And she had warned him. He knew what to expect, and that she wouldn't back down.

As Lelani walked back to the house, the image of her dad slowly moving down the beach still played in her mind. She was glad she had witnessed that—it only fanned her desire to get Emma away. Her dad had enough stress with his demanding wife. Why add a child to the mix? And how about when Emma became a teenager and decided to rebel? What if her father—like his father—died young, maybe as a result from the stress, and Emma was left alone with her grandmother? It was a formula for dysfunction.

"Lelani," called Gil as he ran toward her. "Hurry!"

"What's wrong?" Lelani began to run. "Is it Emma?"

"No," he huffed. "It's your parents."

"My parents?"

"They're having a huge fight."

Lelani was barely on the grounds when she heard their voices coming from the pool area.

"Shut up, you old fool!" screamed her mother.

"No, I will not shut up," he yelled back. "You will listen to me!"

"I knew this would happen. My own daughter has turned you against me!"

"No!" Lelani yelled as she stepped onto the pool deck opposite their face-off. "Daddy loves you more than anyone, Mother. He would do anything for you. No one could turn him against you. It's impossible."

Her dad turned and looked at Lelani with a sad expression. "But it is possible to love my wife and my daughter and my granddaughter. That *is* possible."

"What are you saying?" demanded Lelani's mother.

"I'm saying that Lelani is Kala's—I mean *Emma's* mother, and a daughter should be with her mother. And a mother should love her daughter. Daughters need their mother's love."

"Meaning I don't love Lelani?"

Now everyone got silent. Even the birds seemed to be holding their breaths. Lelani wondered if Gil had gone into the guesthouse to avoid all this. Who could blame him?

"That's what you think, isn't it, Lelani?" she persisted. "You think I don't love you. And that's what you told your father."

"No." Lelani held out her hands. "I do think you love me, Mother, in your own way. Because I don't understand how any mother could possibly not feel a slight bit of affection for her own child. But I also think, if you do love me, you'll let me have my daughter. So that I can love her the way only a mother can."

Lelani's mother's hands were clenched into tight fists as she stood there glaring across the pool.

"I'm too old to be a father to a little girl," said her dad sadly. "Emma deserves better."

"Define *better*," snapped Lelani's mother. "Having an unemployed single mother who lives in a rented room and doesn't even have a car— is that better? And don't you think an old father is better than no father? Really, Lelani, if you love your child, why would you put her in—"

"Emma could have a father." Gil emerged from the shadows. "If your daughter would marry me, I would gladly be Emma's father. If you're worried about money, *don't*. I am perfectly capable of supporting a wife and child. I've been in love with your daughter since the moment I met her eight months ago. And I've watched her be tortured by what this has done to her, being denied her own child. Not only that, but denied your love as well. I am usually a patient man, but I am just about fed up!"

Lelani's dad actually smiled now. He walked over to where Gil was standing and extended his hand. Gil greeted him. But Lelani was speechless. Had Gil just proposed to her, right there in front of her parents? Or was he simply trying to help her?

"Now, hear this!" her father boomed across the pool. "As the man of this house—which I am—I officially declare that *this thing is over*. Lelani is Emma's mother. And she has my blessing to take her child." He pointed over to where Ginger was lurking in the shadows by the back door. Lelani was relieved that Emma wasn't with her to witness the fireworks. "Ginger, as your boss—and don't forget who pays the bills around here—you are to help Lelani gather up whatever it is she needs for Emma, enough for the time being. The rest will be sent to her later." He turned to his wife. "Is that understood?"

She glared at him, spun around, and marched back into the house.

"She'll get over it," her dad assured them. "A little jewelry, trip to Europe, whatever it takes, she will get over it."

Lelani ran over and threw her arms around him. "Thank you, Daddy! Thank you! Thank you!"

"And before you go, I want to talk to you—about your unfinished education."

Lelani felt her hopes surge.

"I always wanted a doctor in the family, Lelani. Please, don't give up that dream."

"I haven't, Daddy. I just got derailed. That's all."

Now he shook Gil's hand again. "I won't hold either of you to what you said out here, son, but I will admit that it gave Alana one less argument."

Gil glanced nervously at Lelani.

"We can sort that out later," she said quietly.

"In the meantime, what are you waiting for?" asked her dad. "Go and get your daughter."

"I will." Lelani was already on her way.

"And tell Ginger that she has two weeks of severance pay, but she better start looking for another job."

Lelani found Ginger in the nursery, quietly packing a diaper bag. Emma was sweetly sleeping in her crib.

"Ginger?" Lelani went over and placed a hand on her shoulder. "I want you to know how much I appreciate you taking care of my daughter. You've done a good job."

Ginger stood and looked at Lelani with tears in her eyes. "I did my best."

"I know you did. And you will never know how much I appreciate it."

She nodded as she stuffed another diaper into the bag. "You know the truth?"

"What's that?"

"I'm glad she's going to be with you."

"Thank you." Lelani hugged her now. "My dad is going to give you two weeks' severance pay. And I'm sure he'll write you a letter of recommendation too."

"Thank you."

Emma woke up and Lelani lifted her out of the crib, holding her warm sweet body close to her. "You're going home with Mommy," she said quietly. Then she kissed the top of Emma's head.

Ginger helped Lelani gather up a few more things that she thought Emma might need and even offered to carry them over to the guesthouse. As they walked over, Ginger quietly confessed that Mrs. Porter wasn't the easiest woman in the world to work for. Lelani thought that was an understatement, but she simply smiled, then thanked Ginger again.

"Good luck." Ginger reached over and patted Emma's head.

Gil and Emma and Lelani stood together in the front room of the guesthouse. "Can you believe it?" she asked him.

"I'm still pretty stunned."

"I've never loved my dad more than I do today."

"That took some nerve."

Lelani looked at Gil and shook her head. "And that took some nerve for you to leap out and say what you did."

"I mean it, Lelani, every word. I can't imagine you'd be surprised. You know I love you. You know I'd marry you in a minute if you'd just say yes."

With Emma between them, they kissed. And Lelani said, "Yes."

Thirty-one

Megan

Although they were on two different flights, they all agreed to meet at the Maui airport terminal around eleven. Marcus and Edmond had already dropped off Megan and Anna plus luggage so that they could check in while the guys returned the Jeep. Killiki dropped off Kendall, Gil, Lelani, and Emma. Megan and Anna watched as Killiki and Kendall said what looked like a very romantic good-bye before Killiki drove away.

"Want me to hold Emma while you check in?" Megan offered to Lelani.

"No way," said Kendall as she reached for the baby. "You'll get to hold her on the way home. But I'm on a different flight."

"But you have a broken arm," Megan reminded her.

"I don't." Anna reached for Emma, saying, "Come to Auntie Anna."

"You need to check in anyway," Lelani reminded Kendall.

"Auntie Anna," said Megan. "That has a ring to it."

"My mother already called me Tia Anna. *Tia* is aunt, you know."

"And how did your mother take the news?"

"She wasn't a bit surprised."

"Seriously?"

"No. I called her a couple of times already, kind of giving her a heads up so that she wouldn't have a coronary if it really happened."

"You knew Gil was going to ask her?"

"I'm his sister. I could see it in his eyes."

"I'm just so happy for them, and for Emma. It's like a fairy-tale ending."

"Well, except that the happy couple doesn't usually drive off with a baby seat in the back of their horse-drawn carriage."

Megan chuckled, then glanced at Gil, who was actually carrying Emma's baby seat over to the checked-bag security area now. She just shook her head in wonder. "How many people go to Maui for a vacation and come back with a baby?"

Soon they were all making their way through the open-air terminal, taking turns holding Emma as they passed through security, then finally settling themselves into the restaurant. They ordered a quick lunch before Megan, Marcus, Lelani, Emma, and Gil's flight boarded.

"I can't believe what a natural Gil is with the baby," said Kendall as she watched him adjusting Emma in the highchair.

"Oh, I learned this little trick at the restaurant," he told them as he tied a bib around Emma's chubby neck.

"And Emma seems fine with everything," said Megan in amazement. "She acts like she's been hanging with this crowd all her life."

"She's a good baby," said Lelani fondly. "I just hope she stays good for the whole flight."

"You'll have us to help with her," Megan reminded her.

"Okay, okay, enough about Emma," said Kendall. "Sorry, but I have to hog some of the limelight before you guys run off to catch your flight."

"So you want us to talk about you now?" asked Anna.

"Yes, and I'm just dying to know what you think of Killiki." Kendall smiled happily.

"Isn't it more important what you think?" asked Megan.

"I think he's wonderful."

"I'm surprised you're even getting on the plane to go home," teased Anna.

"To be honest, it's not easy." Kendall smiled. "But I told him I need to go home and attend to some of my messes."

"You told him about your messes?" asked Megan. "Which ones?"

"All of them. I told him everything—including that I'm pregnant."

The table got quiet and Megan looked at Marcus. Like the other guys, he looked pretty surprised.

"You mean you guys didn't know?" Kendall's eyes grew big. "Oh, you are such good girlfriends. I can't believe you didn't spill the beans."

"You told us not to tell anyone."

"Well, I don't care who knows now. Killiki knows and, guess what, he loves me anyway."

"Sounds like quite a guy," said Marcus with a twinkle in his eye.

"And you know he's a plumber, right?" asked Anna.

"Yes." Kendall nodded. "And I'm proud of it. Plumbers have it made in Maui. They can work when they want and surf when they want."

"This sounds serious," said Gil.

"It is. We're going to e-mail each other every day and see where it goes." She smiled. "Now, enough about me. Have you guys set a date?"

Gil looked happily at Lelani. "It's up to her."

"I've always dreamed of a June wedding."

"Ooh," said Kendall. "Me too! And with all the works!"

"But I don't want a big wedding," Lelani said quickly.

Anna burst out laughing. "Don't forget who you're marrying."

"We can have a small wedding if Lelani wants," Gil assured them.

"I can't wait to hear Mama's opinion on that." She turned to Lelani now. "Oh, yeah, speaking of our mother, she has offered to babysit Emma for you."

"But I thought I could do that," said Kendall.

"You keep forgetting you have a broken wrist," Megan reminded her.

"Oh." She frowned.

"I know," said Anna. "Maybe you could help my mom babysit, and that way you'd learn how to do it at the same time."

"You think I don't know how to care for a baby?"

"Do you?"

"Well, not really. But I've been practicing on Tinkerbell."

"Oh yeah, I just talked to my mom," Anna told her, "and Tinker sends her best."

Now Emma began clanging her spoon loudly on the metal tray of the highchair, and everyone turned to look at her.

"It looks like she wants to make an announcement," teased Gil. "She's trying to get our attention."

"Yes, I think you're right," said Lelani. "I think Emma wants to thank everyone for coming to Maui, and she wants to thank everyone for the role they played in helping to get her back with her mommy. Right, Emma?"

Emma just grinned and cooed and pounded the spoon a few more times as if to show that she agreed.

"And," Megan raised her iced tea as if to make a toast. "We want to officially welcome you, little Emma, to our big happy family. Aloha!"

They all lifted their drink glasses and cheered, "Aloha!"

And, really, Megan thought they were like a family—a family of friends that was growing closer all the time.

... a little more ...

When a delightful concert comes to an end,

the orchestra might offer an encore.

When a fine meal comes to an end,

it's always nice to savor a bit of dessert.

When a great story comes to an end,

we think you may want to linger.

And so, we offer ...

AfterWords—just a little something more after you

have finished a David C. Cook novel.

We invite you to stay awhile in the story.

Thanks for reading!

Turn the page for ...

- **Discussion Questions**
- **A Conversation with Melody Carlson**
- **An Excerpt from *three weddings and a bar mitzvah***

Discussion Questions

1. How does Kendall's pregnancy pull the women of Bloomberg Place together? What do the roommates discover about each other that they might not have fully appreciated before this event?

2. Describe a crisis you faced that had some positive effects on a relationship that was important to you.

3. If you were Kendall's roommate, what advice would you have given her about the decisions she must make regarding her baby? Why?

4. Kendall places a high value on keeping up appearances. What made her finally be so honest about her "messes" with Killiki—and herself? What does it take for you to tell yourself the truth about mistakes you've made?

5. Compare Anna's and Lelani's responses to Abuela Castillo's disparaging remarks about Edmond and Lelani. How would you have responded to such publicly embarrassing remarks about yourself? About your "significant other"?

6. If you'd been in Lelani's shoes, what would have been the most difficult aspect of returning home?

7. Why does Megan have a hard time knowing whether Marcus is a dedicated Christian or not? Are her expectations of him fair, limited, judgmental? What does she come to love about him?

8. Anna and Lelani each have difficult mothers. Why do you think Mrs. Mendez was eventually able to overlook her disagreements with her daughter, while Mrs. Porter was not?

9. What do you think of Anna's advice that Lelani apologize to her mother?

10. Was Lelani right to insist that she have custody of Emma? Was her father right to support her wishes? Why or why not?

A Conversation with Melody Carlson

Some of your characters—like Abuela Castillo or Mrs. Porter—have such shocking worldviews. Do you dream up these women or base them on real life "characters"?

I've actually known women similar to these two. It's possible that their worldviews resulted from things like chemical imbalance or narcissism, but that didn't make them any easier to interact with.

Extended family relationships can be difficult to navigate. What advice would you offer young women who want to have a good relationship with their parents but feel ready to give up on ever having one?

I think everyone has at least one difficult relationship in her life, and often it's with a family member. But usually, with some patience, forgiveness, and maturity, we eventually ease beyond the rough spots. Occasionally relationships turn toxic and disabling and, for survival's sake, we need to create boundaries and distance ourselves. But I do believe that most parents of young adults only want the best for them. It's just not easy letting go.

As Megan observes at the end of the story, the women of Bloomberg Place have managed to create their own extended "family of friends." Would you describe any of your friendships this way?

Absolutely. Like they say, you can't pick your family, but you can pick your friends. Although my husband and I feel blessed to have some wonderful relatives, they don't live nearby. For that reason, we've built up a strong network of friends that feels very much like family. Or, like Scripture says, "A friend nearby is better than a brother far away."

What does it take to create such a "family"?

I think the biggest thing is commitment. Because, like family, friends can rub you the wrong way at times. It's just how life goes. Of course, it's easier to commit to friends when you've already established that you have common interests and compatible personalities, as well as a foundation of honesty, compassion, and love. I believe the best way to have a good friend is first to be one.

Why do you think these kinds of relationships are important to women even when their biological families are pretty healthy?

I think we all need friends that we can let our hair down with. Even when we have healthy family relationships, there will come times when we need to spill our guts to someone outside of the family loop. Whether we're squabbling with a sibling, fretting over a parent, or trying to raise a teenager, there's a certain safety zone in being able to confide in someone who's not related to you.

When you set out to write the 86 Bloomberg Place series, did you expect these women to grow so close? Did any of them surprise you along the way?

I think I hoped they'd grow close, but in the first book, it felt like a major challenge. I mean, you throw four distinctly different women together under one roof, and anything can happen. But that was also part of the fun. Consequently, they've all surprised me in some way. Whether it's unexpected maturity, an act of kindness, or doing something totally off the stupid scale, these four young women are always catching me off guard. Even now as I'm beginning the fourth and final book, I'm not quite sure what will happen next. And, like life, I don't know that everything will wrap up neatly in the end.

An Excerpt from *three weddings and a bar mitzvah*

One

Megan Abernathy

"Okay, then how does the *second* Saturday in June look?" Anna asked her housemates.

Megan frowned down at her date book. She and Anna sat at the dining room table trying to nail down a date for Lelani and Gil's wedding. Megan had already been the spoiler on the first weekend of June, but she couldn't help it. She'd already promised her mom that she'd go to a family reunion in Washington. Now it seemed she was about to mess things up again.

"I'm sorry," she said, "but I promised Marcus I'd go to his sister's wedding. It's been scheduled for almost a year now, and it's the second Saturday too. But maybe I can get out of it."

In the adjacent living room, Lelani shook her head as she quietly rocked Emma. The baby was teething and fussy and overdue for her afternoon nap. Megan wasn't sure if Lelani's frustrated expression was a result of wedding planning or her daughter's mood.

"What time is Marcus's sister's wedding?" Anna asked Megan. "Is it possible you could do both weddings in one day?"

"That might work." With date book in hand, Megan rose and left the table to see if she could take Emma and give Lelani a break.

"Or we could look at the third weekend in June," Anna called from the dining room.

Emma's eyes finally fluttered closed, and Megan watched as Lelani gently eased the baby into the playpen that was set up in a corner of the living room. Lelani pushed a dark lock of hair away from Emma's forehead, tucked a fuzzy pink blanket around her, then finally straightened and sighed.

"Looks like she's down for the count," Megan whispered.

Lelani nodded. "Now, where were we with dates?"

"If you still want to go with the second Saturday," Megan said quietly, "Anna just suggested that it might be possible for me to attend two weddings in one day."

"That's a lot to ask of you," Lelani said as they returned to the dining room. Anna and Kendall were waiting expectantly with the calendar in the middle of the table opened to June.

Megan shrugged as she pulled out a chair. "It's your wedding, Lelani. You should have it the way you want it. I just want to help."

Anna pointed to the second Saturday. "Okay, this is the date in question. Is it doable or not?"

Lelani sat down and sighed again. "I'm willing to schedule my wedding so that it's not a conflict with the other one—I mean, if it can even be done. Mostly I just wanted to wait until I finished spring term."

"What time is Marcus's sister's wedding?" asked Anna.

"I'm not positive, but I thought he said it was in the evening."

"And you want a sunset wedding," Kendall reminded Lelani.

"That's true." Anna nodded.

"But I also want Megan to be there," Lelani pointed out.

"That would be helpful, since she's your maid of honor," said Anna.

Megan tried not to bristle as she reached for her phone. Lelani's choice had put Anna a little out of sorts—especially considering that

Anna was the sister of the groom—but in truth, Megan was a lot closer to Lelani than Anna was. And at least they were all going to be in the wedding.

"Let me ask Marcus about the time," Megan said as she pressed speed dial and waited. "Hey, Marcus," she said when he finally answered. "We're having a scheduling problem here. Do you know what time Hannah's wedding is going to be?"

"In the evening, I think. Do you need the exact time?"

"No, that's good enough." Megan gave Lelani a disappointed look. "I'll talk to you later, okay?"

"You're not thinking of bailing on me, are you?" He sounded genuinely worried.

"No, but we're trying to pin down a time and date for Lelani."

"It's just that I really want my family to meet you, Megan. I mean all of my family. And I want you to meet them too."

"I know. And I plan to go with you."

"Thanks. So, I'll see you around six thirty tonight?"

"That's right." Megan told him good-bye, then turned to Lelani with a sigh. "I'm sorry," she told her. "That wedding's at night. Maybe I should blow off my family reunion so that you—"

"No," Anna pointed to the calendar. "I just realized that the first Saturday in June is also my mother's birthday."

"So?" Kendall shrugged. "What's wrong with that?"

Megan laughed. "Think about it, Kendall. How would *you* like to share your wedding anniversary with your mother-in-law's birthday?"

Kendall grinned. "Oh, yeah. Maybe not."

"How about a Sunday wedding?" suggested Megan.

"Sunday?" Lelani's brow creased slightly as she weighed this.

"Sunday might make it easier to book the location," Kendall said. "I mean, since most weddings are usually on Saturdays, and June is a pretty busy wedding month."

"That's true," agreed Megan.

"And you gotta admit that this is short notice for planning a wedding," added Kendall. "Some people say you should start planning your wedding a whole year ahead of time."

"Marcus's sister has been planning her wedding for more than a year," Megan admitted. "Marcus says that Hannah is going to be a candidate for the *Bridezillas* show if she doesn't lighten up."

They all laughed.

"Well, there's no way Gil and I are going to spend a year planning a wedding." Lelani shook her head. "That's fine for some people, but we're more interested in our marriage than we are in our wedding."

"I hear you." Kendall laughed and patted her slightly rounded belly. She was in the fifth month of her pregnancy now. She and her Maui man were corresponding regularly, but despite Kendall's high hopes, Killiki had yet to propose.

"I really don't see why it should take a year to plan a wedding," Megan admitted. "I think that's just the wedding industry's way of lining their pockets."

"So how much planning time do you have now anyway?" Kendall asked Lelani. "Like, three months?"

"Not even," Lelani flipped the calendar pages back. "It's barely two now."

"Which is why we need to nail this date today," Megan said. "Even though it's a small wedding—"

"And *that* remains to be seen," Anna reminded her. "My mother's list keeps growing and growing and growing."

"I still think it might be easier to just elope," Lelani reminded them. "I told Gil that I wouldn't have a problem with that."

"Yes, that would be brilliant." Anna firmly shook her head. "You can just imagine how absolutely thrilled Mom would be about that little idea."

Lelani smiled. "I actually thought she'd be relieved."

"That might've been true a few months ago. But Mom's changing." Anna poked Lelani in the arm. "In fact, I'm starting to feel jealous. I think she likes you better than me now."

Lelani giggled. "In your dreams, Anna. Your mother just puts up with me so she can have access to Emma."

They all laughed about that. Everyone knew that Mrs. Mendez was crazy about her soon-to-be granddaughter. Already she'd bought the baby all kinds of clothes and toys and seemed intent on spoiling the child rotten.

"Speaking of Emma," Kendall wagged her finger, "Mrs. Mendez was certain that she's supposed to have her on Monday. But I thought it was my day."

"I'm not sure," Lelani admitted. "But I'll call and find out."

"And while you've got Granny on the line," continued Kendall, "tell her that I *do* know how to change diapers properly. One more diaper lecture and I might just tape a Pamper over that big mouth of hers!"

They all laughed again. Ever since coming home from Maui, Kendall had been complaining about how Mrs. Mendez seemed to find fault with Kendall's child-care abilities. In fact, Mrs. Mendez had spent a week "teaching" Kendall the "proper" way to do almost everything. To be fair, Megan didn't blame the older woman. She'd been a little worried about Kendall too. But to everyone's surprise, Kendall turned out to be rather maternal. Whether this was the result of the pregnancy or a natural bent, Megan couldn't decide, but it had been a huge relief.

"Now, back to the wedding date," said Lelani.

"Yes," agreed Megan. "What about Sunday?"

"Oh, no," Anna said. "I just remembered that I promised Edmond I'd go to his brother's bar mitzvah that day."

Lelani groaned.

"Edmond's brother?" Megan frowned. "I thought Edmond was an only child. And since when is he Jewish?"

"Remember his mom remarried?" Anna told her. "And Phillip Goldstein, her new husband, *is* Jewish, and he has a son named Ben whose bar mitzvah is that Sunday." She sighed. "I'm sorry, Lelani."

"But is it in the evening?" asked Megan.

"Good point." Anna nodded. "I think it's in the afternoon."

"So why can't you just do the bar mitzvah and *then* the wedding?" Kendall suggested.

"You're right. That's what I'll do." Anna turned back to Lelani. "And if you had the wedding on Sunday night, you could probably have the reception in the restaurant afterward. I'm guessing it will be late by the time the wedding's over, and Sunday nights aren't exactly busy."

Lelani nodded. "Probably. Do you think your parents would mind?"

"Mind? Are you kidding? This is what they live for."

"But you still don't have a place picked for the wedding," Megan reminded her.

"I have several outdoor locations in mind. I'll start checking on them tomorrow."

"We'll have to pray that it doesn't rain." Megan penned 'Lelani and Gil's Wedding' in her date book, then closed it.

"Should we have a backup plan?" asked Anna. "I'm sure my parents could have the wedding at their house."

"Or here," suggested Kendall. "You can use this house if you want."

Anna frowned. "It's kind of small, don't you think?"

"I think it's sweet of Kendall to offer." Lelani smiled at Kendall.

"I can imagine a bride coming down those stairs." Kendall nodded toward the staircase. "If it was a small wedding."

"I'll keep it in mind," Lelani told her. "And your parents' house too, Anna."

"It might be tricky getting a church reserved on a Sunday night," Megan looked at the clock. "And speaking of that, I better get ready. Marcus is picking me up for the evening service in about fifteen minutes." She turned back to Lelani. "Don't worry. I've got my to-do list, and I'll start checking on some of this stuff tomorrow. My mom will want to help with the flowers."

"And my aunt wants to make the cake," Anna reminded them.

"Sounds like you're in good hands," Kendall said a bit wistfully. "I wonder how it would go if I were planning my wedding."

"You'd be in good hands too," Lelani assured her.

"Now, let's start going over that guest list," Anna said as Megan stood. "The sooner we get it finished, the less chance my mother will have of adding to it." Megan was relieved that Anna had offered to handle the invitations. She could have them printed at the publishing company for a fraction of the price that a regular printer would charge. The plan was to get them sent out in the next couple of weeks.

As Megan changed from her weekend sweats into something presentable, she wondered what Lelani's parents would do when it was time for the big event. Although her dad had promised to come and committed to paying Lelani's med school tuition, Lelani's mom was still giving Lelani the cold shoulder. Make that the *ice* shoulder. For a woman who lived in the tropics, Mrs. Porter was about as chilly as they came. Still, Lelani had friends to lean on. Maybe that was better than family at times.

"Your prince is here," Kendall called into Megan's room.

"Thanks." Megan was looking for her other loafer and thinking it was time to organize her closet again. "Tell him I'm coming."

When Megan emerged, Marcus was in the dining room, chatting with her housemates like one of the family. He was teasing Anna for having her hair in curlers, then joking with Kendall about whether her Maui man had called her today.

"Not yet," Kendall told him with a little frown. "But it's earlier there."

"Ready to roll?" Megan asked as she joined them.

He grinned at her. "Yep." But before they went out he turned around. "Hey, does anyone else want to come tonight? There's a really good band playing."

Megan's housemates thanked him, but it seemed they all had plans. Even so, Megan was glad he asked. And she could tell her housemates were becoming more open to church. Really, the chance they would come one of these days was a matter of timing.

"So, are you nervous?" Marcus asked as he drove toward the city.

"Nervous?" Megan frowned. "About church?"

"No. The big interview."

Megan slapped her forehead. "Wow, I temporarily forgot. We were so obsessed with Lelani's wedding—trying to make lists, planning everything, settling the date—I put the interview totally out of my mind."

"Hopefully it won't be out of your mind by Monday."

"No, of course, not."

"So … are you nervous?"

Megan considered this. It would be her first interview for a teaching job, which did make it a little unsettling. "The truth is, I don't think I have a chance at the job," she admitted. "And, yes, I'm nervous. Thanks for reminding me."

"Sorry. Why don't you think you'll get the job?"

"Because I don't have any actual teaching experience." She wanted to add *duh*, but thought it sounded a little juvenile.

"Everyone has to start somewhere."

"But starting in middle school, just a couple of months before the school year ends … don't you think they'll want someone who knows what she's doing?"

"Unless they want someone who's enthusiastic and energetic and smart and creative and who likes kids and has lots of great new ideas and—"

"Wow, any chance you could do the interview in my place?"

"Cross-dress and pretend I'm you?"

She laughed. "Funny."

"Just have confidence, Megan. Believe in yourself and make them believe too. You'd be great as a middle-school teacher."

"What makes you so sure?"

"Because I remember middle school."

"And?"

"And most of my teachers were old and dull and boring."

"That's sad."

"I would've loved having someone like you for a teacher."

"Really?"

He chuckled. "Yeah. If I was thirteen, I'd probably sit right in the front row and think about how hot you were, and then I'd start fantasizing about—"

"Marcus Barrett, you're pathetic." Just the same, she laughed.

"What can I say? I'm just a normal, warm-blooded American kid."

"Give me a break!" She punched him in the arm.

"Is that your phone?" he asked as he parked outside of the church.

"Oh, yeah. A good reminder to turn it off." She pulled it out to see it was Kendall. Megan hoped nothing was wrong. "Hey, Kendall," she said as Marcus set the parking brake. "What's up?"

"Guess what?" shrieked Kendall.

"I have no idea what, but it sounds like good news." She stepped out of the car.

"Killiki just called."

"That's nice."

"And he asked me to marry him!"

Megan raised her eyebrows and looked at Marcus as he came around to meet her. "And you said yes?"

"Of course! Do you think I'm crazy?"

"No. Not at all. Congratulations, Kendall. I mean, I guess that's what you say."

"So now we have *two* weddings to plan."

Megan blinked. She walked with Marcus toward the church entry. "Oh, yeah, I guess we do."

"And I'm getting married in June too!"

"That's great, Kendall. I'm really, really happy for you. Killiki seems like a great guy."

"He is! Anyway, we just looked at the calendar again. And we finally figured that I should just get married the same day as Lelani, only I'll get married in the morning. That way we'll all be able to go to both weddings."

"Wow, the same day?"

"Otherwise, you'll be at your reunion or Marcus's sister's wedding. Or Anna will be at the bar mitzvah. Or Lelani and Gil will be on their honeymoon."

"Oh, that's right."

"And I want all of you there!"

"Yes, I suppose that makes sense."

"It'll be busy but fun."

"Definitely." Megan thanked Kendall for telling her and said good-bye, then Megan closed her phone and shook her head. "Wow."

"Kendall's getting married?" asked Marcus as he held the church door open for her.

"Yes. Can you believe it?"

"Good for her."

"And her wedding will be the same weekend as your sister's, and the same day as Lelani's."

Marcus held up three fingers with a perplexed expression. "Three weddings in one weekend? That's crazy."

"Yep." Megan nodded. "Three weddings and a bar mitzvah."

"Huh?" Marcus looked confused, but they were in the sanctuary, and Megan knew she'd have to explain later.

Other Fiction by Melody Carlson

Let Them Eat Fruitcake
(David C. Cook)

I Heart Bloomberg
(David C. Cook)

These Boots Weren't Made for Walking
(Waterbrook)

On This Day
(Waterbrook)

Ready to Wed
(Guideposts Books)

Finding Alice
(Waterbrook)

The Other Side of Darkness
(Multnomah)

Carter House Girls series
(Zondervan)

Just An Ordinary Girl
(Revell)

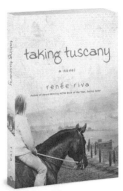
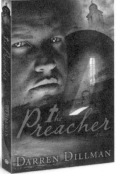